A pair of bright white lights appeared in the distance, grew larger, then diminished in a few seconds, much like opportunities that come and go. He looked at the car that lay motionless in the darkness, pondering why she had invited him to her room at midnight when everyone else had gone home. Although they had spent many late-night hours together, they had never shared any intimacy. He was not clear about what their real relationship was. Friends? Lovers? Something in between? Whatever it was, he felt his blood coursing fast, calling out the desire to hug her from every single cell in his entire body. It was too hot, even on this cold winter night. He untied the top button of his coat, letting in the cold air to help cool him down.

Praise for Li Cai

"Li did a fantastic job of representing life in China and how living in the US often amazed him." Velda Brotherton

The Two

by

Li Cai

This is a work of fiction. Names, characters, places, and incidents are either the product of the author's imagination or are used fictitiously, and any resemblance to actual persons living or dead, business establishments, events, or locales, is entirely coincidental.

The Two

Contact Information: info@thewildrosepress.com

Cover Art by *Kim Mendoza*

The Wild Rose Press, Inc.
PO Box 708
Adams Basin, NY 14410-0708
Visit us at www.thewildrosepress.com

Publishing History
First Edition, 2023
Trade Paperback ISBN 978-1-5092-4985-5
Digital ISBN 978-1-5092-4986-2

Published in the United States of America

Dedication

To my wife and my daughter
This book would not have been possible without their support.

To my parents, brother, and other family members
Thanks for their encouragement.

To my friends
I owe the following people a huge debt of gratitude (alphabetical order). This book would not have been possible without their critique and help.

Writers' Guild of Arkansas
Raymona Anderson, Marilyn Collins, Nancy Hartney, Lorraine Heartfield, Maeve Maddox, Belinda Ostrowski, Madlyn Springston, Gloria Williams Tran, Barbara Youree.

Arkansas Ridge Writers
Ed Barham, Velda Brotherton, Jim Hale, Patricia Heck, Ellen Mueller, Lynne Rich, Vivian Rose, Farla Steele-Treat.

Chapter 1

On a hot summer night, three people sat at a tea table in a small living room without air conditioning, an elderly couple on homemade couches and a young man on a stool. The candlelight in front of them flickered over their faces, creating an air of uncertainty. The elderly man slowly opened a package, pulled out a stack of American dollars with his bony fingers, and set the envelope down on the table. He licked his thumb and index finger and counted the bills, most of them ones and fives.

The full moon cast a dazzling rectangle and the crosshatching of the window grids on the otherwise dark cement floor, as if it had opened a portal to another world. In the center of that cross, two large, fully packed suitcases stood silently, waiting for the adventure to the other side of the earth.

"Xiang, here are two hundred dollars." He leaned forward and held out the thick wad of cash. "Be careful. Don't lose it."

Xiang stared at the foreign currency in the wavering candlelight. "Father, where did you get it?"

"From the black market."

"You shouldn't do that. It's very expensive." The son pushed his father's hand back. "We're already in debt. I can't take this money."

The woman gently pressed Xiang's hand down.

"Your father went through a lot of trouble to get it." She took the money from her husband, carefully slid it into the envelope, and handed the package to her son. "Take it with you."

"No, I can't do that." Xiang did not move. "Two hundred dollars is more than you both make in a year. To send me to the United States, you not only spent all your savings but also borrowed a lot of money from our relatives and friends." He looked down at the airline ticket on the table, feeling guilty for driving the family into huge debt. "This ticket alone is worth more than what Father makes in several years."

The old man adjusted his position and massaged his sore waist. "You don't have to worry about us. As long as you are safe in America, everything will be fine. Your research assistantship will start next month. In the meantime, you need it."

In the faint candlelight, Xiang looked at his parents' frail faces. The lack of nutrition had taken a toll on their health. In order to support him to study abroad, they had saved every penny from their daily expenditures, including their meals, for the last two years.

Mother leaned forward to him. "After you get to the United States, don't worry about us. We can take care of ourselves." She paused for a moment. "Your brother wants to go to America too. You—"

"I know. I will do whatever I can to get him there."

Xiang had decided to live frugally and save as much money as possible so that he could help his parents improve their living conditions and support his brother to study overseas. These were all just the natural, inevitable responsibilities of a Chinese eldest son.

"It's time to go to sleep now." Mother got up. "You

have to catch an airplane in a few hours." She approached the light switch by the door and flipped it on.

The room remained dark.

"Still no power." She shook her head and went back to her seat. "I don't think we'll have electricity tonight. It's the second power outage this week."

Xiang went to his room and lay on his bed, but he was unable to fall asleep. Going to the United States to pursue his doctorate was his and his parents' dream. Everyone had been excited and happy since the moment he had received a letter from the University of Northwest Arkansas, confirming his admission and offering him a research assistantship. Now, a few hours before he was to leave for America, that feeling had vanished.

Rolling over, he saw the moon through the window and remembered a woman.

Two days earlier, he had gone to see her after a long goodbye dinner with his friends. She lived on the top floor of a six-story building with no elevator and broken stairwell lights. Using the moonlight streaming in through the windows on each landing, he groped his way up. When he arrived at her door, he paused to catch his breath and smooth his hair. Then he knocked.

No one answered.

He knocked again, a little harder.

Still no response.

Xiang looked at his wristwatch. Nine-thirty. Believing that she must have gone to bed, he turned to leave. Just then, he heard her voice. "I'm coming."

He waited. After an unusually long time, the door slowly opened, and a woman a little shorter than him appeared at the door crack, crutches under her arms. Her face was partially covered by white bandages, and her right leg was in a cast.

With wide eyes and a dropping jaw, he took a step back and stared at her. For a moment, he even wondered if he was in the wrong place.

"Hi, Xiang." She spoke in a joyful tone and opened the door wider. "Come on in."

He looked at her from head to toe. "Yan, what happened?"

"I fell on the stairway a few days ago." She led him to the living room. She leaned her crutches against the wall next to a couch and managed to sit down. Xiang thought about helping her but was not sure how she would take it.

"How are you?" She smiled at him.

"I'm fine. I'm going to the United States this Friday."

"How nice. What are you going to study?"

"PhD in physics."

"Congratulations." She turned to gaze at a large picture on the wall across the room. "Zhoufei's father also studied physics in America."

Xiang glanced at the photo. It was a family portrait with her daughter Zhoufei and her husband Zhouyi. Zhoufei was pursuing her master's degree in physics in the United States, and her husband had been beaten to death by Red Guards during the Great Cultural Revolution.

From 1966 to 1976, the disastrous political movement swept the nation, and students from middle schools to universities across the country formed Red Guards. They dragged scientists and government officials away from their offices and homes, humiliated them in public, imprisoned them to interrogate them, and tortured them to confess that they were anti-revolutionaries.

Xiang turned back to look at her. "Is there anything you want me to take to Zhoufei?"

"Thank you for asking, but she's fine. Since this is your first time going to the United States, you must have a lot of things to carry." Yan paused for a second. "From her letters, I can tell that she was a little depressed. You are her best friend and classmate, so perhaps you can help her."

"She is probably just homesick, but I will check it out for you."

After chatting with her for a while, Xiang got up to leave.

She limped toward the door with him. "Please don't tell her that I'm injured. I don't want her to worry about me. She needs to focus on her studies."

What a mother. After her husband died, she had overcome many difficulties to raise her child, but now, when she needed her daughter to care for her, Zhoufei lived thousands of kilometers away. She did not even want her daughter to know that she was injured for fear that it would distract her.

A moving light flickered in the dark sky, bringing Xiang back to the present. Through his window, he watched the airplane flying westward, wondering how many parents had been left alone by their children who were pursuing higher education in Western nations.

I will come back after completing my PhD and look after my parents, he promised to the moon that stared at him. *They raised me, protected me, and provided me with the best education they could.*

A stabbing pain in his stomach interrupted his

thoughts. He had developed an ulcer while he was a child in the education camp in the remote countryside during the Great Cultural Revolution. At times, when it struck, he had to rest for a day or two to recover. Although it had become less of a problem in the past few years, it still flared up now and then, and when it did, he had to grit his teeth for hours to endure it.

Xiang pressed his hands to his stomach and became concerned. He had a plane to catch in a few hours. What if the pain became severe? What would he do if it happened on the plane or in the United States?

He did not want to think about it. To move forward, he had to pretend that nothing was wrong and that he would be fine.

Chapter 2

While Xiang was talking to his parents, his younger brother Shan studied in the library without air conditioning at the Xihe University, two thousand kilometers away from Huadu. He prepared for the Test of English as a Foreign Language (TOEFL), a standardized test for foreigners seeking admission to an American university. The room remained hot even after midnight, and he was drenched in sweat. He had thought about going outside several times, but always decided not to. He could not afford to waste a second since the exam would be the next morning. Scratching his head, trying to figure out which answer was correct, he felt someone pat his shoulder. He turned and saw Lei, his best friend and classmate.

"What brought you here?" Shan laid his pen on the desk.

"I've been looking for you." Lei breathed heavily.

"What did you do?" Shan noticed the sweat on Lei's forehead. "Did you just finish your workout?"

"No, I ran here."

"Oh? What's so urgent?"

"I need your help supervising my workers." With his palm, Lei wiped the sweat from his face.

"When and where?"

"Now. I got a project to renovate the East Temple."

"How did you get the project?" Shan blinked in

astonishment.

As a historic landmark built over a thousand years ago, the East Temple had been the symbol of the city for centuries. How could it have awarded the renovation contract to a one-man company that had been registered for only two years?

“Jiangkai gave it to me.”

Shan nodded. That was why. He had heard that Lei’s father knew the CEO of Jiangkai, the city’s largest real estate company.

“Anyway,” Lei continued, “it’s due tomorrow for completion, but the manager got sick and went back home. Now, the workers are idle on the job site.” He paused to take a breath. “The city will inspect the project tomorrow morning. If I don't finish it, I'll let Jiangkai down, and they won't give me anything in the future.”

Shan looked at his TOEFL book and then back at his friend. He had helped Lei several times and would be happy to do so again but not at this critical moment in his life.

As he was about to tell Lei that he would have a language test the next day, Lei spoke again. "I planned to supervise the workers myself, but Chief Wang called and asked me to meet him at East Ocean. I know you are very busy, but I only need your assistance for one hour. Once I finish meeting with him, I'll be back immediately.”

Shan nodded, understanding why his friend needed him. Wang was the CEO of Jiangkai, and the East Ocean was a luxurious bathhouse where wealthy businessmen mingled and conducted business.

“Okay. I’ll help you.” He sighed and closed the book. “I need to go back to our dorm to get my bike.”

"I'll drive you there in my car."

"Drive? You have a car?" Shan looked at his friend, wide-eyed. Although Lei's father was a high official, they shouldn't be that wealthy.

"Yes, I got one last month."

Lei led the way to the black car parked under the streetlight right on the roadside and drove to the East Temple. Half an hour later, they arrived at the site.

As they ascended the broad marble stairs to the temple entrance, Shan noticed the bright round moon staring at him and remembered the expectations of his parents and brother. He stopped for a moment, questioning whether he had made the right decision, and then continued with firm steps. He had agreed to help his friend and should not back down.

After two minutes of climbing, they reached a pair of gigantic dark red wooden doors that led into a vast hall with a huge domed ceiling. A rope hung from a large timbered beam near the apex of the dome, with both ends drooping to the floor. At the far end of the hall, a group of about thirty young men lay on the ground as if sleeping.

They must come from the impoverished countryside.

Ever since the central government had launched an economic reform, a great number of rural youths flocked to the cities, hoping to earn enough money to support their families. With little education, they worked as construction workers, hopping from job to job and working for long hours.

Shan turned to his friend. "What exactly do you want me to do?"

Lei pointed to an unpainted section of a beam near

the ceiling. "That section needs to be completed."

Shan glanced up at it and then at the sleeping young men. "It's midnight now, and they looked very tired. I'm afraid there might be a serious accident if they go there to work."

"I know, but as long as they are cautious, there shouldn't be any problem." Lei led Shan to the rope and shook it. "Look at how robust it is. It—" His beeper went off. He read the text on the gadget and then looked back at Shan. "I have to go now. Let me introduce you to the head of the construction workers before I leave."

He led Shan to a sleeping muscular young man in his early twenties.

Lei tapped the dormant man with his toe. "Zhuzi, wake up."

In an abrupt jerk, the boy's eyes flew open, and his body jolted upright. He blinked and looked around as if trying to orient himself.

"Here, here." With his foot, Lei tapped Zhuzi on his leg to get his attention. "This is Shan, your manager for tonight. Make sure you finish this project before you go home." He then patted Shan's shoulder. "Sorry to drag you into this. I have to leave now. See you in an hour."

After Lei left, Shan knelt, looked into Zhuzi's eyes, and spoke softly. "Could you wake them up? The sooner we finish the job, the earlier we can go home." He used the term we to make himself more acceptable to the young man.

"We have already worked fourteen hours today. Everyone is tired. No one wants to go up there now. It's too risky." He paused for a moment. "I brought them to this city. If they get injured, I can't face their parents. Their families depend on them."

Fourteen hours? They had worked for fourteen hours today.

Shan glanced at the boys who were still sleeping. They looked to be in their late teens, and they were all skinny. His heart sank. If they were injured, it would be catastrophic for their families.

Shan went to the rope, grabbed it with both hands, and gave it a hard yank to test its strength. It seemed strong enough to hold a person safely, but the problem was that these kids were too exhausted to work.

He retrieved a pack of cigarettes out of his pocket, pulled out one, and lit it. With his head lowered, he paced back and forth by the rope like a pendulum. He took a drag on the cigarette.

What should I do? Maybe I should convince Lei to negotiate with Jiangkai tomorrow.

No, he could not do that. He had promised to help Lei, so he had to keep it. His word was his honor. He exhaled the smoke, shaking his head.

Chapter 3

As Xiang lay face down on his bed, squeezing his stomach in an effort to relieve the agony, he heard it growl. After glancing at the clock beside his bed in the dim room, he realized that the pain was most likely caused by hunger because he had not eaten anything for seven hours. He got up and went to the kitchen to find something to eat. While he walked across the living room, he saw his backpack lying on the floor in the moonlight. He unzipped it and took out a crimson booklet with large golden Chinese characters on its cover.

People's Republic of China

Passport

A month earlier, after accepting the offer from the University of Northwest Arkansas, he visited Dr. Liu, the president of the Huadu Institute of Applied Physics, to request a letter. To process his passport application, the Huadu Public Security Bureau required a letter from his employer, verifying his identity and stating that he was permitted to study overseas.

"Sorry I can't help you. You need to talk to Human Resources." Dr. Liu dressed in a dark blue business suit glared at him from behind a shiny red cherry desk.

That reaction was expected. Lately, too many graduate students had left for the United States without finishing their studies. Xiang had heard that the man had complained about being used by those young men and women.

He made a smile at the president and said humbly, "I contacted Human Resources, but they told me that only you have such authority. I'm sorry for bothering you."

"I can't help you. We do not support students quitting their graduate programs to go to America."

"I wish I could wait until I get my master's degree, but the opportunity comes. If I don't go to the United States now, there is no guarantee I will be able to go there in the future."

"That's your problem, not mine. I can't break our policy."

Policy? Since when did the institute have that? Just two weeks ago, your daughter left the institute for France without finishing her graduate studies here.

Thinking of that, he said without carefully choosing his words, "If the institute has such a policy, it is wrong. Our government has adopted an open-door policy allowing students to study abroad at any time."

The moment he had finished, he was surprised at his nerve in rebuking the president.

Dr. Liu's face flickered for a moment like he'd been shocked by electricity. Seeing his wide-open eyes and a dropping jaw, Xiang realized that he was in big trouble. No one at the institute, particularly graduate students, dared challenge the president. Xiang cleared his throat and softened his tone, trying to salvage the situation. "Sorry if I offended you. I didn't think when I spoke. It's not easy to get accepted as a graduate student in the United States. I don't want to miss this opportunity."

"You graduate students are extremely selfish. Our

country has made a significant investment in you and expects you to work for the country after you graduate. However, many of you are leaving the country to pursue luxurious lifestyles in western countries. It is not only a huge financial loss to the country but also a brain drain."

Xiang blinked at the man and nodded.

He has a point. I have received a free college education, and I'm halfway through my master's degree. It would be unfair to the institute and the country if I quit now and go to the US.

He took a step forward. "I'll come back after getting my PhD in America. It will benefit the institute."

"What a nice plan." Dr. Liu sneered. "Are you telling me that we should keep a position open for you indefinitely? I'm sorry. There's nothing I can do for you. The institute has decided not to provide support letters to graduate students." He flipped the documents on his desk closed. "You can leave now. I'm going to a meeting."

Leave? No, no. If I leave this room now, I'll not able to get the letter.

"I want to quit graduate school." Xiang blurted out in a hurry.

Dr. Liu widened his eyes and then squinted at him. "Are you sure?"

Xiang was not certain. If he quit graduate school, his personnel files would be transferred to his local community. Although Dr. Liu could not control him anymore, there was no guarantee that the community service center would write a letter for him. If that happened, not only would he be unable to study overseas, but also he might not be able to find a decent job, let alone return to the prestigious research institute.

Dr. Liu leaned back with his hands crossed under his

chin and spoke with the voice of a father to a son. "Young man, let me offer you some advice as a more experienced person, not as the President of the Institute. It's a terrible idea to quit the graduate program and leave the best research institute in the nation. So many people want to come here, but we only take the best. Think about it twice before you take this step."

The words touched Xiang's heart. "I love this institute, and I don't want to leave. Is it possible for you to write a letter for me? Studying in the United States will have a great impact on our younger generation. I'm sure you know it. Otherwise, you wouldn't send your daughter to France."

How stupid. He wanted to slap himself in the face the instant he finished the last sentence. How dare he compare him to the daughter of the president!

Dr. Liu's face flushed. "No. As I have told you, we do not allow students to go overseas before they complete their graduate studies."

Xiang realized that he had reached the point of no return and he would have no future at the institute. With no other way out, he straightened his shoulders like a hero. "In that case, I want to quit the graduate program."

The president frowned. "If you insist on quitting, you will have to pay back your tuition first."

"I will. How much?"

The president rolled his eyes as if searching for something. "Twenty thousand Yuan."

Are you kidding? Twenty thousand Yuan! Xiang shouted in his mind. *My parents make two hundred Yuan a month.*

****

Another rumble from his stomach pulled Xiang back

to the present. He put his passport into the backpack and went to the kitchen to look for food, but there was nothing ready to eat. Not having time to cook, he drank two cups of warm water to settle his stomach and went back to his bed.

Soon, he drifted off to sleep.

The sun rose, and he arrived at Huadu airport. The lobby looked like a huge football stadium. Thousands of people milled about and laughed loudly. After getting his ticket, he walked to Border Control at the far end of the building. As he waited in the line of a few hundred people, he smelled the delicious aroma of Peking Duck, a popular Huadu delicacy. He looked around and spotted a food counter by the wall.

His mouth watered, and he craved to have one last big Chinese meal before leaving the country, but he could not do it because hundreds of more people had already lined up behind him. He did not want to miss the flight just to have one more taste of Peking Duck. He swallowed and stayed in line. When his turn arrived, Xiang slid his passport through the small slot at the bottom of the bulletproof window and waited for the officer in a dark blue uniform to stamp it.

The man flipped through the pages for a while and then frowned. He gazed at his computer screen for a moment and then raised his head, staring at Xiang's face. "Is this your passport?"

"Yes."

"This passport is fake."

Chapter 4

Shan threw his cigarette to the floor, ground it with his foot, and returned to the rope. He grabbed both ends and pulled himself up as if he were doing pull-ups in a gym. He swung and twisted his body to test its strength.

Pretty sturdy. He nodded and then waved at Zhuzi. "Come here."

The young man got up and approached him.

"I just checked the rope, and it's very strong. It should be safe for people to climb."

"The rope has no problem. The problem is we're very tired."

Shan stared at the young man silently for a moment and then pointed at the group asleep by the wall. "Bring three strong people here."

"Why?"

"Just get them here for me."

The young man left and soon came back followed by three men with bloodshot eyes. Shan grabbed one end of the rope, handed it to them, and wrapped the other end around his own waist. "Grab that basket and brush for me," he said to Zhuzi. "I'm going to paint that beam."

The young man stared at him with wide eyes, as if surprised.

"Go get the basket and brush. If we don't finish it today, you will not get paid, at least not without penalty. You are tired, but I'm not. I can do it."

Shan felt compelled to help them. They had been working very hard on this project and were just one step away from finishing it. This task seemed straightforward, so he should have no problem completing it for them. Besides, the sooner they finished it, the sooner he could return to his dorm for a good night's sleep.

"No, I can't let you do that. You shouldn't take the risk. You're a city man." Zhuzi reached over to Shan, apparently trying to untie the rope. "I'll do it."

Shan pushed his hands away. "You have worked fourteen hours and are exhausted. I'm not tired. It's safe for me to go up there. Go get the things for me. The sooner we finish the work, the earlier we can go home."

The young man looked at him for a few more seconds and then left for the tools. While waiting for Zhuzi, Shan double-checked the rope around his waist, making sure it was firmly fastened. The young man returned with the basket and brush but did not hand them to Shan immediately as if still hesitating. Shan took the items from him and said to the workers, "Now, pull the rope."

No one responded.

"Do it. I'll be fine as long as you hold it tightly."

The young men started to pull the rope, and Shan ascended incrementally. When he was about halfway up, he looked down and instantly felt his leg shaking. The rope seemed to be around his neck, not his waist.

What am I doing? What am I risking my life for? This is Lei's business, not mine. It doesn't make any sense for me to take such a risk.

As the rope continued to drag him up, the thought of quitting grew stronger. With each inch closer to the ceiling, he felt one step closer to death. He did not want to die. He wanted to study in the United States like his brother and then return to his country with glory.

In fear and regret, he looked down, intending to signal the workers for his descent. Instantly, his legs trembled, and his chest tightened. To regain his composure, he turned to stare upward again.

I can't return to the floor with a sweating and trembling body, he said to himself. *That will make me a laughingstock among rural people. It will also disappoint my friend. I'm safe. It's not my time to die.*

Shan closed his eyes, letting himself be pulled up. His word was his honor, and his action his credit.

When he opened his eyes again, he saw several painted Chinese gods looking at him from the dome. Gods, I'm here to beautify the temple, the place where people worship you. Please bless me. He talked to them as though they understood him.

As he reached the ceiling, he focused his mind on the work. With each movement of his arm, he covered his fear with paint. Half an hour later, he finished the job and looked down again to signal the workers to let him descend. To his surprise, instead of four people who had originally pulled him up, a large group of young men was holding the rope. He glanced at the corner where they had rested and noticed that the place was now empty.

He waved at the people looking up at him as he descended from the ceiling. As his feet touched the ground, a young man thrust a bottle of water into his hand, another handed him a towel, and another helped him untie the rope from his aching waist. He felt like a brave astronaut who had just returned from space.

"Thank you very much…" Zhuzi's voice broke.

"You are the only one who has ever helped us." He paused again, tears in his eyes. "In the future, if you ever need us, just let us know. We will do anything for you."

The young man's tears and broken voice moved Shan so deeply that he realized how much his actions must have touched these poor country folks. Coming from the impoverished countryside, they must have rarely received any kind of respect in the metropolis. Feeling sorrow for them, he took some money from his pocket and handed it to Zhuzi. "All of you have been working very hard today. I don't have much, but this will help you buy some food for tonight."

The young man took a step backward. "We can't take that."

Shan grabbed his hand and put the money in his palm. "It's past midnight. Get them some food. They must be hungry now."

Zhuzi took the bills and shook Shan's hand, tears running down his cheeks. "Thank you. I will never forget your kindness. You are the only one who has ever respected us."

"Don't mention it. You were born in poor rural areas and grew up at the bottom of society. Now, you've come to the city to seek a better life for yourself and your family. Without any relatives or friends to help you, you must have encountered many hardships. But never quit. You will succeed in the end."

As they were talking, Lei returned. Upon learning that Shan had done the work for him, he looked at his friend with wide-open eyes. "Thank you very much." He turned to the workers. "You guys can go home now."

On the way out of the building, Lei asked Shan, "Why did you do their job?"

"They have been working long hours today and were exhausted."

"You are a college student from an intellectual family, but they are poor farmers from the impoverished countryside. When you did that for them, you lost their respect. Besides, it's too dangerous to go up there at midnight."

Shan smiled. "It's okay. I'm still alive."

Lei patted Shan's shoulder. "Buddy, I owe you one. Let's go have a drink. I know of a very nice bar near here."

Chapter 5

Xiang looked at the officer with wide eyes, his heart pounding in his chest. "It's not possible. I got this passport from the Huadu Public Security Bureau."

He saw the officer speak but could not hear a word. He shook his head and looked at the officer again, only to find everything blurry and fading away. In a second, the world became black.

"Oh, my eyes!" Xiang screamed out loudly, but he could not hear it. He attempted to rub his eyes, but his hands could not move.

"No!" he shouted again and woke up.

He glanced around and realized that he was not at the Border Control, but in his own bed. Sitting up and leaning against the wall, he tried to recover from the nightmare. A few minutes later, when he heard his stomach growling, he got up, put on his clothes, and headed to the kitchen to get some water to calm it down. As he opened the door, he saw his father squatting by his luggage and attempting to put something into it.

"Father, what are you doing?"

"I'm trying to squeeze this jacket into the luggage." Father turned to look at him. "You need it during the winter."

"You shouldn't do that. You need it for yourself. I can buy one in the United States after I get my research assistantship."

"In China, things are cheaper. Come help me put it in."

Xiang squatted down next to his father, and together they forced the jacket into the fully packed suitcase.

"Very good." Father stood up slowly, walked over to the small dining table, and sat down on a wooden chair. "Have a seat."

Xiang sat next to him and then heard the sound of water running in the kitchen. He turned to look at it over his shoulder. "Is Mother in the kitchen?"

"Yes, she's making breakfast for you."

Xiang glanced at the wall clock. It was four-twenty. "Did you two sleep?"

"A little. Don't worry about us. We will go back to sleep after you leave for the airport." Father shifted his weight. "Since you will be on your own in America, you should be really careful about your health. You should try to prepare your own meals. American food is not very healthy. Also, don't walk outside after dark. The crime rate in America is very high. Nothing is more important than your safety and health. If—"

"Breakfast is ready." Mother came out of the kitchen with a plate of stir-fried tomatoes and scrambled eggs. She set it on the dining table and then returned to the kitchen to get a bowl of hot milk and fried peanuts. On her third trip, she brought out a homemade sticky rice cake.

"Mother…" Xiang stopped, looking at his mother sitting across the table. What could he say? Nothing. No words could express how he felt. They had rarely had such a lavish breakfast. Steam bread, rice porridge, and a small dish of pickled vegetables were their usual meal.

"They are your favorite." Mother choked lightly. "I

will not be able to cook for you—"

Seeing tears in her eyes, he leaned forward. "Mother, cheer up. I'm going to the United States, not a reeducation camp in the countryside. I will return in five years with a PhD."

Over the past twenty years, Xiang had only seen his mother cry twice. Ten years before, his parents were sent to different rural areas thousands of kilometers away from each other for reeducation. His mother sobbed as she said goodbye to his father. Although Xiang did not understand why she wept, he later learned from his father that it could have been a permanent separation.

To avoid ruining his final moments with his family, he brought his recollection back to the present and began eating his breakfast. A third of the way through the meal, he pushed his chair back. "'I'm full."

He was not. He could finish all the food in no time, but he wanted to save some for his parents. They had not eaten well for a long time and probably would continue to live a frugal life. Even if he sent money back, they would put it aside to support his brother to study in the United States.

"Why do you eat so little?" Mother glanced at him.

"I'm just not hungry so early in the morning."

After chatting for a few minutes, Xiang got up and started to move his luggage to the stairway. Without an elevator, he carried two fifty pounds suitcases one floor at a time. His father lugged the small suitcase and his mother the backpack. When they descended to the first floor, Xiang saw a gleaming car under the streetlight. His girlfriend dressed in a pink shirt and a pair of blue jeans leaned against the driver's door like a movie star.

She approached his mother and reached for the

backpack. “Ayi, give it to me.” Ayi was a respectful term by young people to address middle-aged women.

“Mother, she is Miaomiao.” Xiang gestured at his girlfriend.

Mother removed the backpack from her shoulder and handed it to her. “Glad to see you. Xiang talked about you many times. He said that you are a sophomore in the Department of Music at Huadu University.”

“Yes.” Miaomiao took the bag.

“Thank you for taking him to the airport,” Mother said, looking at her without blinking as if trying to decide what kind of girl she was.

Miaomiao turned to Xiang’s father and then back at his mother. “Xiang will be away from home for some time. If you need any help, please let me know.” She handed a piece of paper to Xiang’s mother. “These are phone numbers for my home and my dorm.”

She then helped Xiang put the luggage into the trunk of the car.

“It’s a nice car,” Xiang said.

“It’s my dad’s.”

Miaomiao’s father was the president of a trading company.

After loading, Xiang approached his parents. “I'm leaving now. Take care of yourselves.” He turned to his father. “Father, you don’t need to save money for Shan. I'll get my assistantship next month, enough to support him to study in the United States.” He then looked at his mother. “Mother, I’ll come back to see you next year.”

“Don't return until you have earned your PhD,” Mother said softly. “If you do, there is no guarantee that you will be allowed to go back to the United States.”

“Your mother is right,” Father added. “The risk of

coming back to see us is too high. We will be fine, and you don't need to worry about us."

"We will see." Xiang nodded. "I have to go now."

He entered the car and waved to his parents through the open window until the vehicle made a turn at the end of the building.

An hour later, they pulled off the road into the airport parking lot and dragged their luggage toward the brightly lit terminal. They passed through the lobby and slowly walked toward the security checkpoint, the place that would separate them into different worlds.

At the entrance, Xiang held his girlfriend's face with both hands. "Don't cry. I'll write to you once I arrive in the United States."

She nodded quietly.

"Don't forget to sign up for the next TOEFL. Even though you have two more years to graduate, it wouldn't hurt to take it earlier. The scores are valid for five years."

She nodded again and wiped her tears from her face with her palm. Her mouth moved as though she tried to speak, but no sound came out. Xiang hugged her gently at first, then tightly, as if trying to squeeze her into his chest so that he could take her to the United States.

Chapter 6

The airplane took off from Huadu International Airport. Through a small window, Xiang saw the city shrinking and moving away from him. He waved to the land where he had lived for twenty-three years since he was born, promising to return in five years with honor and glory. As the white clouds blocked his view, he pulled down the window shade and leaned back with his eyes closed. An hour later, he heard someone speak and opened his eyes to see a female American flight attendant handing out drinks.

"What would you like to drink?" She smiled at the young Chinese woman sitting next to him.

"Apple juice."

The attendant poured the juice into a cup, handed it to her, and then turned to Xiang. "Would you like something to drink?"

He glanced at the cart for a second. "Origin juice, policc."

"Excuse me?"

"Origin juice, po-lice," he repeated his words slowly to make sure she understood him.

After blinking for a second, she turned to the girl beside him as if seeking assistance.

"I think he meant orange juice, please."

"Sorry, my hearing isn't very good today." Smiling, the flight attendant poured him a cup of juice and moved on down the aisle.

He set the drink on his tray table and thanked the young woman next to him. She looked like a college student in her early twenties. Her large eyes and her well-kept black hair reminded him of a Saturday night before he had quit the graduate school at the Huadu Institute of Physics.

It was in the graduate dorm, and all his roommates had gone home for the weekend. He sat at a table in his dorm, staring at a poster on a desk.

Do I really want to mount it on the University Triangle? What if my friends find out I did it?

He turned to stare out at the dark night through the window, tapping his fingers on the desk.

He shouldn't do that. That's way over the line. Xiang rolled the poster to store it but stopped in the middle. He couldn't quit. He had to do it. It was about his future.

Xiang continued rolling the poster. Instead of putting it away, he inserted it into his backpack, ready to leave for the Triangle. While he was getting up, he glanced at the old mechanical clock on the table to see what time it was. Eleven forty.

Too early. He shook his head and sat back. The library had just closed, and students were everywhere.

From his drawer, he pulled out the *Guide to Surviving in the United States* and read it. However, he had trouble focusing since his mind kept wandering to the poster and possible outcomes. Twenty minutes later, he heard the door rattle and turned. When he noticed someone unlocking the door, he immediately tucked his backpack under the desk.

The door opened, and his roommate Jiping came in, carrying a large cardboard box.

"I thought you had gone home for the weekend." Jiping set the box down on the table.

"What's in the box?" Xiang pointed at it.

"Posters advocating political reform." His roommate wiped the sweat off his forehead with his arm. "We're going to post them on the University Triangle message board. Would you like to join us?"

"It's too late now." Xiang shook his head, feeling lucky that he had not gone there. Otherwise, he would have run into his roommate.

Since China had opened its doors to the world, western political ideas and philosophies had infiltrated the country and influenced college students. They took to the streets, demanding political reform. At Huadu University, the University Triangle was the hottest spot where students expressed their political views and shared the news on a large bulletin board. Every day, hundreds of students visited the site.

Jiping took out some posters and then slid the box under his bed. "I have to leave now. I'm going to have a meeting and may not come back. Have a good night."

Xiang continued reading the book after his roommate left. A few minutes later, the door opened again, and his roommate Dong came in with a giggling girl. As soon as they saw Xiang, they stopped laughing.

"Sorry, I didn't know you were here," Dong said and then turned to the girl. "This is Xiang, my roommate. He is going to the United States."

Her eyes glowed with admiration.

"Xiang, this is my girlfriend, Lan." Dong put his arm around her shoulders. "She is a sophomore in the Art Department."

Xiang blinked. Which one is his real girlfriend, this

one or the girl from the Huadu Academy of Fine Arts?

Dong went to the windowpane to grab his cup with a toothbrush and toothpaste in it, took some clothes from his bed, and left with his arm around Lan's waist. He stopped at the door and looked back at Xiang over his shoulder. "Don't forget to write to me. After you settle down, we can set up a joint venture and do some international business together."

Thinking that Dong had been trading contraband TVs for the past few months, Xiang joked, "Don't tell me you want me to smuggle a color TV from America for you."

Dong laughed and left with his girlfriend, leaving Xiang sitting by the window alone. Gazing at the full moon, he contemplated his roommates and himself. They all graduated from Huadu University and were graduate students at the Huadu Institute of Physics, and all of them came from intellectual families. If China had not opened its doors to the West and instituted economic reforms, they might have lived very similar lives. Yet, the tide of unprecedented change was sweeping them in different directions, which would drastically alter their futures.

Xiang waited in the room for another thirty minutes and then left for the university with his backpack on his shoulders. After biking for twenty minutes, he arrived at the south entrance of the school. Two campus security guards checked everyone's IDs at the gate. To ensure the university's safety, only students, faculty, and other university personnel were permitted to enter. Even though Xiang had graduated, he had managed to keep his student badge.

After passing through the gate, he proceeded to the

University Triangle, which was located at the northwest corner of the busiest T-intersection leading to the main library, classrooms, and student dormitory compound. At the Triangle, a five-yard-long wooden board stood in a flower bed and was covered in posters and papers of all colors and sizes all year long. Many viewpoints were deemed to be westernized, unfitting for the country. Any time of year, whether it was freezing winter or scorching summer, there were always throngs of students on both sides of the board, some taking notes, while others chatting or even debating. A few lost-and-found notes and commercial flyers were posted on the bulletin board but were quickly covered by new political posters or thrown into the trash can next to the flower bed.

As he approached the intersection, he saw six students reading messages on the board. Not wanting to draw their attention, he made a right turn and headed toward the library. He pedaled around campus for twenty minutes and then returned to the Triangle. This time, the board stood alone in the night under the yellow streetlights.

No one was in sight.

He stopped in front of it, tacked up his poster in the most visible location, and then quickly pedaled away into the darkness.

On the way back to his dorm, he could not stop thinking about the content he had handwritten on the poster.

I graduated from Huadu University this spring, and I will be going to the United States to pursue my doctorate in the fall. Currently, I am single and looking for a girlfriend. If you are interested in knowing me, please contact my friend at...

To hide his identity, he used his friend's name and address. Two days later, his friend gave him a letter from Miaomiao, a junior student in the Department of Music at Huadu University.

Chapter 7

After more than thirteen hours of flying, the aircraft landed at San Francisco International Airport. Xiang passed through U.S. Customs and dragged his carry-on luggage through the crowded terminal, running toward the Arkansas gate. When he reached the waiting area, there was no one at the check-in counter. He rushed down the corridor and boarded the plane.

The moment he entered, he stopped and backed up a step, believing that he was in the wrong place. An American airplane couldn't be that small.

"May I help you?" A flight attendant smiled at him.

"Does this go to Arkansas?"

"Yes." She nodded.

Xiang had imagined that he would be in a big, crowded airplane with hundreds of people, but... Perplexed, he passed through the door and dragged his suitcase down the narrow aisle to his seat. Sitting alone, he studied the aircraft, trying to understand why it was so small and why so few people were on board. It was an American airplane, and he was going to Arkansas, a beautiful state. He knew it. He had seen its pictures in the brochure that the school had sent to him.

Unable to find an answer and disappointed, he closed the window shade and leaned back to rest. Gradually, he drifted off to sleep.

About three hours later, he was awakened by an

announcement that they were about to arrive in Fayetteville. He opened the window shade and gazed down. Instead of seeing skyscrapers and highways, he saw miles of dark green mountains, which reminded him of the impoverished countryside where his father had been sent for reeducation during the Great Cultural Revolution. As the airplane descended further, a small airport became visible. It looked like farmland in the middle of nowhere.

His heart sank. He sat back and closed his eyes again, refusing to believe what he had witnessed. He was going to study for his PhD in Arkansas, not to become a farmer in the countryside.

The intense vibration of landing on a small runway rocked him as if telling him to wake up from his delusion. After the airplane came to a stop, he followed the other passengers to the exit. The moment he saw the outside, he froze. Instead of connecting to a terminal, the plane parked a few hundred yards away from a small building that looked like a neighborhood grocery store in Huadu, and the whole airport was surrounded by steel wires.

Is this America? Is this where I am going to pursue my PhD? It can't be.

Hoping that the airplane had landed somewhere for refueling, he glanced around. His heart sank even further when he saw the Fayetteville Airport sign outside the steel wires.

Are you kidding?

He looked up at the sky as if questioning God.

No wonder the Chinese government has been telling us that millions of Americans are living in poverty. Compared with the magnificent Huadu airport, this one looked like a shabby museum depicting last-century aviation.

In extreme disappointment, he descended the stairs and followed the other passengers toward the small building. Rather than entering, they stood outside, looking at the airplane.

What are they doing? Why don't they go inside to get their belongings?

Xiang joined them and glanced at the wide-open field, unsure of what to look for. After a few minutes, a cart full of luggage pulled up in front of them, and the other passengers began to gather their suitcases. He grabbed his and followed the others out of the airport through a narrow opening between the steel fence and the building.

Before him, a two-lane road curled from east to west, disappearing on both sides behind forests and mountains. On the other side of the street, a gravel parking lot with a few old vehicles looked like a giant junkyard. It felt as if he had worked extremely hard, only to climb down instead of up the food chain. Seeing the bleak future ahead of him, he blamed his father for forcing him to come to such a horrible place.

While in China, he had applied to several graduate schools in the United States. The University of Northwest Arkansas was the first to accept him and offer him a research assistantship. It asked for a response within one month. He did not reply immediately because he was waiting to hear from other universities. However, after receiving multiple rejection letters, he gave up and accepted the offer. Three weeks later, he received good news from a better university and changed his mind.

“Don't do that,” his father told him. “Once you have

committed to the University of Northwest Arkansas, you should not change your mind just because you get a better offer. It's a matter of integrity and credibility. Your word is your honor."

He took his father's advice. After all, the University of Northwest Arkansas is an *American* university.

While he was regretting his decision, he heard someone calling his name. It was a young Chinese man.

"You must be Xiang." The man extended his hand. "I'm Yitan, a graduate student in physics. The Chinese Student and Scholar Association asked me to pick you up."

"Yes. Thank you very much for picking me up."

The handshake shook away the dark cloud in Xiang's heart.

Yitan grabbed one large piece of luggage and led Xiang to a black car parked along the roadside. They loaded all his belongings into the trunk and drove to the university.

Xiang gazed out of the side window. In the vast grassland, the road stretched for miles, and there were no tall buildings, no bustling commercial centers, nothing but horses and cows roaming about. After ten minutes, he noticed a long, white, one-story building without a single window in the middle of nowhere. With brownish rust all over, it looked old and shabby.

"What is that?" He pointed at it.

"A chicken farm."

"A chicken farm?" Xiang frowned.

"Yes. There are thousands of chickens inside. You'll see a lot of them. "Chicken farming is one of Arkansas' biggest industries."

Xiang remembered the reeducation camp he and his

father had been sent to during the Great Cultural Revolution. Not far away from the pigpen where they lived, there was a filthy chicken farm. The stinging mixed smell always made him nauseated.

He sighed and shook his head.

What a mistake! I gave up everything I had in Huadu and moved to the land of chickens.

Yitan perhaps sensed Xiang's feelings. "When I first arrived in Arkansas two years ago, I had difficulty accepting that I had spent so much time and money to come to such a small town. However, after living here for a month, I began to love this place. The people are very friendly, the cost of living is low, and there are no heavy industries. No pollution, but beautiful mountains and lakes."

That's a nice way to describe the backward countryside.

What he had seen not only disheartened him but also embarrassed him. He had promised his family and girlfriend that he would send them photos once he arrived at the university. Now, he had difficulty keeping his promise. The rural area would disappoint all of them. Miaomiao might even suspect that he raised chickens in Africa instead of studying for a doctorate in America.

Chapter 8

The next morning, Shan woke up a hungover with a headache. As he reached for his cup of water, he noticed his TOEFL book on the floor and remembered that he was supposed to take a TOEFL test at nine o'clock. He sat up abruptly to look at the clock on his desk. It was 9:30. Instantaneously, his headache throbbed as if it were about to explode.

Oh, no! What have I done!

He slumped back like a rock and buried his face in his hands, regretting going to a bar with Lei the night before the exam. When most students had gone home for the summer, he had stayed in the school to study for his TOEFL exam. Now, he had missed the test.

What was he going to say to his parents and brother?

He lay motionless in his bed. A moment later, he sat up again, checking his TOEFL preparation book to see if there would be another test before the deadline for graduate school applications. Lucky. There was one in three months.

He picked up the book from the floor, dressed, and headed to the library. From now on, he would fully devote himself to studying for the test and would not allow anything to distract him.

****

Summer break came to an end, and school began. In China, students are divided into classes according to their majors in the last two years of college. His class was going to have an outdoor activity at the beginning of the semester.

On the first Sunday, they went to Three Moon Lake, the largest lake and most beautiful sight in the province. Over the water, there was an island connected to the bank through an arched bridge. After hiking and boating for four hours, they went to the pavilion on the island to rest.

It was an ancient Chinese-style structure with a golden roof and six long, deep red poles that ran from the ceiling to the ground. The poles and the benches were woven together in a hexagonal pattern. Tired and hot, the students sat idly in the pavilion, some talking in small groups and some quietly staring out at the lake. Still too early to return to school, the class president asked everyone to suggest an activity that would engage the group so they could continue to enjoy the outing.

After several ideas were rejected, Shan stood up. "How about I show you my secret power?"

"What is that?" the class president asked.

"I can hear written words."

There was a loud buzz, then a huge hullabaloo of laughter.

"No, you don't." A girl chuckled.

"I'm serious. Did you watch the TV show, Hear Handwriting, last week? A young man demonstrated his power to a panel of scientists, and one of them said that one in ten thousand people has that ability."

"Yes, I did, but I don't think you can," she replied.

"Of course, I can. If you don't believe me, I can prove it to you."

"Show us," another girl urged.

"All right, I'll show you." Shan had prepared for this

game before the trip. He took a stack of paper and a bundle of pencils out of his pocket and handed them to the other students. "To hear your handwriting, I need a quiet environment. How about this? I'll sit here, and you sit there." He pointed to the benches far away from him. "Each of you writes one word or two on a piece of paper. Then fold it twice, write your name outside the paper, and place it here." He tapped the bench beside him. "I will listen to each of them one at a time."

"No. We don't trust you. We must watch you closely, so you won't be able to fool us." A student objected.

"If you don't believe me, you can take a video of me and examine it in slow motion later."

"Let him do it his way," the class president said. "We have thirty pairs of eyes watching him. I don't think he can fool all of us."

Shan sat down. "Good. Let's get started."

The pavilion became quiet, and the students began writing. After everyone put their writing near him, he picked up a piece of folded paper. "I'm going to start. Please do not make any noise during this process." He looked at the name on the paper and then at the group. "This one was written by Yanyan."

"Yes!" A pretty girl leaped up from her bench, jumping and clapping.

People looked at her, laughed, and yelled. After a few moments of excitement, she sat down, and everyone's attention returned to Shan. They watched him like detectives.

Shan pressed the paper against his left ear, then his right ear, and then his left again as if struggling. Several seconds later, he set the paper aside and looked at

Yanyan. “The word you wrote is *war*. Please don’t say yes or no. Let me hear the rest of them and then tell me if I got yours right.” He glanced at the other students. “And you as well. Please maintain silence until I finish hearing all the words.”

As he talked, he noticed the girl's disappointment. He ignored it and continued with the rest until he had finished. “Now raise your hands if I have gotten yours right.”

Everyone raised their hands except for Yanyan. Laughter and shouting erupted, and the students started debating.

“I have told you before that people can hear text,” a male student with glasses said to the people around him. The eyes, ears, and nose are all connected to the brain. Since different people have different connections, it makes sense that people can hear writing.”

“Agreed. I do believe he is able to hear our handwriting,” another student said. “I watched him very carefully throughout the entire process without blinking.”

Several girls flocked to Shan.

“How did you do that?”

“Did you trick us?”

“Is that real?”

Rather than answering the questions, Shan simply smiled at them.

Chapter 9

Shortly after they left the airport for Northwest Arkansas University, it began to rain. With raindrops falling from the sky and wind howling, the world seemed to be sobbing.

Who would not cry?

He had worked extremely hard to apply to graduate schools in America and left one of the most prestigious Chinese research institutes in hopes of a better life, only to discover that he would be living in the middle of nowhere with cows and chickens.

Refusing to accept the reality, Xiang closed his eyes, but he immediately opened them again and turned to face Yitan. “May I rest for a while? I’m exhausted.” He lied, afraid that his behavior would offend his new friend.

“Of course.”

As he tilted his head to the right, he saw a herd of large cows eating peacefully in the pasture.

How nice to be a cow. Nothing could disturb its life, not the dreary rain nor the depressing dark clouds.

Again, he closed his eyes, refusing to see anything. After quite a while, the car suddenly jerked, and he opened his eyes. The vehicle had stopped under a traffic light hanging from a cable like a criminal dangling from a rail.

Seriously? Is this really America? Traffic lights in Huadu are far better than these. They are held up by strong arms that reach out from sturdy poles.

"We are almost there." Yitan pointed to several old two-story buildings on the other side of the intersection. "I live there. Let's go to my home first. My wife has been preparing dinner for you."

Having dinner with his family? No one had ever invited him to a family dinner in his life.

Xiang turned to look at the new friend. In a foreign country thousands of miles away from home, a Chinese man picked him up from the airport and invited him for dinner. For a moment, he felt like he was in China rather than in America.

When the traffic light changed, Yitan turned left onto a two-lane street with a few buildings on either side. "We are at the university now."

What?

Xiang blinked and looked out through the window, trying to locate the campus' walls and gates, but they were nowhere to be seen.

That wasn't possible. Even China's universities were surrounded by concrete walls, with security guards posted at their gates. People had to show their school IDs to enter. America was a far more advanced country, and its universities should be much better protected than those in China.

Confused, he turned to his friend. "When did we enter the campus? I haven't seen a gate."

"It has no gate. In the United States, universities are not surrounded by walls. It is open to the general public. When I first arrived here, I was surprised too."

Yitan made a right turn, pulled into the parking lot of a residential complex, and led Xiang into an apartment. The moment Xiang stepped into the room, he heard piano music and saw a little girl about five years old playing piano across the living room. Her fingers fluttered over the keyboard like butterfly wings.

He had never seen a real piano before. In China, it was a luxury for the rich. He glanced around the room, trying to figure out how wealthy the family was. In the living room, a nine-inch TV sat on a wooden stand facing a worn couch, and an old dining table held several dishes. It appeared that the only valuable item was the piano.

A woman wearing a blue T-shirt emerged from the kitchen and extended her hand to Xiang. "Hi, I'm Fei. How was your trip?"

"Pretty good." He shook her hand.

"You must be hungry now. Food is ready." Then she turned to the girl. "Bonnie, time to eat."

Xiang followed her to the table. The large plates of tomato, egg, and black pepper, as well as beef and green pepper, made it seem like a holiday feast.

"Thank you so much for inviting me to dinner. This is so luxurious."

"Not at all. This is our usual meal." She looked at him. "Food in America is cheap if you cook it yourself. Then you spend only about ten percent of your income on food."

Really? Xiang blinked, thinking that Chinese families spent more than half their income on food, yet the quality wasn't as good as this.

"Housing is cheap too," Yitan spoke. "Ours costs two hundred dollars a month. "Yours is a hundred dollars."

A hundred dollars?

Xiang calculated quickly in his head. His research assistantship was ten thousand dollars. With the inexpensive food and housing, he should be able to save about seven thousand dollars per year. The saving would help him pay off his family's debts, improve his parents' living conditions, and sponsor his brother to study abroad. He smiled in his heart, feeling better for coming to this low-cost rural area.

During dinner, he learned that Yitan supported the whole family with his graduate research assistantship, and his wife stayed at home to care for their child. They spent most of their money on the girls' piano, violin, ballet, painting, and other activities.

What a lucky child.

Xiang cast a glance at her, remembering his childhood. At her age, he barely had enough food because of the nationwide Great Famine. Some claimed that it was caused by natural disasters, while others attributed it to government mismanagement of the economy.

Soon after dinner, the rain stopped, and a rainbow streaked across the clear sky. Yitan took Xiang on a ride around the campus to help him become familiar with it. In contrast to the disappointing countryside he had seen on the way to the university, Xiang found that the school was much better than he had expected. The azure sky and white fluffy clouds reflected off the glass walls of the buildings, and the well-maintained grassland with its ancient trees was everywhere. It seemed to him that he had entered a kind of fairyland. For several times, he was compelled to get out of the car and lie down on the grass, breathing the fresh air and looking up at the clouds.

After driving for a while, Yitan pulled into the parking lot of the six-story building. "This is your dorm."

"My dorm? I thought I would live in an apartment

with a new Chinese student.” Xiang blinked at his friend.

“I’m sorry, I forgot to tell you. As your apartment won't be ready until tomorrow, I've reserved you a room here for tonight. I'll take you to your apartment tomorrow.”

They exited the vehicle and walked to the rear. Yitan took out Xiang’s carry-on suitcase and backpack from his trunk. “Do you want to take the large luggage with you or keep it in my car?”

“If it is okay with you, I would like to leave it in your truck since I will only stay one night.” Xiang took the backpack and suitcase from his friend.

“Here is your key. It will open your room's door as well as the building's.” Yitan glanced at his wristwatch. “I have to go now. We're going to the movies tonight.”

After saying goodbye, Xiang rolled his suitcase toward the building's entrance. The moment he opened the door, a gust of cold air greeted him.

Wow, air conditioning.

Having never been in an air-conditioned room before and being tired from nearly twenty hours of travel, he was thrilled by the prospect of sleeping comfortably on a sweltering summer night.

He entered the building and came to a complete stop, his eyes wide and his mouth slightly ajar. He had never seen the lobby of a student dorm so grand, so high-ceilinged, and so clean. It reminded him of the luxury hotel he had seen in a movie. After a brief moment of shock, he gathered himself and dragged his suitcase toward the corridor that led to his room, keeping his eyes on the surroundings—the paintings on the walls, the couches, and the tables. He felt as if he were walking through a museum.

When he stepped onto the carpeted hallway, he felt softness under his feet, as if he were wearing a brand-new pair of sneakers. He took several steps on the carpet to relish the sensation before moving on. As he reached his room, he paused, trying to guess what it looked like.

At Huadu University, he and six other students had shared a room with a cement floor and two naked bunk beds on either side of the door. Their luggage was stacked on the top of one of the bunks. Outside the window parked hundreds of bicycles.

Xiang unlocked the door and pushed it open. The room was larger than his at Huadu University and had a desk and a bed with a thick, soft white mattress on each side. The golden evening light poured through the half-opened blind, creating large, distinct stripes on the carpet. As he looked out the window, he saw trees, green grass, and blossoming flowers.

The stark contrast between the simple, small airport and the rural country road and the fancy dormitory made him feel so much better. He took out his camera from his backpack and began to take pictures inside his room and in the lobby. He would send them to his family and girlfriend, showing them how wonderful his life was in the United States.

After returning to his room, he set the camera on the desk and dragged his suitcase to a bed. He took out his clothes, stacked them together to make a pillow for him, and then stretched out on the bed, reading *The Guide to Surviving in the United States*, the book that he had brought with him from China.

Gradually, he felt cold and developed goosebumps.

The air conditioner was blasting freezing air over his sweaty body. He got up, set the book on the desk, and followed a humming noise to a rectangular white box by the window, which was blowing cold air through its thin slots. He examined it from top to bottom and from side to side, trying to locate its power switch to turn the machine off. Unable to find it, he considered unplugging the cord but decided not to. The plug was behind the air conditioner, hard to reach. He was afraid that he could break the plug if he tried to pull it out of the wall or damage the equipment without properly shutting it down. It was his first day in America, and he did not want to cause any trouble.

Xiang went back to his suitcase and dug through it to find long-sleeved clothes, but he could not find one. All of them were in the large luggage in the trunk of his friend's vehicle. He sighed and walked to the window, staring at the red evening clouds and thinking about contacting his friend. However, he did not have Yitan's phone number and had no idea how to get to his apartment.

Hopelessly, he grabbed the shorts and T-shirts that were being used as a pillow and put them on. He jumped in the room for a few minutes to warm his frozen body and then settled down at the table to read *Out of Africa*, another book he had brought with him. Maybe the torrid African continent would warm his body.

Chapter 10

Xiang continued reading *Out of Africa*. The vivid descriptions of the scorching sun and desert warmed the chilly room. He no longer felt cold. As he fully immersed himself in the book, he felt something under his nose. He touched it with his finger and then looked at it. Snot. His nose itched, and he sneezed loudly.

He froze, not from the cold but out of fear. In the past, whenever he had caught a cold, his body had reacted with a fever, and it had taken him a week to recover. That was in China, and he could see a doctor and had time to rest. Currently, he was in the United States. He had no insurance, no money, and no time.

He could not let the frigid room bring him down, and he had to act.

Xiang got up, grabbed a 300-page novel from his suitcase, and headed back to the air conditioner. He tore a page off the book, crumpled it, and squeezed it into a slot that was spewing cold air. Then he removed another page and sealed another groove. He repeated the process until all the slots were filled. After that, he ran his hand around the air conditioner to check the airflow. No more.

Satisfied, he returned to his bed and curled up like a dead lobster with a small blanket partially covering his body.

Slowly, he drifted into a dream, in which he walked barefooted in a mountain covered in deep snow that stretched for miles and miles into the distance. The cold crept up to his legs, his waist, his chest, and his entire body.

Sneezing loudly, he woke up.

Xiang got up and checked the air conditioner again and found out that between the wall and the back of the box, a blast of icy air blew. He grabbed a few shirts and stuffed them into the cracks, and then jumped in the room and jogged in the hallway to warm his body. A few minutes later, he stopped. After nearly twenty hours of traveling across the world, he was exhausted and needed to rest.

On the way back to his room, he went to the bathroom and noticed a row of showers. Wondering whether there was any hot water, he stood to the side and turned on a shower.

It was cold.

He turned off the shower and walked away. Disappointed, but not surprised. Since the school had not opened yet, it made sense that there was not any hot water. In China, student dormitories did not have hot water at all.

As he walked down the hallway, a thought occurred to him. *Maybe I should let the water run a little longer.* He returned to the bathroom and turned on the shower again, feeling the water with his finger. One second passed, two seconds, and three seconds, and it was still cold.

Patient, be patient, he said to himself. Patience changes the world.

The world did not change, but the temperature of the water did. He turned off the shower and rushed back to his room to grab a towel and get changed. When he returned, he turned on the hot water and let it run down his head, neck, back, legs, and feet. As his body warmed up, he started to whistle *I Am Happy*, a Chinese melody.

America was America. Even in the rural countryside, students could take hot showers in their own dormitories. Chinese students did not have such luxuries. In a Chinese university, there was only one central bathhouse, and students had to walk quite a distance to get there. After enjoying the best moment of the night, he went back to bed and quickly fell asleep. When he woke up in the cold again, he took another hot shower. He repeated the same actions several times throughout the night.

By the time the sun broke the darkness, he got up and left the building for fresh, warm air. He stretched in the empty parking lot for a while and then ran along a trail. The dancing sunlight and the singing mockingbirds in the trees congratulated him for having survived a dark and freezing night.

He stopped at a small creek, stepped onto a boulder in the rushing water, and squatted down to watch the fish and shrimp swimming in the crystal-clear brook. They fled immediately as if they had been scared by his foreign face. He walked to the bank, picked up a dead tree branch, and returned to the rock, poking around to see if any more shrimp or fish were hiding in the grass or underneath the gravels, as he had done in his childhood.

Sixteen years before, his parents had been sent to different reeducation camps thousands of kilometers apart. His father and he went to the impoverished countryside in the east, and his mother and his brother to the poor mountains in the west. Near the shabby, small cabin where he and his father lived, a shallow, crystal-clear river ran from east to west. He was told that if he followed the river, he would be able to reach his mother. During the summer, after helping his father care for pigs, he walked west in the water for hours until he was stopped by the waterfall. Then he entertained himself by playing with fish and shrimp hiding beneath the rocks.

Laughter disrupted his recollection. He glanced back and saw two beautiful college girls jogging along the trail with their blonde ponytails swinging over their shoulders. So pretty and so energetic.

After they passed, he got back on the path and continued walking. Twenty minutes later, he reached the top of the hill. On the horizon was a red European-style building with a big bell tower. He had seen the picture of it on the cover of the brochure that he had received from the university where he was in China. It served as a symbol for the university. Further east, the crimson sun gilded the mountain peaks, piercing through the summits. As he watched the landscape, the bell rang, reminding him of his promise to write to his family as soon as he arrived in the United States. Hurrying back to his room, he sat down at his desk and wrote to his parents, his brother, his girlfriend, and his other friends. When he was finished, he put the letters into the envelopes he had purchased in China and walked out of the dorm to the post office in the Student Union.

"Good morning, may I help you?" A young woman behind the post office counter smiled at him.

Xiang had never seen a beautiful American girl from such a close distance before. Her blonde hair was neatly brushed and fell to her shoulders. Her blue eyes, crimson lips, rosy cheeks, and long, upward-turned black eyelashes reminded him of Hollywood actresses. She looked like one of the girls who had jogged in the trial. With his heart pounding like a drum, he glanced away, trying to avoid direct eye contact, but he still could not block out her existence. As her perfume drifted across the table and reached his nostrils, he wished he were invisible so he could gaze at her for as long as he liked.

"May I help you?" Her sweet voice brought him back to the present.

He placed his letters on the counter, smiling at her. "Oh, yes. I want to buy sex stamps."

"Excuse me?" Her face turned red, and her eyes widened.

"I want to buy s-e-x stamps." He spoke slowly and clearly, making sure she understood.

Chapter 11

The woman scowled at Xiang for a moment before walking over to a young man seated at the computer table a few feet away. She bent over and spoke to him in a voice that Xiang could not hear. The man peered at Xiang from time to time like a detective.

With wide-open eyes, Xiang stared at them, puzzled.

What happened? Why did they talk about him that way?

The man said something to the woman, then stood up and walked to the counter, trailed by her. "May I help you?"

"I…" Xiang took a deep breath, cleared his throat, and pointed at the envelopes. "I want to buy sex stamps for them."

The man stared at him for a moment before picking up the envelopes and counting them. A few seconds later, he raised his head to face Xiang with a friendly expression on his face. "Do you mean you want to buy six stamps?"

"Yes, yes."

Almost imperceptibly, the girl giggled. Following the stamp sale, the young man extended his hand to Xiang. "I'm Steve. I'm a student in business school. What's your name?"

"Xiang."

They shook hands.

"It's nice to meet you. Where are you from?"

"China."

"Welcome to America. A friend of mine is from China too. Are you a new student?"

"Yes, I came yesterday." Xiang considered asking Steve what happened a moment ago but decided against it.

They probably just didn't understand my accent.

"There is a church across the highway from the school," Steve said. "It offers free English classes to international students every Saturday morning. Would you like to come?"

Free English lessons? Why? How could a capitalist church offer anything for free? Something wasn't right.

Xiang had been taught since he was an elementary school student that religions were evil and that capitalists always exploited people.

Perhaps noticing his hesitation, Steve continued, "You don't have to attend Bible studies or listen to testimonies. You can just come to study English. By the way, I teach there."

That's why he invited me. He looks like a nice guy.

Xiang smiled at Steve. "Thank you for the invitation. I would love to attend the class. When is it going to start?"

"The Sunday after next." Steve wrote the church's address and his phone number on a post-it note and then handed it to Xiang. "Call me if you need a ride. I can pick you up."

"Thank you very much." Xiang folded the paper carefully and tucked it into his pocket.

"The class starts at ten and ends at twelve," Steve

added. “After that, we'll have a free lunch.”

Free lunch? No, no, no. There is no such thing. Even in communist China, there is no free food, let alone in capitalist America. Steve must have a hidden agenda.

Xiang became alerted.

After leaving the post office for his dormitory, he kept wondering why the nice girl had given him an enraged look. Suddenly, a thought struck him.

Sex.

The word sex flashed before his eyes like stars, as if he had been hit in the head.

Oh, No!

His face turned red hot.

What I have done!

He wanted to go back to explain to her that he did not mean sex, but six. However, he had no face to see them. Taking out the piece of paper that Steve had given to him, Xiang threw it in the trashcan nearby and ran back to his dorm.

In his room, he stood at the window, staring out at nothing with an empty mind. After a long while, he sat down at his desk and studied *The Guide to Surviving in the United States* so that he would not make foolish mistakes again. A few minutes later, his stomach growled, reminding him that he had not had breakfast. He ate two small packs of pretzels provided by the airline and continued to read until his friend arrived to help him move to his apartment.

His apartment was a white two-story building with a manicured lawn and a large tree. Two squirrels chased each other on the grass, sometimes only one yard away from Xiang as if he did not exist.

Lucky squirrels. If you were in China, you might

have been at the dinner table.

As he watched the little creatures playing, he heard his friend say. “Your room is on the second floor.”

He looked up at the window about twice the size of the one in his parents' apartment, feeling guilty for living in such a lavish place. “Are you sure the rent is one hundred dollars per month?”

“The total rent is two hundred dollars,” his friend explained. “You and your roommate will split the bill. He is a master's student at the Agriculture Department, and he will be here in two days.”

However, his roommate did not arrive as scheduled. On the first day of school, Xiang had a quick breakfast and left for the physics department. In the front yard, he ran into the landlord.

“Good morning, Xiang,” she greeted.

“Good morning.” He forgot her name. American names were difficult to remember.

“Your roommate can't come because he is having difficulty getting a visa.”

“Oh…” He blinked at her, mouth open and heart sinking. What should I do if she asks me to pay the whole rent?

She seemed to notice his concern. “Don’t worry. You'll only pay one hundred dollars regardless of whether he comes or not.”

He felt relieved, but also confused. How was it possible for people in this capitalist country to be so kind? He thanked her and headed toward the school again. When he reached the classroom, he saw several students, mostly international students, sitting quietly. Because of his poor listening skills, Xiang chose to sit in the first row so that he could hear the professor more clearly.

Minutes later, a middle-aged man in a red T-shirt, dark blue shorts, and sneakers walked into the room with a folder in his hand. He placed it on the podium and spoke slowly like a turtle walking.

"Good morning. My name is Nelson, and I will teach you thermodynamics."

Was he a professor or a substitute?

Xiang had not expected an American professor to dress like that and have trouble speaking. While feeling sorry for the teacher, he told himself that he had had a really lucky day—he had understood every word the professor had said.

As he was thinking, Nelson continued, "Since many of you are new to the country, I will speak slowly for the first two weeks so that you will be able to understand the lecture and get used to my accent."

Which country am I in? Xiang blinked at the professor. *Is this the United States? How could it be that people in this capitalist country are so nice?*

America, the land of greed, began falling apart in his mind and was replaced by the smiling faces of kind people. The contradiction between what he had witnessed in the past few days and what he had been taught for over twenty years left him confused. For a moment, he even wondered whether he was dreaming.

Three days later, while walking along the hallway of the physics department on his way home for lunch, he overheard two students talking to each other.

"Do you know there is free food today?"

"Where?"

"Student Union."

Xiang threw a glance at them, blinking.

Free lunch again? How was that possible?

Although he had difficulty believing it, he decided to check it out. It would be nice to have a free lunch. However, on the way to the Student Union, he felt embarrassed. In China, decent people did not go after free food, only beggars did. He was a PhD student in physics, and he had his dignity and self-esteem. He considered changing his course, but curiosity and the need to save money for his family compelled him to keep going.

Chapter 12

Shan had thought that the students' excitement over the game that he had played on hearing written words would fade away after a night of rest, but it did not. The next day, it returned in full force and continued for days. His popularity increased each day as more girls became fascinated by his special ability and grew interested in him. The story of his amazing aptitude quickly circulated across the Electrical Engineering Department. Even professors asked him about his unique talent.

The thrill of fame made it difficult for him to concentrate on his studies. Even when he was preparing for the TOEFL, he could not help but delight in the admiration he received. In the end, he decided to avoid the other students by leaving his dorm early in the morning and returning late at night.

One evening three weeks later, as he walked back to the library from a student dining hall, someone called him from behind. It was his friend Meng, the head of the Communist Youth League in his department.

Meng waved him down. “Shan, where have you been? I’ve been looking for you since yesterday.”

“Oh? Why?”

“There was an election for a new student body president.”

“Oh.” Shan patted his forehead. “I forgot all about it. Who won?”

"You."

Shan chuckled. "Don't make fun of me."

"I'm serious."

"How could anyone vote for me? I didn't even run for president."

"We're surprised too. Although you were not on the ballot, you still won the election. "We've never seen anything like this before." Meng took a breath. "Since you didn't run for the presidency, we need to know whether you're interested in the office."

Am I?

Shan hid his true feelings with a stoic expression on his face. He knew that his friend spoke to him on behalf of the Communist Youth League, which would make a final decision on the election outcome.

He had never dreamed of being the president of the student government. It was like an unreachable star in deep space. Shan had not run for it not because he was uninterested in it, but because it was too lofty for him. Now, the star had fallen into his hand. It would be a lie to say that he did not want the position, but he could not show his thrill as that could be interpreted as power-hungry. Besides, he was unsure whether he should take it. The good thing came at the wrong time as the next TOEFL was only two months away.

As he was thinking, his friend said, "Just to let you know that Wei placed second. If you don't want to be the president, he will be." Meng stepped forward a little and lowered his voice. "The following is off the record. Many students don't want him to serve another term, and neither do we."

Shan did not like Wei either. After winning last year's election, that man managed to get himself a private room while the rest of the students shared a room with six others.

Hating the idea that Wei might be reelected, Shan asked, "May I think about this tonight and get back to you tomorrow?"

"Sure."

They chatted for a few minutes more and parted ways.

Shan changed his direction. Instead of going to the library, he went to Little Moon Lake, one of the favorite spots among the students. Each morning, they went there to study, and every evening, they strolled around the lake in groups, relaxing and enjoying the scenery.

As he walked along the shoreline trail, he pondered the issue. His preparation for the next TOEFL exam was so tight that he could not afford to waste even a single thought on the possibility of becoming president. However, the position was so alluring that he could not stop himself from considering it.

Accept it? Yes or no?

It was so difficult to decide. Rationally, he should stay away from it and focus on applying to study in the United States, but emotionally, he wanted it. Popularity appealed to him, and he enjoyed the feeling of being surrounded by people. It was so difficult to decide. Rationally, he should stay away from it and focus on applying to study in the United States, but emotionally, he wanted it. Popularity appealed to him, and he enjoyed the feeling of being surrounded by people. The presidency provided both.

When he reached a large boulder by the water, he stepped on it and gazed at the reflection of the setting sun and the red clouds in the calm water. A moment later, he picked up a pebble and threw it into the sky. It flew toward the sun, curved in the air, and then splashed into the water, creating vibrant ripples that danced in the crimson sunlight around its landing spot.

How nice it was to be the center of attention. As he stared at the scene, the waves gradually faded away, and the water returned to its former state as if nothing had happened.

Shaking his head, he returned to the trail. The presidency was a lot like the rock that had created a center around which ripples cheered. Sadly, the moment lasted only a short time, and now it was buried in mud at the bottom of the lake. No one even knew it ever existed.

That was not what he wanted for his life. Going to the United States to get his PhD was what he should do.

He made the decision and headed back to his dormitory to tell Meng about it. When he approached the campus bookstore, he saw from a distance that Wei was chatting with several female students who were holding ice cream and laughing by the table right outside the building.

He took a detour without thinking. As he strode away from them, the girls' giggling and Wei's howling laughter grew louder in his ears.

Shaking his head, he tried to get rid of them, but it did not work.

Perhaps because of jealousy or something he did not know, Shan decided to be the president. He had convinced himself that he could prepare for the TOEFL and manage the student government at the same time and was confident that he could accomplish both as long as he worked efficiently.

Thus, he became president. In the weeks that

followed, he threw himself into his duties in the hope that, once the organization was up and running, he could devote himself again to his studies. He spent all his spare time recruiting new members and organizing parties and other events. Gradually, in the excitement of his new life, he completely forgot about the test until he received a letter from his brother. It said that a professor at the University of Northwest Arkansas would be willing to admit him as a graduate student if he met the school's minimum TOEFL requirements.

What great news. Although Shan had been preparing for the TOEFL, he had been worried about the fierce competition. As so many people sought to study in the United States, the universities had become incredibly selective, only admitting those with the highest TOEFL scores.

The letter dampened his enthusiasm for the student government. He thought about rearranging his priorities, resigning from the council, and devoting his time and energy to achieving TOEFL success, but he rejected that idea. It would make him look untrustworthy.

The next day, he convened a meeting of the student council. "Thank you for giving so much of your time and energy to the student government over the past few weeks. We have accomplished many very good things. Now it's time for us to form committees, with each of you serving as chairman. This will allow you to reach your full potential."

The proposal was unanimously approved, and committees were established. Following the meeting, he created a large poster listing the committee chairmen's names and responsibilities and pinned it to the dormitory bulletin board in the hope of establishing public accountability for the chairmen, which would motivate them to carry out their duties and relieve him. All the committees functioned perfectly well without him, and he was able to focus on the TOEFL. Although glad to be out of the busywork, at times he felt a little wistful as if he were an unnecessary appendix to the organization.

One day, he was called in to see Mr. Gudong, the associate chair of the Communist Party Committee at the Department of Electrical Engineering, responsible for monitoring student ideology.

Unlike other school officials, he actively sought out opportunities to interact with students. He ate in the student dining hall at least twice a week and attended many student activities. Despite this, there was always an invisible barrier between him and the students. They found him impenetrable. He exhibited no emotion, not even a smile or a twitch of the eyebrow. Even when students burst out laughing, his face hardly moved, and he remained as stiff and unbending as a tree.

"How are you doing?" Mr. Gudong motioned for Shan to take a seat across the red-brown table from him.

"Pretty good." Shan sat on the edge of the chair, leaning slightly forward with his hands crossed under the table, wondering about the purpose of the meeting.

On the desk, two small red flags of China and the Chinese Communist Party were joined at a golden pole, forming a V in victory.

Mr. Gudong glanced at them, then back at Shan. "Last week, we had a long discussion about you."

About me?

Out of nervousness, Shan rubbed his sweating hands under the table.

"We have contacted your high school classmates

and teachers, and we have sent people to your parents' employers to learn more about your parents, their histories, and their current circumstances."

Why did they do that? What did they want?

Shan's palms began to sweat as he became more nervous.

"We studied your grandparents' personnel files."

My grandparents? Why? Why did they do all of these? What are they after?

Shan felt a jolt of fear in his chest, and he heard his heart pounding.

One of his grandfathers had been a senior member of the Nationalist Party that had ruled China before the Communist Party had taken over. The two parties had fought each other for thirty years, resulting in millions of deaths. After the Communist Party won the civil war, the offspring of the defeated nationalists were denied access to higher education and jobs. During the Great Cultural Revolution, many of them were branded as counterrevolutionaries and beaten to death. Although the country had changed, fear of punishment still lingered among many nationalist descendants.

Shan glanced out the large window behind the associate chair. Dark clouds roiled the sky, and crimson leaves on the trees were whipped by the wind like blood.

He sensed that a storm was approaching.

Chapter 13

The courtyard of the three-story Student Union was packed with students. On the side, opposite to the entrance of the building, was a makeshift black stage, on which several people were playing guitars. On the other two sides of the courtyard, students sat at tables, talking to their visitors. A hundred yards away from Xiang, there was a long line from a table piled high with large brown boxes. Two girls were handing out food from the boxes.

Instead of joining the line immediately, he walked into the crowd in front of the stage and pretended to listen to the music. Through the corner of his eyes, he peered at the food to see whether it was free. It would be extremely humiliating for him to wait in the line only to discover that he would have to pay for his meal. Xiang could not afford to eat out. He had to save money to pay off his family's debt, improve his parents' living condition, and sponsor his brother to study in the United States.

At the table, one of the girls picked up a thin slice of bread from an open box and placed it on a food tray being held by a young man. He said something to her and left without paying. Xiang continued to watch until he was convinced that the food was indeed free.

How is that possible? This is America, a capitalist country.

Carrying the question in his mind, he joined the line,

keeping his head low so that no one would recognize him. Going after free food was embarrassing. In China, no decent person would do that. He wished the line would move faster so he could grab the food and get out of there as soon as he could.

When he reached the table, one of the girls smiled at him. "Which pizza would you like?"

Which one?

Having never eaten pizza before, he did not know which tasted better.

"Would you like one of each? We have pepperoni and cheese pizza."

"Oh, yes. One of each."

After receiving his two slices, he walked away from the table into the shade of a big cottonwood tree, where he devoured the pizza like a wolf and finished them in no time. Then, he went to the nearest table to check what was going on.

"Hi, how are you?" He greeted a man standing there. "What is going on here?"

"We are recruiting for our amateur basketball club. You're welcome to join us."

Was he kidding?

Xiang looked up at the students behind the table, all of whom were about a head taller than him. He thanked the student and moved to the next desk.

"How are you? What do you guys do?"

"We are a student newspaper," a man sitting at the table answered. "We are currently accepting applications, and you are welcome to join us."

By this time, Xiang understood that each table represented a student organization, and they were recruiting new members. He stopped at one after another, trying to decide which one to join.

"Hi, how are you?" he asked a group of three girls. "What do you guys do?"

"We're a sorority," a girl answered.

"What's sorority?" He had never heard of such a thing.

She stood up and explained in a thick Southern accent.

Although he had difficulty understanding her, he still nodded and smiled. After she finished, he asked if he could have some of the materials on the desk. He wanted to learn more about the club to see if he would fit in.

She handed him four sheets of paper, and he stuffed them into his backpack before walking over to the last table.

"How are you? What do you do?" He looked at a tall, muscular male student in a black T-shirt.

"We are…."

Xiang had trouble understanding him. He could not tell if it had been the student's accent, or the speed with which he spoke, or the choice of unusual words, or all of the above.

After finishing speaking, the student extended his hand. "I'm Owen. What's your name?"

"Xiang."

As they shook hands, Xiang felt the warmth and strength of the student's handshake.

"We … movie tonight … free … Would you … us?" Owen added.

From a few keywords, Xiang deduced that the club would host a movie night and he had been invited. Although he was hesitant because he had a lot of homework, he accepted the invitation. It was an excellent opportunity to make some American friends and improve his English.

Owen wrote something on a piece of paper and handed it to Xiang. "… my phone number …."

Xiang inserted the paper into his pocket, thanked the new friend, and left for the physics department, rejoicing. The sky seemed bluer, the clouds whiter, the wind softer, and even the squirrels were friendlier. They scurried about in the grass near him, fear-free.

Was this a capitalist, money-greedy America or a land of free food, free movies, and free from fear? Xiang became more confused as if he was trying to piece together a jigsaw puzzle through a pair of distorted glasses.

Forget about it, just enjoy your life.

He worked in his lab until evening, then ate a quick, simple dinner, and headed for the Student Union. When he reached the movie theater on the third floor, the door was closed, and no one was around. Assuming that everyone was probably already inside, he pulled the door. It did not open.

Why was the door locked?

Xiang frowned and looked at his watch. It was fifteen minutes before the film started. He went to the empty lounge, sat down at a nearby table, and pulled out his physics textbook from his backpack. He tried to study, but he kept glancing around to see if anyone had come. Five minutes passed, then ten, then twenty. Still, no one showed up.

What was going on? Did they cancel the movie?

He finally stood up, took out the note that Owen had given him, and read it. Too bad. He had made a wrong assumption. The movie was not playing at that theater but in a different one. He hurried out of the building, asked for directions three times, and arrived at the location.

What was this?

He fixed his gaze on the gray four-story building, a structure that looked more like a dormitory than a movie house.

How was that possible?

A second later, he convinced himself that Owen had intended for them to meet at the dorm and then go to see the movie together.

He entered the building, followed the directions to a room on the second floor, and knocked. The door opened, and Owen smiled at him. “I'm so glad you came. The movie has started.”

What? A movie in this tiny room?

Rather than walking in, he stood still in the doorway, regretting that he had not found more about this before accepting the invitation. He wanted to watch a movie in a real theater, not in some student's dorm room. He considered leaving, but that would be too rude. He had no other choice but to watch the film with them.

He stepped into the darkness, and the door closed behind him. The light from the small screen lit up the room enough for him to see the other students huddled together on couches. While he waited for his eyes to adjust to the dimness so that he could assess the situation, he saw two men on the screen sitting on a sofa in a luxurious room, drinking wine and talking. A moment later, they set their glasses aside and began hugging and kissing each other.

The blood shot up to Xiang's head, and he felt dizzy

and out of breath. He turned toward the door, trying to flee, but Owen was leaning against it.

Chapter 14

In the dark, Xiang's eyes had not adjusted to see who was in the room and what they were doing, which increased his fear of being attacked at any moment. His chest started pounding fast, and he could feel sweat coming off his forehead and hands.

I must get out of here before it's too late.

He turned to Owen, who was blocking his path. "Excuse me. I have to go to the bathroom."

Owen gazed at him for a second and then stepped back from the door. Xiang opened it, and through the hallway light, he saw Owen's face twitching. As he slipped out of the door, he heard the student say. "Thank you for coming."

Xiang sensed that he had hurt Owen's feelings, but that was the least of his concerns at that moment. He had to leave the room as soon as possible.

While outside, he bent over and rested his hands on a large tree, repeatedly opening his mouth as if about to vomit. Nothing came out. His stomach turned, and his head throbbed. He leaned over the tree for some time before walking to the physics department. He needed something to calm him down, to erase the memory of the dark room and the movie. Doing research was his most effective remedy. He could find peace and forget about everything unpleasant in the lab.

He rambled down the street with his head lowered,

unaware of his surroundings until he heard a woman's voice. Xiang looked up and saw his friend Cecelia standing by her red car in the parking lot of the physics building. She was a blonde girl from California who was pursuing her master's degree in physics. Her sporty figure and large eyes were more striking than ever.

"Are you all right?" she asked.

"Yes, I'm fine. I'm fine."

Xiang caught a whiff of her scent and felt compelled to hug her. He had never touched her, not even thought about it, but now every single cell in his body needed her.

"I'm going swimming. Do you—"

"Sure," he replied before she had time to finish her sentence. He knew what she was going to say because they had gone swimming together many times.

He climbed into her car and leaned back on the soft leather seat. Like a suffocated person taking in oxygen, he inhaled eagerly the aroma of her perfume. He wished that she would take all the wrong turns and never arrive at their destination so he could sit beside her forever.

Cecelia, unlike in the past, did not talk as she drove. Ten minutes later, they pulled into the parking lot of the recreation center. After swimming for a while, they competed as they usually had done. He swam the butterfly, splashing the water as if an eagle were trying to escape from an alligator attack. For the first time, he miraculously beat Cecelia.

When they finished the competition and took a break at the end of the lanes, she removed her goggles and looked at him. "What happened to you tonight?"

"What do you mean?"

"You looked awful when I saw you in the parking

lot."

He related the incident with Owen to her, and she listened silently.

"Are there gay people in China?" she asked after he finished.

"I don't think so."

"I'm sure there are. The public just doesn't know about them. Most homosexuals are nice, good people. The only difference between straights and homosexuals is how their genes develop."

"I'm not against them, but I don't feel comfortable being with them."

Cecelia's face jerked as if she had been stung by a needle.

"Are you all right?" he asked.

"I'm fine. I forgot to tell you that I'm a lesbian."

Xiang's jaw dropped. "I'm sorry. I didn't mean to offend you. I'm so sorry."

"It's all right." She shrugged. "I understand how you feel. In high school, I hid my sexual orientation from everyone, thinking that it was shameful and disgraceful, but not anymore."

After that night, the word homosexuality no longer frightened Xiang, and he and Cecelia grew closer. They swam together more often and even had dinners at each other's apartments.

Christmas break approached, and most students left for the holidays. As a teaching assistant, Xiang had one more lesson to teach. After setting up the equipment for the planetarium show, he sat in the room, waiting for a group of elementary school students to arrive and thinking about what he would do for his first Christmas.

Twenty minutes later, he stepped out of the room to

the window, gazing down at the snow-covered parking lot below. He wondered whether the students had changed their schedule and failed to inform him. After all, Christmas was coming, and it had been snowing.

He returned to the room to turn off the equipment, but when he touched the switch, he stopped. He had nowhere to go. His empty apartment would make him homesick and depressed. Rather than shutting off the power, he started a program and sat in a chair, watching the stars and galaxies swirl across the domed ceiling. The white stars streaked across the black sky like snowflakes, reminding him of the story of *The Little Match Girl*, who froze to death on a white Christmas.

After half an hour had passed, he turned off the equipment and walked out of the planetarium, ready to leave. At the door, he saw two women and a group of kids approaching.

"I'm terribly sorry we're so late," a short brown-haired woman said. "Our bus had a problem,"

"That's okay." Xiang felt lucky that he had not gone home. Otherwise, he would have disappointed them.

"Can we still watch the planetarium show?" the woman asked. "It took us five hours to get here."

"Five hours?" He uttered it, not meaning to question her.

"Yes. We are from Jonesboro."

Xiang was speechless and deeply moved. Children had traveled several hours to see the planetarium show on the snow day. He let them in. Instead of showing them only one program as he was supposed to, he showed them two and encouraged them to ask questions.

After the show, the brown-haired woman approached him. "Thank you so much. It's very educational for the kids." She extended her hand. "I'm Eva. Where are you from?"

"China." He shook her hand.

"That's a wonderful country."

After chatting for a moment, they left, leaving Xiang alone in the empty planetarium. He turned off the machine, checked the room to ensure everything was in place, and then walked out. As he descended the stairs, he saw the women come back.

"Did you forget something?" He reached for the keys in his pocket and was ready to go back to the room with them.

"No," Eva said.

No? Then why does she come back? Why is she looking at me like that?

Chapter 15

The wind picked up, and the crimson leaves outside the windows swayed furiously. Mr. Gudong opened a folder and flipped papers before pulling one out. He read it briefly and then looked at Shan. "According to the file, your grandfather was a high-ranking member of the nationalist government."

The words reminded Shan of his cousin, who had been expelled from college after the school discovered that his grandfather had been a senior nationalist official.

What are they going to do to me?

He gazed at the associate chair, waiting for the verdict, throat dry.

Mr. Gudong sipped tea from a white mug imprinted with the red Communist Party flag. "It's not your fault to have a nationalist grandfather. You can't choose your grandfather."

Shan felt a rush of relief but was more perplexed as to where all this was leading to.

The associate chair set down his cup. "Yesterday, after a long discussion and serious consideration, we decided to invite you to join the Chinese Communist Party."

What? Did he say that they want me to become a member of the Communist Party? No, it was impossible. I must have misheard.

The party membership was by invitation only and

was a priceless ticket to high social status. The earlier a person joined the party, the higher the person could climb, and college was the earliest possible time to join.

Perhaps noticing the perplexed look on Shan's face, Mr. Gudong said again, “We have decided to invite you to become a member of the Chinese Communist Party.”

Despite that assurance, Shan still found it hard to believe.

One year before, on a stormy Chinese New Year’s Eve, his brother had told their parents during a family dinner that he was thinking about joining the Chinese Communist Party.

As soon as he said it, a bolt of lightning ripped through the black sky, and thunder rumbled through the house as if the heavens were startled.

“Why?” Mother stopped eating and gazed at Xiang. A potato fell from her chopsticks onto the table.

“If you are not a member, your career will go nowhere. Look at the country. All leaders are party members.”

Mother picked up the potato and put it in her bowl. “Earning a doctorate in the United States is more important. It will help you get a good job.”

“That's not good enough. I may become a professor at a prestigious university, but to advance my career, I must be a member of the Communist Party.”

Mother stared at him for a second. “Don't —”

Father interrupted. “Let’s talk about it later.”

Throughout the dinner, nobody brought up the subject again.

Shan’s first assumption was that his parents had discouraged his brother because his grandfather had been beaten to death during the Great Cultural Revolution.

After he overheard their conversation, he understood the real reason.

"I've ruined Xiang's future." Mother said sadly to Father in their bedroom. "He will never be allowed to join the Communist Party." A long pause. "When I was in college, I tried to join it, but no matter what I did, I was never invited because my father was a nationalist congressman."

Mother's emotions and words were deeply engraved into Shan's heart. He realized that neither his brother nor he would ever be able to get into the elite organization. He understood why his parents had pushed them so hard to go to the United States. They simply did not have a future in China.

While he was thinking, Mr. Gudong sipped his tea quietly, as if giving him time to process the information. After a while, the associate chair put down his cup and looked at Shan. "I know this comes as a shock to you. We didn't make this decision lightly. We have observed all students since they started university."

He froze, taken aback for a moment by the realization that he, like the other students, had been watched from the start, then relieved that he had not yet done anything that would come back to haunt him.

The associate chair continued, "We are glad to see that you have a high moral standard and the ability to lead. As student government president, you continued to live in a shared dorm room with other students instead of moving into a private room, as your predecessor did. You set up several committees and have successfully run the student government with little participation." Mr. Gudong paused for a second. "We believe you will be a great addition to our party."

Shan was delighted to have been invited to join the ruling party, but something still bothered him. It all had happened too fast and too easily. He felt as if he had been given a big prize without having to earn it. Too good to be true.

Mr. Gudong picked up a sheet of paper from a light brown folder on his desk. He glanced at it briefly and then looked at Shan. "I heard that you have been applying for graduate studies in the United States. Is that right?"

"Yes." Shan wondered where the conversation would lead.

"Given the opportunities that are available to you here and your leadership potential, you will have a much brighter future in China than in the United States." Mr. Gudong placed the paper back into the folder. "The Great Cultural Revolution has created a leadership vacuum. Most of our government officials are in their fifties or older, and they will be retiring in the next ten years. It will be a once-in-a-lifetime opportunity for you. After joining the Communist Party, you will become one of the few young members with a college education. If you stay here, you will have a much better chance of being promoted to a high position than others in your generation. However, if you go to the United States, your chances will be much slimmer. After you get your degree and return to China, you'll find that many of the key positions have already been filled by other young people." The associate chair stopped, reaching out to the red party flag and speaking to it. "We are rebuilding our country, and we need the younger generation."

Shan nodded while he listened. Maybe Gudong was right. China was undergoing a historic economic transformation, which provided him with tremendous opportunities to make a difference. Perhaps he should remain in China and ride the wave of change that was sweeping the country. He did not enjoy research anyway.

He gazed at the red flag that was within his arm's reach for a few seconds and then turned to the associate chair. "Thank you for your advice. I will stay in China."

The moment he told Mr. Gudong about his decision, he saw two birds flying out of the red trees and pecking furiously at the window as if warning him.

Chapter 16

Eva said to Xiang, "We would like to invite you to spend Christmas with us."

He was not sure whether he had heard it correctly. In China, people did not invite a stranger into their homes.

"You said that you had no plans for the holiday, so we'd like to invite you for Christmas," she added.

Xiang was excited at the prospect of spending his first Christmas with American families rather than alone in his apartment. As he was about to say yes, he remembered the incident of attending a homosexual club activity. Although his opinion about homosexuality had changed, he had learned to think twice before accepting an invitation.

They barely know him. Why were they inviting him to their homes for Christmas? What was their real purpose? America had the highest crime rate in the world. What if—

While he was thinking, a little blond-haired boy came running up to Eva and stood next to her, looking up at Xiang with large green eyes.

"This is my son, Benjamin." Eva wrapped her arm around the boy's shoulders.

Xiang recognized him. During the planetarium session, he had asked where the center of our galaxy was, how far away it was from Earth, and which star was the furthest one that the human eye could see without a telescope. He was always polite and respectful, raising his hand before asking questions and thanking people afterward.

The family must be decent. Otherwise, they wouldn't have such a good boy.

Without further hesitation, he accepted the offer.

“Thank you.” Eva smiled broadly as if she were invited by Xiang.

She wrote something on a piece of paper and handed it to him. “This is my phone number. I’ll pick you up on Christmas morning.”

On the morning of Christmas Day, Xiang sat alone by the window in his living room, watching the snowfall and waiting for Eva. Gazing at the fluffy white world with no footprints, he remembered the previous Chinese New Year in Huadu. It had been a heavy snowy day, and his family had gathered around their small dining table to make dumplings.

“This is your favorite.” Mother looked at Shan while wrapping dumpling dough around blended red tomato and yellow eggs, the color of the Chinese flag. “Do you remember the first day you came home from Grandpa’s? I made a dozen different kinds of dumplings for you. But unlike your brother, who liked chives-and-pork dumplings, you only ate the ones made with tomatoes and eggs.”

Shan was born in the city but was sent to live with his grandfather in the countryside soon after his birth because raising two children during the nationwide famine was too expensive. In 1958, the Chinese government launched the Great Leap Forward, an economic and social campaign aimed at modernizing the country and building a robust communist society. To placate their higher-ups, local officials claimed they had boosted grain production a hundredfold. They forced the peasants to uproot their crops and relocate them to areas where the central government would visit. All crops died after the inspectors left, but the local officials were promoted.

The following year, the country was ravaged by a severe famine. Government officials said that it was the result of natural disasters, while many people believed that the Great Leap Forward was responsible. Over ten million people died of starvation during the three-year Great Famine.

While Xiang was thinking, a black van pulled off the street and created two long, parallel tracks on the pure white snow all the way to his apartment. Eva came out of the vehicle with Benjamin and a big man. Xiang carried his luggage down and met them at the door.

“Merry Christmas, Xiang.” Eva gestured at the man. “This is Andrew, my husband.”

After a brief exchange of greetings, Andrew pointed to two large suitcases. “You don't have to bring so much stuff. Just bring your clothes and personal items. We have everything else you need.”

Xiang returned the luggage to his room, came back with a small suitcase, and then entered the van, heading toward Jonesboro.

Three hours later, Andrew pulled the car off the freeway onto a narrow, bumpy dirt road in the woods. Sitting in the vibrating vehicle and watching the zigzag path disappear a few yards ahead, Xiang felt as if he were in an ancient world, isolated from modern society. The feeling of unease crept into his mind. He wondered why they lived in such a primitive land. Twenty minutes later, a one-story house appeared at the far end of a large gravel yard. The baby Jesus and his mother Mary glowed in the darkness near the front door.

The scene reminded him of a movie in which a character wandered into a strict religious area and mysteriously died. His unease grew stronger.

The car stopped in front of the house, and he followed the family inside, keeping a watchful eye on the surroundings. In the hallway stood a cabinet with two glass doors, two rifles on the right side and one on the left. Xiang stared at the guns, wondering why there was only one rifle on the left side and why the family possessed weapons. In China, it was illegal to own a gun.

While he was thinking, he noticed a long case with a big bottom leaning on the wall next to the cabinet. It was solid black and large enough to fit a rifle inside.

Here it was. That explained why there were only three guns in the cabinet.

The glowing religious figures outside the isolated house and the weapons, especially the one in the dark case, chilled him from the inside out. Massive goosebumps broke out all over his body. He regretted coming to this house in the middle of nowhere without consulting with his American friends first, or at least, telling them where he was.

As he was thinking, Benjamin turned to look at him over his shoulder and walked back next to him, pointing at the weapons. "They're my father's."

"Why does he need so many guns?" Xiang asked, regretting the words as soon as they were out of his mouth, afraid that he had asked the wrong question at the wrong time in the wrong place. He remembered a proverb *curiosity killed the cat*.

"He likes to collect guns," the boy answered. "It's his hobby. He believes everyone should have the right to own guns." He paused. "But my mom disagreed. She says that guns are the source of all the killings in this country."

The boy's explanation and his innocent expression relieved Xiang's worry. He proceeded to follow Benjamin into the living room.

"This is the fireplace." The boy pointed at the fire as if he were giving a museum tour. "It is my father's favorite place. He reads here all the time."

Xiang glanced at the flames, remembering the piles of lumber he had seen outside the house.

Which century was it now? They still used wood to heat the house.

When he glanced away from the fire, he noticed three large red socks hanging from the mantel.

Why did they hang such big red socks over here? Who had such huge feet? The family was so strange.

Chapter 17

"Would you like to look at your room?" Benjamin asked.

"My room?" Xiang was surprised that he would have his own room during his time with the family. In China, his family never had spare rooms for guests. When relatives had come to visit, he and his brother had to sleep on the floor in the living room.

"Yes. It's for guests."

The boy led him down the hall to a room with a queen-size bed and a wreath hanging on the wall high above the pillows. "My mom vacuumed the room and washed all the bedding for you."

"Thank you." Xiang stared at the green wreath with red balls and then at the white bed and pillows under it, afraid to step into the room. In China, when someone in the family died, the loved ones dressed in white and arranged wreaths around the deceased's room.

Who died in here? Was that bed used by the dead person?

While he hesitated, he heard Eva call for dinner. As he followed the boy to the dining table, he kept glancing back at the room, afraid that he would have to sleep there for the next few days. It was ominous to live in a place where someone had died.

After they sat down at the dining table, Benjamin asked, "Have you ever had a Christmas dinner?"

"No, this is my first time."

Glancing at the table with golden roasted turkey, mashed potatoes, gravy, cranberry sauce, and many other dishes, Xiang remembered the best meal he had ever had fifteen years before.

During the Great Cultural Revolution, he had followed his father to a reeducation camp in the remote countryside, where they barely had meat or eggs in their daily diet. One stormy summer morning, his father woke him up before sunrise. "Do you want to eat fish?"

Xiang rubbed his eyes, checking whether he was dreaming.

"Do you want to eat fish?" his father asked again.

"You got fish?" He jumped out of his bed.

"We'll go to catch some."

"Where?" He sat down, disappointed.

"In the East Lake."

"Dad, how can we catch fish? We don't have tools." Xiang looked out at the water pouring from the sky. "Besides, it's raining so hard."

"That is why we will catch some today. It has been raining for many hours. The lake must have overflowed. If we go now, we will have a good chance of catching some."

They put on their raincoats and departed, carrying a basin. At the East Lake, they stopped at a crack from which clear water poured out. Father glanced at it. "Let's wait here. This is a good place to catch fish."

Twenty minutes later, a fish about a foot long was flushed out of the crack and bounced across the grass, thrashing violently. Father kicked it further away from the lake, preventing it from bouncing back in. Instead of seizing it right away, they waited until it lay still. Then they put it in the basin and took it home. They boiled the fist with water and salt, turning it into the most delicious dinner Xiang had ever tasted. After they returned to Huadu a few years later, Xiang tried many times to prepare fish in the same manner as they had done that night, but he had never been able to match the taste.

While he was thinking about it, he heard Andrew say. “Give me your hand.”

Why? Xiang turned to look at the man whose hand was waiting for his. What did he want to do? Palm reading?

He glanced at the others. When he saw that they were all holding hands, he remembered a movie in which a religious group in a remote tribe had roasted a wild pig around a campfire. They held hands in a circle, danced, and yelled, thanking God for giving them the food.

That would be interesting, he thought and put his left hand in Benjamin's and his right in Andrew's, expecting to stand up with them, hopping around the table, shouting and cheering. However, they did not rise. They remained seated, with their heads bowed.

“Let's pray,” Andrew said solemnly.

Everyone closed their eyes except for Xiang, who was curious to look at the family. He had seen people pray before meals in movies, but he had never witnessed it in real life. He inspected their looks, feeling funny.

“Thank God for….” Andrew began.

After a few seconds, thinking that his behavior was quite disrespectful, Xiang bowed his head with his eyes closed. Having worked extremely hard and lacking sleep in the past few days, his head got heavy the moment he shut his eyes. It grew heavier with each word Andrew spoke. The rhythm of Andrew’s voice was like an old nursery rhyme, droning on in a lullaby. The longer it went on, the heavier Xiang's head got, and his chin dropped wider toward his chest. He jolted awake as he lost his balance. Embarrassed, he glanced at the family to see if they had noticed. Fortunately, all of them were still praying, eyes closed.

Not wanting the same thing to happen again, he lowered his head and closed his eyes, biting his lip to let the pain keep him awake. After what seemed like a perpetual prayer, he heard the word *Amen* and felt Benjamin and Andrew release his hands. He took a deep breath and opened his eyes.

As the meal started, Xiang watched Eva, mimicking what she did. He sliced three pieces of the turkey, placed them onto his plate, and then popped one into his mouth with a shining silver fork. He wrinkled his nose. The meat was not nearly as appetizing as he had anticipated, and it was also far too dry.

Looking at the large golden bird, he wondered why the two countries were so much different, even in their holiday meals. In China, dumplings are served as the main course at Chinese New Year’s dinners. They are small and made by wrapping meat and vegetables in flour dough. However, a turkey is big and starch is enclosed by meat in the form of stuffing.

As he was thinking, he heard Eva ask, “Do you like the turkey?”

He raised his head and saw everyone looking at him, apparently waiting to hear his opinion.

“Yes, it’s delicious. I love it.” He lied to make the family happy.

Although the meal was not as delightful as he had expected, it was the best one he had ever eaten in the

United States. After dinner, they sat near the fireplace and a Christmas tree, sipping coffee and chatting. Sitting across from the mantel, Xiang kept glancing at the red socks dangling above the fireplace and wondering why they were so big.

Even Andrew, the largest person in the family, did not have feet that size. Besides, they were far too colorful for a man.

"Do you like the stockings?" Benjamin looked at him.

"Yes, they're pretty," Xiang complimented. "Whose socks are they?"

The boy laughed. "Nobody's. They're for Santa Claus. He'll come at midnight."

"Why does Santa Claus need the socks? Why do you put them there?"

Xiang realized that he had asked a stupid question. Of course, those socks were hanging there to dry. What else could they be doing?

"We hang them near the fireplace because Santa Claus will come into the house through the chimney. It is easier for him to put candies in the stockings."

Ha, another stark contrast between the two countries.

In China, people set off fireworks at midnight to scare away the monster Nian. They believe that the beast comes out to steal their poultry on Chinese New Year's Eve. In America, however, people hang socks on their fireplace for Santa Claus, who comes to fill them with presents at midnight on Christmas.

Two bright yellowish lights outside in the dark woods caught his attention. They moved across the yard and stopped at the window.

"Let's go. Henry is here." Andrew put on his heavy coat, picked up the dark case next to the gun cabinet, and walked out.

Xiang had not expected that they would go out at night, let alone with the weapon.

Where are we going? Why do they need a gun on Christmas night? Who is Henry?

He wanted to ask where they were going, but he dared not speak for fear of giving himself away. As he was alone with the family in the middle of nowhere at that hour of the night, he had no choice but to follow them to the door. As he stepped into the frigid darkness, the only things he could see were snowflakes falling in front of the two bright beams and Andrew with the black case in his hand.

Chapter 18

Shan had a strange dream, in which he was wandering through a mountain wilderness in search of a treasure called the Future. After months of climbing up and down and crossing swift-flowing rivers, he came to a fork in the road. Five large golden stars blazed down from the dark sky, illuminating the crimson forest to the left. Fifty small white stars sparkled from the inky black space, beaming down on the blue prairie to the right. Taken aback by this bizarre world, he stopped and stared at the scene that looked like the flags of China and America.

Where should I go?

"This way." A young woman beckoned to him in the blue woods.

"Don't listen to her. This is the right path." An elderly man on the left waved. "Trust me."

The man looked familiar to him, so he took a step forward and instantly fell into a bottomless abyss. He awoke, gasping for breath.

Not wanting to disturb his roommates, he crept out of the room softly with a pack of cigarettes. In the hallway, he lit a cigarette and took a drag, pacing back and forth and thinking hard.

Should I pursue a doctorate in engineering in America or stay in China to ride the wave of economic reform? It's a pivotal moment in my life, and it will determine my future. I can't afford to make a wrong decision.

He exhaled smoke and kept thinking.

Universities had been shut down during the ten years of the Great Cultural Revolution. To reconstruct the country, the government was urgently searching for talented future leaders from current college students. It was rumored that a delegation from the central government visited his school a month ago, looking for potential hiring of a graduate with an engineering background. If he stayed in China after graduation, he would have a good chance of working for the central government. That would be a fantastic start to his career.

He paced to a window and continued to think as he gazed at the moon.

But, what about his parents? They were expecting him to go to the United States, just like his brother, and they had kept telling him that becoming a scientist was the best and safest career path for him.

Unable to decide, he decided to toss a coin. If it faced up, he would stay in China, otherwise, he would go to America. The coin landed face-up on the floor. That was it.

The next afternoon, he went to see Mr. Gudong, telling the man that he would not go overseas to study but remain in China to participate in the great reconstruction of the country.

"You have made the right decision." The associate chair nodded and then walked up to his bookshelf. He pulled out three books and handed them to Shan. "I suggest you thoroughly study them. Having a natural leadership talent is not enough to make you a future leader. You must have a solid theoretical foundation."

Shan looked at the books. Two of them had been written by the founding father of the communist government, Chairman Mao, and the other by Shaoqi Liu, the second-highest official in China until the Great Cultural Revolution. Then, he had been branded as the number one anti-revolutionary in the country and died miserably on a bare wooden bed with decubitus all over his body and human waste beneath him. After the Great Cultural Revolution, the government restored his reputation, proclaiming him a great communist.

Shan solemnly took the books with both hands, as if they were weapons with which he could protect his country.

From that day forward, he read each book line by line, underlining important words and jotting down thoughts and questions in the margins. Every night, when he left the library with the book in his heart, the moon shone brighter, the sky was clearer, and the air was more pleasant.

By the time he had finished reading all of them, he was a changed man, strong, resolute, and fearless. He believed from the deepest core of his heart that communism was the best system for humankind, in which everyone was treated equally, and people would get whatever they needed. He had discovered the meaning of his life.

At the party's induction ceremony, Shan raised his left fist and pledged through his heart and teeth to a red flag of the Chinese Communist Party that he would devote his life to the great course of Communism.

The wave of excitement overwhelmed him the whole day and well into the night. Unable to sleep, he wrote to his family at two o'clock in the morning.

Dear parents,

I have some exciting news for you. A few hours ago, I joined the Chinese Communist Party. I'm the only student party member in the physics department.

I'm sure you will be proud of me or even find it difficult to believe, but it is true that I'm a member of the Chinese Communist Party. I know that both of you tried to join it but failed because my grandfather was a congressman of the nationalist party before the communists took over the country. I know neither of you believes that your children can join the elite organization, but I made it. The country has changed, for the better and for the best.

A few days later, he received a call from his father. "Shan, we have received your letter. Mother and I congratulate you, but—" He paused. "but, the next TOEFL is critical for you. You have failed the test once. Please don't make the same mistake twice. Don't let anything distract you from the right path."

"Don't worry. Joining the Communist Party will not affect my studies." Shan did not tell his father that he had decided not to go to the United States out of fear of disappointing them.

"You should stay away from politics," Father continued. "Don't forget about what happened to your grandfather. Before 1949, he was the president of Jianghong University and a nationalist congressman. Shortly before taking over the country, the Communist Party persuaded him to remain in the mainland by offering him a more prestigious position in the new China. Therefore, he did not go to Taiwan with the other nationalists. Several years later, however, he was ousted from his post in a political movement and tortured to death during the Great Cultural Revolution. Don't trust any promise from anyone."

"I knew that. But it's history. Our government has already declared the Great Cultural Revolution a disaster and will never allow it to repeat."

"You never know," Father said. "You are too young to understand politics. History always repeats itself. In politics, any promise is meaningless. Besides, as a politician, your career advancement is determined by whom you follow rather than how much you offer to society. If you are on the winning side of a power conflict, you get promotions. Otherwise, you will end up in prison, regardless of how much you contribute to society."

"Then, I will follow the right person."

"In many cases, there is no right or wrong. It's just a power struggle among factions. When you get a job, you have to listen to your immediate supervisor. If you don't, your career will stagnate. However, if you follow him, and he loses a power fight, you'll go down with him. We are ordinary people, and we don't have connections. If you get into trouble, no one can help you. Go to the United States to get a PhD. That's your best choice."

"Father, you worry too much. The country is changing, and the trend is irresistible."

Shan ignored his father's advice and warnings. He was determined to dedicate his life to the good of the party and the country. He had been sworn to a communist flag, and his personnel files had been sent to the upper echelons for clearance. It was just a formality that he had to go through. Nothing could go wrong. He would become an official member of the ruling party in one month.

As he had expected, three weeks later, he received a letter from the Communist Party committee of the electrical engineering department. Excited like a bull before bullfighting, he opened the envelope, drew out a piece of paper, and read it.

After careful consideration, the communist party committee of the electrical engineering department at Xihe University has decided not to admit you as a party member.

What?

Shan froze, blood rushing into his head and his heart ceasing to beat. *Impossible, it's not possible, how can it be?* His head buzzed, and his entire body trembled so violently that he had to grip the edge of the table to steady himself.

Chapter 19

Xiang entered the minivan and slid into the seat next to Benjamin. The van followed the white car out of the yard and into the dark woods, jolting along the rutted road. Snowflakes glittered in the beams of the car's headlights, obscuring the view. The engine purred and the windshield wipers swished hypnotically back and forth, brushing away the snow from the glass. Through the side window, Xiang stared out at the black winter world, questioning why they went out in the middle of Christmas night with a rifle and the real reason for inviting him for Christmas. It was not uncommon for outsiders to be used as scapegoats for illegal activities.

As he was thinking, he heard Eva singing *Jingle Bells*, then all of the family together. The cheerful rhythm blew away his cloud of suspicion. Even the mundane movement of the windshield wipers came to life, swinging back and forth like two batons leading the family chorus.

The dramatic change in his mood surprised him with how powerful music could be. He felt an impulse rush inside him, an urge to join in, to share in the holiday spirit, but, he was unable to do so. All of the songs he had learned were to express gratitude to the Chinese Communist Party and Chairman Mao. He sat quietly and listened, wishing someday he and his family could travel in a car and sing holiday songs.

When the music stopped, Benjamin turned to him. "Would you like to sing with us?"

"I don't know how to sing American songs." He sighed in the darkness.

"Do you play an instrument, like a guitar?"

"No." He shook his head.

To Xiang, musical instruments had been something of a fantasy. He had never before had the opportunity to even lay his hands on one. When he first started elementary school, the Great Cultural Revolution swept the country. He spent most of his time fighting on the streets or running to assemblies to watch government officials or scientists being humiliated in public. After his family was sent to the countryside for reeducation, he helped his father raise pigs or ran around in the mountains with his dogs to hunt for anything edible.

Benjamin's family sang again, and this time, it was *We Wish You a Merry Christmas*. The music reminded Xiang of a news broadcast on the Chinese Television Network, in which several young people wearing Western-style clothing sang the same song in celebration of Christmas. In the middle of it, a group of middle-aged people emerged from nowhere. They chanted, "Down with Christmas!" and "Resist Christmas!", as they waved large placards proclaiming that Christmas was a Western cultural invasion.

"Here we are," Andrew's voice broke Xiang's thoughts.

He looked out through the window again and saw that the vehicles were pulling off from the country road. When they stopped thirty yards from a one-story house decorated with Christmas lights, two adults and two boys came out of the white car. The boys pulled out two large dark cases from the trunk, and Benjamin took his black case from the van and joined the other boys. They stood side by side, facing the house, with their parents behind them.

What are they doing?

He remembered a movie in which a firing squad stood side by side and shot people standing against a wall. He stared at the boys and the cased rifles in their hands, his heart racing, afraid to blink. The boys set the cases on the ground and took out long objects.

No!… Xiang screamed inside.

He trembled, gasped, and glanced around, trying to identify the direction to flee.

Loud sounds broke the silence. It was not gunshots, but Christmas carols being played by boys on guitars.

Xiang took a long breath, hands on his chest.

The yellow lights at the apex of the porch were turned on, and an old couple came out slowly. Standing at the front door, the aged man supported the woman with one hand and leaned on a pillar with the other. Together, they looked at the group quietly.

Xiang felt a surge of warmth rush through his body and wanted to join the group, but he did not know anything about the Christmas music. Standing behind the two families, he listened to music and admired the house's decorations, allowing the holiday spirit to permeate his body and his heart.

Following the singing, the two families waved Merry Christmas and Happy New Year to the old couple and got back into their cars, driving into the darkness. A few minutes later, they stopped at a distance from another building and performed holiday carols again. In the snow and wind, they traveled from family to family, playing Christmas carols for them.

After they came back from the trip at midnight, Xiang took a hot shower and lay on his cozy bed. Although he was exhausted, he could not fall asleep. His Christmas night experience conflicted with everything he had been taught his entire life. If he had not experienced it himself, he would never have believed that the capitalist Americans were willing to stand in the snowy night to bring happiness to others.

He rolled over, trying to clear his mind and get to sleep, but another scene popped into his mind.

A few days before Thanksgiving, feeling lonely and in no mood to study, he had attended a dance party at the Student Union. When he arrived, the party was already in full swing. Leaning against the wall, he watched people dance. In the dark, white, red, blue, and orange dots flickered everywhere, on the floor, on the wall, and on the people. If no one else had been present, he would have chased the dots to release his loneliness.

Four beautiful blonde girls entered the room, walked past him, and began dancing, swaying, and stepping a few yards away from him. Their revealing necklines, exposed thighs, and the perfume drift created by their motions were transformed by the music into a powerful sensation that penetrated into his flesh, his bones, and his soul. Every single cell in his body had been stimulated and was vibrating in synch with their movement. It reached the point where he could no longer bear being so close to them. He turned and walked away.

As he reached three yards from the loudspeaker, he closed his eyes and swayed to the beat of the music, one piece after another, until someone lightly tapped his shoulder. He turned and saw a tall American young man.

“Hi.” The man smiled at him.

“Hi.” He stopped dancing.

“How are you?”

“Good,” he responded, believing that the person was trying to stop his craziness.

“I'm Chad. Would you like to join us?” The student gestured to a group of four young women and three young men standing a few yards away.

“Sure.” Xiang had no idea why he had been invited, but it did not matter to him. Making new friends would relieve him of loneliness.”

He spent the rest of the night with them and discovered that they were all undergraduates from different colleges and that they attended the same church.

Xiang's Thanksgiving and Christmas experiences warmed his heart even more. How wonderful, how kind, and how thoughtful these Christians were to strangers like him. In the warmth of his heart, he felt safe and cherished. He closed his eyes and soon drifted asleep like a baby in his cradle. He had a dream, a sweet one, in which he got married and had children and grandchildren in this kind, sunny country.

Chapter 20

Two days before the start of the spring semester, Eva's family drove Xiang back to his school. At the driveway in front of Xiang's apartment, Eva hugged him goodbye. “Thank you for spending Christmas with us.”

“Thank you for having me. It was a wonderful experience.”

Eva looked into his eyes. “Do you know why we invited you for Christmas?”

“No, why?” Xiang had asked himself the same question throughout the winter break.

“Before Christmas, on our way to the planetarium at the university, I heard God tell me that I would meet someone and should invite him for the holiday. When we were listening to your show, I realized it was you.”

Xiang felt funny. There was no God. He had been taught for more than two decades. Yet as he watched Eva’s disappearing car, he felt as if God were right there with him, and like Santa Claus, so nice and so friendly.

That night, he had a dream, in which he saw an old man and a young man, both dressed in green military uniforms with red armbands, stomping into an ancient temple.

“There is no God. Religion is opium.” The old man pointed at a statue of Buddha, a Chinese god. “This should be destroyed.”

The young man swung a large club with his full

strength and knocked off the head of a ceramic Buddha. He kicked the head across the floor, where it slammed on the wall and shattered.

"See, it isn't God. It's a piece of porcelain." The old man laughed.

Another person came down from the sky. She looked like Eva. "There is a God. God loves us and wants us to care for each other."

"No, there is no God. It was created by a special group for the purpose of controlling humankind." The young man smashed the remains of the Buddha into scraps.

"No!" she screamed, trying to stop him. "Don't do that. Respect God."

"Don't be stupid. God does not exist," the old man shouted.

The escalating controversy awoke Xiang.

"Stop it!" Xiang sat up with a splitting headache. "Could you two stop it? I don't know whether there is a God, but if there is, it is my PhD advisor who awards me my degree."

Xiang did not have time to investigate the truth about religion. He had to rest. He would have two classes the next morning and would have to go to his lab in the afternoon to make up for the lost time during the winter break. After having too much fun over the holidays, it was time for him to get back to work, not to ponder God.

To fall asleep, he counted numbers in his mind and finally drifted off to sleep with one dream after another. Sometimes, he flew in the sky, asking an eagle whether there was a God, and other times, he dove deep into the ocean, discussing religions with a whale. He even went into space, searching for God.

After a long and busy night, he awoke fatigued at 6:30 in the morning. He took a shower to refresh himself, ate breakfast to replenish his energy, and then headed off to school, still preoccupied with the questions about religion.

At the door of a classroom, he noticed several new students sitting quietly. Without thinking further, he walked to the back and sat in a corner, continuing to think about God. A few minutes later, he noticed a professor walking into the classroom, a different one.

He stared at the blackboard absent-mindedly. Sometimes he thought that there must be a God. Otherwise, how can we explain the perfect order of the universe? The earth rotates around the sun, the moon orbits the earth, and electrons revolve around a nucleus. At other times, he rejected the idea. If there is a great and all-powerful God, why can't he prevent starvation and brutal wars? Why can't he design human beings who can live forever in perfect health? Why can't he create a world in which animals don't have to eat others to survive?

As he was thinking, a student who looked like an undergraduate raised her hand and asked a question. Xiang blinked at the equations on the blackboard and realized that he had made a mistake. He stood up and headed out of the room with his head low. As he passed the professor, he whispered, "Sorry, I'm in the wrong class."

In the hallway, he remembered Jing and felt terrified about himself.

Jing had been his classmate at Huadu University. They took quantum mechanics together in their junior year. Jing had difficulties understanding why, instead of changing continuously, the state of matter changes at intervals in the quantum world. He kept thinking about it day and night. The harder he thought, the more confused he became. His appetite went away, he lost weight dramatically, and he could barely sleep. Finally, he dropped out of school for one year.

Xiang did not want to become Jing. He could not afford to take a year off, not even a semester. He needed the assistantship and, more importantly, he must maintain his student status. Without it, he would have to return to China.

To get out of the terrifying state of mind, he decided to skip classes that day and went back to his room to relax. However, the fight between the atheist and the believer in his head continued. To distract himself from the mental struggle, he vacuumed the floor, wiped the furniture, and reorganized his belongings, but none of this worked.

Hopelessly, he reached for his book *Guide to Surviving in the United States* on the bookshelf, trying to read it, hoping that would distract him. When he opened it, a photograph of his family fell from within. As he bent over to pick it up, he met his father's gaze, which reminded him of a conversation with his father.

"I'm stressed," he had said to Father. "I don't know what to do."

"Let your feet help you make the decision," Father said.

"What?" Xiang blinked at him.

"Even though feet and heads are at opposite ends of a person's body, they are connected," Father continued. "The brain serves as the command center, and the feet help generate wisdom. In Chinese medicine, there are many acupuncture points on human feet, and each is linked to a specific organ. For example, several points on your toes are connected to your eyes, ears, nose, and even your brain. If a person suffers from a headache, a doctor can relieve the pain by massaging the patient's feet. If people are weary, instead of getting a full body massage, they go to foot services to have their feet massaged." Father stopped for a second. "In western countries, health specialists have listed walking as the most effective exercise because it burns excess calories, but that was only part of the whole story. The other part was that during walking, the acupuncture points on our feet got massaged, which stimulated our brains and enhanced our subconscious thinking. So, walking allows us to tackle challenging problems from different angles."

Thinking of his father's advice, Xiang decided to take a walk on campus, letting his feet do the thinking for him. As he passed two American students on a quiet trail, an idea struck him. Instead of debating whether God existed, he should learn about American culture first and let the rest take its course. Living in a student dormitory with an American roommate would be the best way to start.

The next day, rather than cooking his own lunch, he went to a fast-food restaurant a few blocks from the campus. Most people thought that the Statue of Liberty represented the United States, but he disagreed. He considered the statue the symbol of the American political system, but fast food represented American culture.

He marched down the street to the restaurant and ordered two big combos. He knew that they were a little too much to eat, but he purchased them anyway. A ceremony was a ceremony. It had to be powerful and exaggerated. He would eat them all to demonstrate his determination to embrace American culture. He devoured the first meal. Tasted great. He managed to finish the second hamburger, feeling more than full. He stared at the second order of fries and drink, wondering what to do with them.

He thought about taking them home but declined the idea. He had to finish them. It was a ceremony. Leaning back, he ate the fries piece by piece and sipped the drink. After finishing everything, he rested for a while, letting his stomach digest, and then walked out of the restaurant, heading straight to the housing department.

The housing office was located on the other side of the campus. At lunchtime, the room was almost empty except for a middle-aged lady with dark brown hair sitting behind a wooden counter.

"May I help you?" She gazed at Xiang through her glasses.

"Yes. I'm a PhD student in physics. I'm living off-campus. I wonder whether I can move into a student dormitory."

"Of course. We still have some openings." She paused for a second as if hesitating. "But we don't have a graduate student dorm. If you want to live on campus, you may have to share a room with an undergraduate."

"I'm fine with that."

She took a campus map, explained each dorm to him, and then asked, "Which one do you like?"

Xiang studied it for a moment and pointed at a co-ed dorm. "This one."

He signed a contract, paid for the rest of the semester, and left the office for his apartment in a cheerful mood. The sky looked bluer, and the clouds whiter.

After walking for a few minutes, he began to feel a stabbing sensation low in his abdomen. He hunched his shoulders and walked on, but soon the pain overwhelmed him. He stopped and sat under a tree with his hand pressing against his lower stomach. His face was wet with sweat, and his head swam. He feared he might faint. This level of pain had happened before, twice, and each time he had almost been hospitalized.

Chapter 21

Shan leaned back against the wall of his dormitory, gasping for breath. His body shook, his mouth was dry, and his throat itchy.

How was this possible? How was this possible?

He asked himself over and over and considered every possible explanation, but none came to mind. Desperately, he went to see his friend Meng, hoping to find out what had happened.

"Can you tell me why I was rejected by the upper committee?" he asked. "What caused it to overturn the decision of the lower committee?"

"I'm afraid I can't tell you. This information is strictly confidential," his friend replied.

Shan blinked at Meng, surprised that his friend was attempting to distance himself from the issue. Whatever the problem was, it must be extremely serious.

Meng paused for a moment, took a step closer to Shan, and spoke in hushed tones. "This is off the record. Someone made an accusation against you to the committee."

"Accusation? What accusation?" Shan's eyes went blank as he scanned his memory for anything that would disqualify him from joining the Communist Party. Nothing.

"You should talk to Mr. Gudong. He has more information, and he likes you."

Wasting no time, Shan rushed to Mr. Gudong's office.

The man sat behind his desk with his door open, reading the newspaper and drinking tea. When he noticed Shan, he beckoned for him to enter, close the door, and sit down. "I knew you would come to me. Is it about the rejection letter?"

"Yes." Shan nodded. "Why did the upper committee reject me? It rarely overturns a decision made by the lower committee."

"You're correct, but in your case, the situation is a little more complicated." The associate chair shook his head and then stared into Shan's eyes with a blank, unblinking gaze. "Did you ever say anything against the Chinese Communist Party?"

"No, why did you say that?" Shan was astonished by the question.

"In the last two weeks, three students have come to us on separate occasions, reporting your anti-revolutionary comments. They told us that they represented a large number of students who were afraid to speak up."

"What?" Shan was taken aback, his eyes wide open. "That's ridiculous. Who said that?"

"I'm afraid I can't tell you. We must protect them."

"Can you tell me what they said? There must be some kind of mistake."

"Yes. At midnight two weeks before, you said all members of the Chinese Communist Party are either idiots or liars."

"That is absurd!" Shan burst out. "I have never said anything like that. I am a member of the communist party myself. It makes no sense for me to —"

Shan abruptly stopped, goosebumps covering his entire body. That conversation about Chinese Communist Party members had taken place past midnight in his dormitory room. No one else was there except for his roommates, but he could not imagine that any of them had any reason to do this to him. They were all close friends.

His gaze slid to the window. Outside, the wind rattled the leaves of the red trees, and a curtain of dark clouds rolled over the campus. The scene reminded him of the great spectacle of millions of red flags waving frantically during the Great Cultural Revolution. It had been a time when people denounced their colleagues, friends, and even family members out of fear for their own lives, or jealousy, or to gain political advantage.

His thoughts wandered back to three weeks before. After the school turned off the lights in all dormitories, he and his roommates, like many other college students in China, talked in the darkness in their beds. Their topics ranged from arts to science, from politics to everyday issues. Sometimes, the conversations devolved into heated debates, but that did not affect their friendship.

“Shan, I heard you joined the Chinese Communist Party. Is that right?” his roommate Wei, one of the smartest students in the school, who loved reading almost everything, asked.

“Yes, I did,” Shan replied proudly from his upper bunk bed across from his roommate.

“Why on earth would you want to join the Chinese Communist Party? I thought you were better than that.”

“What are you talking about?”

“Anyone who joins it is either a liar or an idiot.”

“Wait a minute.” Shan rolled over to look in Wei's

direction. “Why do you despise it so much? Was anyone in your family executed by the government?”

“It has nothing to do with my family.”

“Then, why did you say that?”

“Because it is true.”

“True?”

“Of course. When people join the Chinese Communist Party, they swear an oath under a communist flag that they will devote their lives to the cause of communism. Do you believe any of them truly mean it? Are they even remotely prepared to die for it? No. They just want better jobs and a higher social status. So, they are liars.”

“You're far too extreme. Many Communist Party members are willing to give their lives for the cause. I'm one of them.”

“Then you're a moron. Communism is a pipe dream. The Party says that in the future, people in the Communist utopia will be able to receive whatever they need. It sounds great, but it's a lie. What if other people want your wife? Can they get her?”

Shan's thoughts were interrupted by the ring of the phone on Mr. Gudong's desk. The associate chair picked up the phone and held it to his ear.

“Hello … Yes … I understand … Okay, I'll make it.” He hung up and looked at Shan. “I need to leave in ten minutes. Is there anything else you would like to say?”

Shan told him what had happened that night without revealing the identity of his roommate. After hearing the story, the associate chair leaned back. “It would have made your life a lot easier if you had told me about this earlier.”

"That was just a late-night chit-chat. I think people should be allowed to express their views, especially in private."

"I understand," Mr. Gudong nodded. "But without knowing the fact, I could not defend you when people used it against you."

"People who told on me behind my back lied to the committee. Did the committee look into the allegation?"

"Do you think we took the matter lightly?" The associate chair looked into Shan's eyes. "We investigated. Even though we have some reservations about that accusation, we can't risk ignoring it. We are the country's ruling party, and we must maintain its purity."

Considering that incident could impact his whole life, Shan asked, "Is it possible for the committee to reconsider its decision?"

"I'm sorry, but we can't. The decision has been made." Mr. Gudong raised his head, looked at the ceiling for a second, and then back to Shan. "Now, the only thing I can do for you is to make sure this never goes into your permanent record, so that you can start your new life after graduation free of any taint." The associate chair took a notebook from his drawer and stood up. "You were a rising star with the possibility of working for the central government. Don't you think someone was jealous of your success and tried to bring you down? I have persuaded you to stay in China, but now I believe that pursuing a doctorate in the United States should be your best option."

They walked out of the office and parted ways at the stairs. Mr. Gudong climbed to the upper floor, and Shan went down.

At the exit of the building, he was stopped by the bad weather. Rain poured down from the sky, thunder rocked the earth, and lightning split the world. With the heavy rain lashing down, it was difficult for him to see the road ahead. Even though the Great Cultural Revolution had passed, the ingrained habit of telling tales behind people's backs still lingered on.

Who did that to him? One by one, he thought hard about all of his roommates but was unable to identify any of them.

Chapter 22

As Xiang leaned against the tree trunk, recovering from his stomach pain, five crows landed on the branches of a tall pine and the road near him. A sixth joined them. They watched him silently from a distance as if they were waiting for his death so they could enjoy a lavish feast.

He frowned. In China, crows were a bad omen. If a person saw five crows, he would get sick. If he saw six, death was near. Although he did not believe in superstition, the arrival of the black birds at this particular time bothered him. He waved at them, trying to scare them off, but instead of fleeing, they remained where they were, fixed their beady eyes on him, and cawed. He picked up a small rock and threw it at them. They flapped a few feet down the road and took up new positions among the trees and electrical poles, cawed again, and waited.

Xiang kept pressing against his stomach with his palm to relieve the pain, regretting eating too much fast food. Born into a Chinese family and living in China for more than twenty years, he had developed a stomach for Chinese food and hot drinks. He started to question whether it was a good idea to move into a dorm and eat American food and drink cold drinks for every single meal forever. Of course not. Between the American PhD degree and the intangible American culture, even an idiot could tell which was more important.

The winter wind blew into his face and cooled his head. He realized how insane he had been to consider living in a dormitory. Here in the new land of endless challenges, he needed to learn which things were essential and set his priorities straight.

Understanding the culture was important, but it would have little use after he graduated and returned to China.

He rested until his stomach recovered and then headed toward the housing office to cancel his contract. As he arrived at an intersection, the traffic light turned red. He stopped, stared at it, and hoped it would change soon because the housing office was about to close. However, the red light stared back at him as if urging him to think twice about his decision before crossing the road.

There was nothing to reconsider. He had made his decision, and nothing would change his mind. He was the type of person who knew what was important and what was not.

The traffic light was more stubborn, refusing to change to green. Idly, he looked around and noticed a two-story student dining hall with a large glass wall facing the street. Many students sat at tables by the windows, some talking and laughing, and some dining alone.

Perhaps I ought to go in and check out the cafeteria before canceling the contract. Maybe American food isn't as bad as I think.

He changed his course, entered the building, and stood at the end of the line in front of the check-in cashier. Looking around at the dining area and seeing students carrying food trays with hamburgers, salads, and cold drinks, he believed that this was not the place for him. However, out of curiosity, he still wanted to see what else was available. When it came to his turn, he smiled at the girl with red hair behind the counter. "Can I go in and just look at the food? I'm not going to eat here. I just want to see what kind of food you serve."

"Sure." She let him in.

The dining hall was four times the size of the fast food restaurant near the campus. He approached a long food counter. The first one he saw was a salad bar. He passed it, shaking his head. In China, people eat cooked food. Only rabbits eat raw vegetables.

He continued to walk. Hamburgers, then pizzas, then fried chicken. They were okay, but he could not eat them every day. He continued further. Ah, mashed potatoes, cooked green peppers, and purple onions. Not great, but at least they were real food. While he was looking at them and wondering if he could survive the semester with them, familiar aromas reached his nostrils. He turned to look to the right over his shoulder.

Wow, noodles and Chinese cuisine.

Stepping forward, he stared down at the chicken soup and thanked the traffic light for stopping him. There was no need to look any further. He exited the building and walked across the street. Rather than heading for the housing department, he walked toward the Student Union to check his mailbox. He had not been there in nearly two weeks.

On the wall of the west wing of the Student Union, there were thousands of small mailbox cubicles. He went over to his and peered through the tiny glass window. The mailbox was full. He retrieved the materials, carried them to a nearby table, and shuffled through them, hoping to find the letters from his family or his girlfriend, but there was nothing.

Disappointed, he dropped himself into a chair like a broken balloon falling from the sky. Through a window, he watched two students, a male and a female, walk down the cement path leading away from the building. Their disappearing figures made him feel deserted by the whole world.

Don't be too sentimental, he said to himself. In this world, in this new country, some people care about you. They write to you regularly, and some of them even contact you every month, never missing one.

He turned to the pile of the letters again and started searching for the ones that had contacted him on a monthly basis. He found one, opened it, and started reading.

Dear Xiang,

We are pleased to inform you that you have been selected for a special offer for a trip to Florida for only $300....

He ripped the letter into pieces and threw them in the garbage can next to the table. He reached for another envelope. From its return address, he knew that the sender cared about him most and wrote to him every month. He opened it, withdrew a neatly folded piece of paper, and spread it out. Large, bold words caught his eye.

New Balance: $43.71. Due date....

He set it aside and went through the rest of the mail, making sure he had not missed anything important. At the bottom of the pile, he discovered two letters stuck together. One had familiar handwriting. His girlfriend's. He grabbed it and held it to his chest, gazing up at the cloudless sky through the big windows. Two birds flew together in the empty blue expanse. In the lonely world, that letter was like a ship to a person trapped on an uninhabited island in the middle of a vast ocean. Without even reading it, he could feel the warmth of her words and love. After enjoying a long moment of happiness, he tore open the envelope and retrieved the letter.

He stopped and stared silently at the paper. Something was strange. Instead of being neatly folded, it was full of wrinkles, as if it had been crumpled by someone before being folded and sealed in the envelope.

How could that be?

He looked back at the sky again. It was still blue, but the birds had disappeared. Glancing at the swaying tree branches, he seemingly saw that his girlfriend wrote him a passionate love letter, but hesitated to send it. She stuffed it into an envelope, took it out and read, inserted it into the envelope, and took it out to read again. Over and over she did this, causing the paper to crumple and distort.

With a happy smile, he unfolded the letter and read.

Dear Xiang,
I'm sorry. I'm so sorry that I can't continue—

Without reading any further, he slapped the letter face down on the table, his palm pressing on it as if to prevent it from flipping over on its own.

Why? Why does she break up with me when she knows how much I need her love?

His heart was pounding, and his head spinning.

Chapter 23

The next evening, after dinner, as Shan was wandering aimlessly around the campus, he heard someone call his name. He turned and saw Lei striding toward him.

"Where are you going?" His friend caught up with him.

"I don't know."

"Would you like to take a walk around the lake?"

"Sure."

People said the lake was filled with tears, both joyous and sorrowful. Students went there when they fell in love, letting the beauty of the setting fortify their relationship, binding them together, and infusing them into each other to become one. When the love ended, they would go to the lake and cry into the water, hoping their tears would wash away their sorrow and heal their broken hearts. Shan needed the lake. He had so many tears inside of him, and he wanted to shed them. The day before, he had been expelled from the Communist Party, ending his own unrequited love for that organization.

As they walked toward the lake, Lei said, "I'm sorry for what happened to you."

Sorry for me? For what? Shan looked at his friend, wondering whether his friend had heard what had happened to him. No, he shouldn't. No one else was supposed to know about it except for the committee members and himself.

“Don’t look at me like that.” Lei patted his shoulder. “Everyone knows what happened to you.”

“How is that possible? That information is confidential.”

“Don’t be naïve. If there is a need, nothing is confidential. Someone must have leaked it on purpose.”

“On purpose? Why?”

Instead of answering his question, Lei asked, “You think that you are the victim in this incident, don't you?”

“Of course, I do.”

“Do you believe the reason they gave you?”

“Yes, of course. What else could it be?”

“Buddy, don’t be so naïve. You're a small fish and not worth their time. Their real target is Mr. Gudong, not you.”

“What are you talking about?” Shan blinked, totally confused.

“Have you heard that a central government delegation visited our university a few months ago?”

“Yes?”

“Do you know why they came here? Did they come here for fun? Did they come here because they were bored at their offices? No. They visited the university to recruit new graduates.”

“What does that have anything to do with me?”

“It has a lot to do with you. Gudong wanted to send you to the central government, but his opponent wanted someone else. So, they must prevent you from joining the communist party. By doing so, they kill two birds with one stone. First, they can send someone else to the central government. Second, they can humiliate Mr. Gudong and weaken his leadership in the hope of eventually ousting him through a series of incidents. You're their bullet."

"You know I was wronged. I didn't say that Communist Party members are either liars or idiots. It was Wei who said that."

"Of course, I know. It doesn't matter if you said it or not. Your fault is that you were elected as the president of the student body. On top of that, instead of moving into a private room like your predecessor, you lived in the same room with six other students. Your fault is that you accepted the invitation to join the Communist Party at the wrong time."

Shan stared at his friend speechlessly.

"Buddy, you have made a lot of enemies. By becoming president without even running for it, you have turned people who have campaigned hard to win the election into your enemies. By living in your seven-student-shared room, you slapped the face of the former president, who still has a lot of supporters, and you prevented future presidents from enjoying their privileges. Think about it. How many enemies have you created? The worst of all, when the other faction of the communist committee intended to send their person to the central government, you accepted the invitation to join the Communist Party, which took away their opportunity if you succeeded."

Astonished, Shan could not say a word. No wonder his parents had opposed him getting involved in politics. It was far more complicated than he had ever imagined.

They stopped at a big rock by the water. Lei stepped up on it, pointing to the lake. "Look at it. The water appears clean and peaceful, but underneath, there is a lot of mud and constant fights for survival among many species."

Shan glanced over the placid surface of the lake, troubled by the thought that he was dragged down into the depths by invisible creatures. He looked back at Lei, wishing his friend could give him the answer to the question that had been bothering him. "Do you know who reported our midnight talk to the committee? The only people who should know about the conversation are our roommates, but I can't think of anyone who would have done that."

"I've been wondering the same thing." Lei bent over, picked up a small rock, and weighed it in his hand. "How far do you think I could throw this?"

Shan didn't respond. He had no interest in how far his friend could hurl a rock.

Lei took a few steps back and then dashed toward the water. He tossed the stone into the air and watched as it arced into the lake. Clapping his hands to get rid of the filth, he turned to Shan. "You need to throw that question away, as I just did to the rock, and then move on. I doubt you'll ever find out, and I can almost guarantee that none of our roommates did that. Maybe someone overheard your argument with Wei in the hallway and told the committee. Or maybe one of your roommates mentioned the debate to a friend who then mentioned it to someone else. As words travel from one person to another, they get twisted and exaggerated, intentionally and unintentionally. As far as—"

Lei's beeper went off. He pulled it out of his pocket, read the message, and looked back at Shan. "I've got to go. I'll see you later." He patted Shan on the shoulder. "You should forget about it. Go to America like your brother. That's what you should do."

Go to America? That was the second time in two days that he had been given that advice. Maybe his parents were right all along that he should get his doctorate there, like his brother, and then come back and work in the academic sector. He was too naïve and too idealistic for the ugliness of politics.

For the rest of that week, he had trouble sleeping and lost his appetite, eating only one meal a day. To cope with the stress, he decided to go to Devil's Mountain to clear his mind and think about his future.

The mountain was the highest peak in the region, twenty miles south of the university. It was said that five thousand years before, a devil had come to the nearby village and become a ruler by inciting violence with his eloquence and merciless teeth. He recruited one hundred muscular men as his bodyguards by promising them gold and women and had them spy on the populace, torturing or even killing anyone who disapproved of his rule. To ensure that his dominance was unshakable, he instigated prolonged fighting among the villagers so that they blamed each other for their misfortunes.

During his reign, thousands of people died, and countless families were destroyed. Starvation and illness became ordinary parts of life. Slowly, people woke up from his lies and realized that he was the source of their misery. They rebelled. However, the devil was too powerful to be defeated. He retreated to the top of the mountain along with his bodyguards and continued to rule his kingdom. This uprising lasted hundreds of years, and the blood formed rivers. When he was about to win, a massive stone fell from the sky and knocked him to the ground.

Despite knowing it was a myth, many people still

visited the mountain to touch the huge boulder in hopes that it would provide them with the strength to overcome their problems.

Shan biked toward the mountain, pedaling furiously, sometimes zigzagging between other riders and sometimes dashing down the car lanes. The daring maneuvers distracted him from the immense stress that he had been experiencing for the past few days. His life had been peaceful and enjoyable until the political infighting in the upper committee had turned it upside down.

The Devil's Mountain was one of the most popular tourist destinations over the weekends and holidays, but it was quiet during the week, particularly on the mountaintop in the early morning. When Shan arrived, there was no one in sight. He walked to the giant rock more than two meters high and laid his hands on it, eyes closed as if it could indeed transmit the powerful energy of the universe into his body. As the wind howled and blew in his face, he remembered his brother.

In 1969, the third year of the Great Cultural Revolution, after his parents were detained by the Red Guards in the national laboratory, his brother Xiang took care of him, especially by cooking for him. One evening, after hanging out with his friends, he returned home for dinner, but the meal had not been prepared, and Xiang was not there as usual. Shan walked to the window and scanned the people on the street below, searching for his brother.

Where was Xiang? Was he in trouble?

The door flew open, and his brother tumbled into the room with swollen eyes and a bleeding face.

"What happened to you?" Shan looked at his brother

in horror.

“I got into a fight with that bastard.” Xiang wiped the blood from his face with his hand.

Shan knew who his brother was talking about.

The previous afternoon, on the way home from school, Hundan, a big kid, had blocked his path. “Give us your money!”

“Why?” Shan looked at him and the two others behind him.

“Why? There’s no why. If you really want to know, I can tell you.” The big kid grabbed Shan by his collar. “You are the son of an anti-revolutionary. We are from the working class. That’s why.”

In the Great Cultural Revolution, every organization was governed by a revolutionary committee, which consisted of representatives from the army and workers. Hundan's father served on the national laboratory governing committee as a worker representative.

Shan backed up a few steps, clutching his book bag tightly. It contained ten Chinese cents from his parents, his monthly allowance.

Hundan reached for his book bag. “Give me that bag.”

Shan twisted his body, trying to free himself. The big kid shouted, “I'll say this just one more time. Give me your bag!”

“No.”

He tried to run, but the Hundan knocked him down and kicked him in the side, in the head, in the legs, everywhere. They grabbed the book bag and spilled its contents on the ground, then took the money. They kicked Shan again, spat on him, and left with hysterical laughter.

When Shan arrived home, his brother looked at him with a surprised expression. “What happened to you?”

“Hundan and his friends beat me.” With tears in his eyes and a broken voice, he told Xiang about the incident.

His brother stood up, veins popping out in his neck. “Tomorrow, I'll teach them a lesson. A big lesson so that they'll never dare to touch you again.”

“Don't. They outnumber you. They'll hurt you.”

“Don't worry.”

Shan did not know how fierce the fight between his brother and Hundan was because his brother refused to tell him. The only thing he knew was that the big kid never bothered him again.

A bird flew west past Shan and brought him back to the present as if telling him to go overseas to pursue a PhD. He knew that his brother was helping him get into a graduate program in the United States, and now all he needed were acceptable TOEFL scores.

With that thought, he descended the mountain and rode his bike to the school. He grabbed his TOEFL books from his dorm and went straight to the library.

The library was a six-story white building with a large study hall on each floor, which could seat more than a hundred students. He went to a corner on the second floor and started a mock test to assess his readiness for the exam. After struggling and sweating for four hours, he finished the test. Without taking a break, he compared his responses to the correct answers.

His heart sank.

He scored far below the minimum requirement for graduate school admission in the United States. His time was running out. It was barely a month until the next

TOEFL exam. He knew that he would not be able to pass the test no matter how hard he studied. Sighing, he gathered his books and walked out of the library. There was no point in continuing to prepare for the TOEFL.

Chapter 24

With the letter under his palm, Xiang stared at the cloud through the windows, trying to make out its shape, but it was no more than a subtle bulge in the vast blue sky, nearly invisible to the world.

While in China, he had imagined the United States to be a place of pleasant experiences and happy life. After all, it was the world's most powerful and wealthiest nation, and he had a good assistantship that would allow him to live comfortably. Yet at that moment, he felt neither happiness nor pleasantness, just dazed, empty loneliness.

Following a few minutes of stillness, he folded the letter, tucked it into his pocket, and left the building for his dorm. Although he did not know what was in the letter, he did not want to read it at this time. He was not in the mood for any more bad news.

As soon as he got back to his apartment, he packed his belongings and cleaned out his room in preparation for moving into the dorm and starting a new chapter in his life.

The following evening, his Chinese friend helped him move his luggage to his dorm before rushing off to fulfill another commitment. He dragged his two large suitcases into the three-story brick building. As he walked down the hallway toward his room, he kept wondering if he would be welcomed and whether he would be able to fit in with the community as the only international student.

His room was located next to a brown wooden gate that divided the hallway into two sections, girls' and boys'. At the open door, he was greeted by loud music. Inside, there was a regular bed on one side and a bunk bed on the other, and his American roommate dressed in a deep orange T-shirt and black shorts was dancing to the tune while folding clothes on the lower bunk. Xiang knocked on the door. The student stopped dancing, turned to him, and smiled broadly.

"You must be Xiang." His tall, broad-shouldered roommate with an oval face and dark brown hair approached him with an extended hand.

"Yes." Xiang shook hands with the roommate.

"Welcome. I'm Robert. I heard you're a graduate student."

"Yes, a PhD student in physics."

"Wow, a PhD student in physics!"

Six other American students appeared at the door, and one of them asked, "Robert, are you ready to go now?"

"Come on in." Robert waved at them. "This is Xiang, my new roommate. He is a physics PhD student." Then he introduced each of his friends to Xiang. "…, and this is Lulu. She lives next door to us…"

Xiang looked at her, his heart pounding, amazed that such a beautiful girl lived right next door to him. Lulu, dressed in red, was an inch or so shorter than him and had big blue eyes and chestnut brown curls.

After introducing his friends, Robert said to Xiang, "We're going to a party. Would you like to come with us?"

Xiang was certain he wanted to join them, but he was not able to. He was a PhD student, and a PhD student was not supposed to have fun during the weekdays. "Sorry. I wish I could, but I have an experiment to do tonight."

"What about tomorrow?" Robert asked. "We're going to have a picnic. How about joining us?"

For Xiang, weekends were the perfect time for research. With no one else in the lab, he could spend an entire day there without interruption. However, not wanting to disappoint his new roommate twice on the first day they met, he agreed to join them.

Robert left with his friends for the party, and Xiang went to the physics department. About three o'clock in the morning, he finished his experiment and walked back to his dorm on the street with no one else but stars in the deep sky, himself, and his shadow created by the yellow streetlights.

When he reached his room, trying not to disturb his roommate, he opened the door quietly and tiptoed to the windowsill to retrieve his toothbrush and toothpaste. After finishing cleaning in the bathroom down the hallway, he went to bed, ending another long day in the dark and quiet room filled with gentle snoring from his roommate.

The next morning, around ten o'clock, he and Robert carried a large cooler to the parking lot, where a group of students waited for them. Robert loaded the container into his Ford and then waved at Lulu and a male student nearby, inviting them to his car.

Xiang and Lulu sat in the backseat. On the way to the picnic area, he learned that she was a freshman in music who had recently moved to Arkansas from

Oregon.

After an hour of driving, the students pulled their vehicles off the road into a gravel yard in front of a one-story wooden house at the top of a forested mountain, facing a lake that was covered in white snow. Since arriving in the United States, Xiang's life had been a monotonous pendulum swinging back and forth between his apartment and the physics department. He had never thought that Arkansas had such a beautiful landscape.

Out in the front yard, he helped Robert unload groceries from the hatchback onto the porch. Then he mingled with the students, trying to make new friends, but he soon found that he had difficulty communicating with them. They had problems understanding him because of his accent. Despite their nods and smiles as he spoke, Xiang could tell they did not get what he was saying. Sometimes, they asked him to repeat himself, but even after he had done so multiple times, they still got him wrong. Likewise, he had trouble following their conversations because their vocabulary was beyond his range, which was primarily limited to physics. His lack of knowledge of American culture exacerbated the matter. When they got excited or laughed, he had no idea what they were talking about.

Feeling that he was burdensome to them, he excused himself and walked into the house to a large TV near the fireplace, where two students sat on a long couch, watching football. He had no ideas about the rules of the game and was not interested in it, but he pretended to watch it. In his head, however, he thought about his experiment data and planned his next research.

Twenty minutes later, Lulu came and invited him to go hiking. Gladly, he followed her and seven other students out onto the snow-covered trail. Hiking in the winter was not as cold as he had expected, especially with Lulu walking alongside him. When they reached a plateau, he paused to gaze down at the white lake below the mountain.

"Beautiful, isn't it?" He heard Lulu say.

"Yes." He turned to look at her but shyly averted his gaze the moment his eyes met hers.

When they returned to the cabin two hours later, the delicious aroma of grilled steak had filled the air on the porch. Some students were lined up for food, while others congregated by the fire with their food plates in hand. Xiang followed Lulu to the line. When it was their turn, she took some salads, bread, and a piece of steak. When he reached for the steak, he frowned. The meat had black grill marks.

How could Americans eat something like this? Didn't they know that burnt meat can cause cancer?

He looked around to see what other students were carrying. When he that saw everyone else had steaks, he picked up one piece of the roast and added some vegetables and fruits to his plate. Then he grabbed a bag of potato chips and followed Lulu to a nearby table.

Sitting next to her, Xiang mimicked her, pressing the steak with a fork in his left hand and cutting a small piece of it with a knife in his right hand. When he picked up the piece with a fork, he noticed that the steak was still red in the middle. He stopped, examined it for a moment, and put it back, turning to look at Lulu, who was about to eat hers.

"Don't eat that." He urged her. "There's blood on the inside."

She stopped, glanced at him, and then at her food,

appearing puzzled.

"Don't eat it. You will get sick. The beef is still raw." He pointed at her steak. "Look at that blood."

She looked at it, then laughed. "This is called cooked rare. Unlike other types of meat, steak doesn't contain bacteria. Many people prefer rare steaks because they are tender and juicy."

He nodded as if he agreed, but in his mind, he thought otherwise.

These crazy Americans. They burned the surface of their steaks and left the bloody insides.

His stomach revolted at the thought of consuming rare flesh. He set it aside and picked up the bag of potato chips.

"If you don't like rare steak, you can get hot dogs," Lulu said.

Xiang went to the food counter and returned with two hot dogs, wrapped in a napkin. He sat down, opened the napkin, and spread ketchup, mustard, and the bits of pink pineapple between the meat and the bun.

Lulu giggled. "I have never seen anyone eat hotdogs like that."

He smiled back and then used his fork to mix ketchup, mustard, and pineapple as if he were cooking Chinese food. He took a big bite of his weird hot dog and then nodded. "Tastes good."

That day, Xiang had the most fun he had ever had in his life, and it revolutionized his whole perspective on the world. All of the scientists had been wrong. For the first time, he realized that time was not constant at all in everyday life. It could be changed dramatically, hours shrinking to seconds, by Lulu. Before he had fully enjoyed her company, it was time for them to return home.

After returning from the picnic, he went to the physics department to study, but he could not concentrate. No matter how hard he tried, his mind always drifted away from his textbook to Lulu and her large, beautiful eyes. After struggling to study in vain, he stood up and paced the room, attempting to push her out of his mind. A few minutes later, he remembered his girlfriend and her letter. This was the perfect time to read it. If she had decided to completely end their relationship, he would not get hurt badly. He had Lulu in his mind. He reached into his pocket for the letter, but it was not there. Blinking, he realized that he had done laundry the night before and had forgotten to take it out of his pants.

Oh, my God.

He tossed his book bag over his shoulder and dashed across the campus to his dorm. He took the pants out of his drawer, lifted them, and rummaged through the pockets. He discovered the letter, a scrambled piece of paper with blue ink smeared across the page like a watercolor.

Chapter 25

A few weeks after moving into the dorm, about two o'clock in the morning, Xiang dreamed about his solar cell research. While he was excited about his record-breaking data, the sky turned into dazzling brightness, and a tremendous sound shook in the lab.

In shock, he opened his eyes and realized that he was in his bed with two glaring white fluorescent lights staring down at him from the ceiling and loud laughter coming from the doorway. He knew that Robert had come back from a party with his friends again. Not wanting to make his roommate feel bad for having disturbed him, he lay motionless, hoping that Robert would not notice that he had been awakened by the noise and lights.

"Your roommate is sleeping." He heard someone say.

"I know." It was Robert's loud voice. "I got some new music. Would you like to listen?"

Xiang frowned, irritated by his roommate's lack of regard. If he were Robert, he would have immediately let the others leave and turned off the light. It was two o'clock in the morning.

While he was thinking, the loud thrum of rock and roll blared through the small room. From the corner of his eye, he saw Robert swaying to the beat with his hips thrusting and his eyes closed.

Why did he do that? Why did he still play the music after his friends had told him that Xiang was sleeping?

Frustrated, he wanted to scream at his roommate, but he restrained himself. Robert had been friendly to him from the first day they had met and was proud to have a PhD student in physics as a roommate. Robert had invited him to attend various activities and told his friends that Xiang was a physicist. His roommate had a small refrigerator containing beers and other beverages, and anytime he had opened it, he offered Xiang a drink.

Hoping that the undergraduate roommate would soon cease dancing and the others would leave, Xiang pretended to be asleep. It was not a weekend, and everyone would have classes the next day. After quite a while, his patience was finally rewarded. When the music ended, everyone left. Although the room was still as bright as in the daytime, it had become quiet. Xiang rolled over and went back to sleep.

Exhausted from his research and studies, he quickly drifted into a state of half-sleep and half-awake. In the last few days, he had not gotten much sleep because he had to work extra hard and was frustrated. A piece of equipment had failed during his fabrication of solar cells, which had ruined the samples that he had been working on for weeks.

Just as he was about to drop into a deep sleep, his roommate came back and turned on the television. The music, gunshots, and loud shouting jolted him awake.

That's ridiculous! Why is he doing this to me? He knows I'm sleeping.

Since coming to the United States, he had frequently heard people talk about racial discrimination. Robert's behavior made him feel disrespected, and he believed that if he were white, his white roommate would not behave in such a manner.

Yes, he has been nice to me, but that doesn't mean he respects me and views me equally. People can be nice to their dogs.

The more he thought about Robert's actions, the more convinced he became that his roommate was nothing but a racist, and the more his anger swelled inside him. With the rage building up, he started to feel agony.

Calm down, he warned himself. He is not that bad. He is just a freshman, a little kid.

Xiang took a deep breath and considered plugging his ear with his fingers to reduce the noise. Just then, he heard a man yell. "You, idiot Chinaman, go back to your country."

Even though he knew it was a movie line, the words still stung like a wasp. In fury, he popped up like a spring and wanted to shout at his roommate. However, his brain took over his emotion. He sat in his bed with his eyes closed, telling himself not to speak. Considering his state of mind, anything he said would ruin their relationship and turn the room into a chilly winter for the rest of the year. He kept reminding him that friendship took a long time to build but could be destroyed instantly.

"Ah!" The roommate sounded shocked. Apparently, the man had been startled by his sudden moment.

Xiang continued sitting on the bed without opening his eyes, awaiting Robert's further reaction.

Nothing. His roommate seemed to have vanished. The room became so quiet that he could hear his own breathing.

Where was Robert? What happened to him?

Xiang remembered the phrase *frightened to death* and wondered whether his roommate was harmed. As he was thinking, he felt his mattress dip and a hand touch his shoulder.

"Xiang, are you okay?" It was his roommate's voice, soft and kind.

Robert was fine. He was still alive. Relieved, but more puzzled, Xiang wondered what kind of person his roommate was. Robert is so wired.

"Xiang, what happened?"

What the hell was that question? Didn't he know what he had been doing? Did he have any common sense? Didn't he understand that it was wrong to play loud music and watch a movie with the volume turned all the way up after midnight when his roommate was sleeping?

Not wanting to hurt his roommate's feelings, he remained silent.

"Xiang, you have to tell me what happened. You're my best friend. If you don't tell me, I'll feel really bad."

Xiang's heart was warmed by the words.

I misjudged him. He was not being disrespectful. His brain simply operates at a different frequency from mine.

Given the unexpected reaction from Robert, Xiang had to find an excuse for his action. He could not tell Robert the truth. It was too hurtful.

"Xiang, tell me what happened, please."

"Sorry to scare you. I had a nightmare." He lied without opening his eyes.

"It's okay. You'll be fine. "It was just a bad dream." Robert sounded like a mother to her baby. He hugged Xiang and then returned to the couch to continue watching the movie.

Xiang sighed and shook his head. He lay down on his bed, stared at the ceiling, and tried to make sense of his roommate.

Perhaps it was just a cultural difference. In China, people were taught to be more considerate of others and to put our communities first. In America, individualism was encouraged. With that philosophy, Robert's behavior was logical and fair. He had paid the same rent as Xiang did. Thus, it was his right to do whatever he wanted within the bounds of the law and regulations.

With this new perspective on the situation, Xiang relaxed and gradually drifted off to sleep.

Two days later, Robert came into the room after midnight, switched on the lights, and turned on the television. When Xiang woke up to the noise, he realized that his roommate had simply not changed his habits. To live in harmony with the American guy, he would have to adjust his schedule.

From then on, he stayed late in the physics building, working until three o'clock in the morning. When he came back to the room, he walked lightly, like a cat, trying not to disturb Robert. As a result of his long hours of work, his research progressed more quickly than he had anticipated. His professor was pleased and told him that he would receive a salary raise the next semester.

In a letter to his parents, he said that he had made a wonderful discovery. A great scientist with good pay had to have an inconsiderate roommate.

Spring break had arrived, and all the other students in the dormitory had gone home, at least he thought so. After returning to his dorm from his lab at midnight, he took a shower and got into bed, ready to sleep. Just then, the phone on the wall jangled.

Who was calling so late?

He glanced at the phone for a moment before picking it up. “Hello?”

He heard Lulu's voice. “Xiang, what are you doing?”

“Nothing. Just came back from the lab.” He was so glad that she was calling from home.

“Would you like to watch a movie with me?”

“Where?” He blinked, confused.

“In my room.”

“What? You're not home?”

“No, I'm staying here for spring break.”

His heart pounded, his temples throbbed, and the back of his throat felt parched. He wanted to sit down and think this through. He and Lulu were the only two students in the building, and she had asked him to come to her cozy room long after midnight. Picturing her slender body in her blouse and shorts and her large blue eyes fixed on him, he felt a surge of blood rush to his head.

What did she really want?

Chapter 26

Xiang and Lulu lived on the same floor, but to see her, he had to go out of the building and enter it from the door on the other side of the dormitory because the gate in the middle of the hallway was locked.

He walked out of the dorm. In the parking lot, Lulu's white car reflected moonlight like a beacon in the vast ocean. Xiang had been in that car with her many times. Since the picnic at the beginning of the semester, they had become good friends. Sometimes, he felt like more than friends. Whenever he could have dinner at regular dining hours, they sat together at one of the long dining hall tables with their other friends. He was so used to eating with her that if she did not show up, it felt like something was missing. He could sense that she had the same feeling for him too. Many times, when he was late getting to dinner, he noticed that she kept looking at the entrance of the dining hall until she saw him.

A pair of bright white lights appeared in the distance, grew larger, then diminished in a few seconds, much like opportunities that come and go. He looked at the car that lay motionless in the darkness, pondering why she had invited him to her room at midnight when everyone else had gone home. Although they had spent many late-night hours together, they had never shared any intimacy. He was not clear about what their real relationship was. Friends? Lovers? Something in between? Whatever it was, he felt his blood coursing fast, calling out the desire to hug her from every single cell in his entire body. It was too hot, even on this cold winter night. He untied the top button of his coat, letting in the cold air to help cool him down.

He made a left turn and headed for the girls' side of the entrance. As he passed a large maple tree, he saw the six-story Johnson Hall rising above the crest of the hill in the distance and remembered a night.

One Friday night three weeks before, Lulu had called him after he had come back from the physics department. "What's your plan for tomorrow?"

"Nothing," he lied. He had a busy research schedule for the whole weekend, but Lulu was more important.

"Would you like to have breakfast together? I want to show you something."

"Sure. What time?" He wondered what this was about. It must be something important, otherwise, she would not have called him so late."

The next morning, he met her at the student cafeteria across the street from Johnson Hall. Throughout the breakfast, she never mentioned that *something*. Xiang even suspected that it was just an excuse for having a meal together.

"What's your plan?" he asked after they finished breakfast.

"Would you like to go to Johnson Hall?"

"Johnson Hall? Sure."

He did not know why she wanted him to go there, but it did not matter. He would go anywhere with her.

They crossed the street, entered the building, took the elevator to the top floor, and climbed a narrow stairway toward the roof. As he climbed behind Lulu and admired her brown ponytail swinging side to side, he remembered a movie, in which a boy led a girl up to the roof of a building and proposed marriage.

Was it the reason she was taking him up to the roof? No, it couldn't be. Proposing marriage was a man's job. Besides, they were not even close to that point.

In a minute, Lulu reached the end of the stairway and pushed open the metal door. From behind her, he saw a large cement space like a parking lot. He followed her out of the dim staircase into the bright daylight and walked with her under the blue sky and puffy clouds to the concrete wall on the east.

"Isn't it beautiful?" She pointed at the distance.

Far to the east, a band of golden sunlight lay along the horizon, tinting the mountain peaks brilliant orange, as if an artist had brushed it on with a large brush.

"Yes, it is."

He took a deep breath of the fresh air and glanced down the main street of the campus, which ran east along with the newly constructed engineering and science buildings. With its vast expanses of grass and trees, it was not hard to imagine that the campus would turn into a giant garden once spring arrived and flowers bloomed.

He turned to look at Lulu. She was gazing at the scene with her elbows on the wall and her hands under her chin, as if in deep thought.

As he reflected on the past, he arrived at the entrance on the girl's side. The door was propped open by a small rock jammed into the corner of the door frame. He pulled the door open but did not step into the building immediately. At midnight, the gravitational pull of the beautiful full moon elevated his excitement to the sky. He was afraid that with such high emotions, he might do something wrong and make a grave mistake.

He stood still, letting the winter cool his head.

As a physics PhD student, he was supposed to be more logical and less emotional. He stood in the wind, analyzing the situation.

He had heard that American girls did not usually like to date Asians. Compared to American men, most Asian guys were shorter, less muscular, and knew far less about American culture. Considering that he had all of those weaknesses, he could not understand why Lulu liked him and what had bound them together. He did not know whether they had any future, even if they loved each other. After graduation, he would return to China. Was she willing to follow him? Could she survive in China?

Marrying an American girl would make him the envy of many Chinese, but having an American wife would also cap his career in China. Having a doctorate from an American university would position him well in the competition for the few coveted positions at top Chinese universities. He could find a job quickly and soon rise to a department head and then a college dean. If he played his cards right, he might even become chancellor or higher. But an American wife would make these leadership positions unreachable. In China, no one with a foreign wife held a government position, no matter how qualified he was. It was how the political system had been working and one of the ways the government had tried to limit the influence of foreign countries.

The rational thought calmed him down. For him, the future was more important. He tried to release the doorknob and go back to his room, but his hands seemed to be glued to it. He tried to step back, but his legs refused to take the order from his brain.

What was he going to do? Should he go forward, or turn around and go back to his empty room?

Isn't it obvious? A voice in his head said. Look. On one side of the door, it is a dark, chili-filled night. On the other side, there is a brightly lit hallway with a red carpet leading to Lulu's room. Even a moth knows which way to fly.

The choice was a no-brainer. A career was far in the sky, but Lulu was right there. He entered the building, kicked the rock into the grass, and closed the door behind him. He walked down the carpeted corridor to her room at the end, with a Chinese symphony of *March On* ringing in his head.

When he reached her door, he stopped. Before him, was the entryway to a different world. Once he stepped through, his life would never be the same. He could already envision it. When spring break was over, Lulu and he would go to the library together, go to the student recreation center together, and do everything together. He would attend her graduation, and she would go to his.

He took a deep breath and playfully knocked on her door eight times. Eight is a lucky number in China.

The door opened and there was Lulu, wearing a pink T-shirt that came down to her naked thighs, giving him an instant picture of her without pants or underwear.

His blood turned to steam. He wanted to grab her, hug her, and kiss her. Right away.

"Come on in." She stepped aside. "What took you so long?"

Lulu lived by herself. He did not know whether she was lucky, or if she had paid double rent, but none of them mattered to him. What mattered was that he was with her, alone in their own small universe.

The room had one bed on each side. One of them was piled with stuffed animals, and the other had a pink quilt. At the far end of the sleeping bed stood a desk, on top of which was a TV.

“I got a new movie.” She went to her bed and turned on her video player with her remote control.

“Oh, what is it?”

“The Emperor.”

He had heard of this movie. It was about the last emperor of China. Xiang pulled a chair up by the bed and sat down next to her.

The movie started. She watched it attentively, but he could not concentrate. He kept glancing over at her out of the corner of his eye. She leaned forward, with her naked legs crossed. They were so close to him that he could reach out and touch them at any moment. Her light perfume drifted to him, enfolded him, filled his nostrils, and entered his lungs. The scent diffused into his bloodstream like a high concentration of alcohol and controlled his brain. With his arm rising in concert with his blood pressure, he wrapped it around her shoulders.

“Please, don't.” She twisted her body and pushed his arm away.

What? He stood up and blinked at her with his jaw-dropping open.

“Sorry, I’m not attracted to Asians.” Her voice was emotionless.

What did she say? He shook his head and blinked.

Why did she say she wasn’t *attractive* to Asians? She was more than attractive. She was beautiful. She was gorgeous.

Xiang suspected that her lack of confidence came

from having been hurt by someone. As a man, he was obligated to protect herself from then on. He would hold her tightly in his arms and shield her from all danger. No one would hurt her again.

One knee on her bed, he leaned over her, his arms open and his chest warm.

“You’re very attractive.” His voice trembled along with the rest of him.

Chapter 27

Shan ate a quick breakfast and then headed over to the university auditorium to take the TOEFL test, relieved that the day had finally come. When he arrived, he found that the room was already packed, and many students sat quietly. At the doorway, he took a deep breath and then entered. Soon after he sat in the back row, a middle-aged woman walked in with a stack of test handouts.

A tall, serious woman glanced over the crowd. "Hello, I'm going to distribute the exam. It will last for three hours. You can go to the bathroom during the test, but the clock will not stop. So, if you need to use the bathroom, now is the time."

Seeing no one left, she started to hand out and returned to the podium. "You may start now."

Shan darkened the circles that he believed to be correct and left the others without trying to guess. Once he was finished, he randomly marked the rest of the answers. In less than an hour, he handed in his test and walked out, holding his head high.

At night, he wrote to his brother, inquiring whether he could go to the United States without TOEFL scores. He knew that the question was nonsense, but it did not hurt to ask. A month later, he received a package from his brother, which contained application materials from the Department of Civil Engineering at the University of

Northwest Arkansas and The Arkansas Language School. Xiang encouraged him to apply to both schools. If Shan's English was the graduate school's primary concern, they might accept him on the condition that he first took some courses at the language school.

Three months after submitting his applications, Shan received two packages. One was from the Civil Engineering Department, informing him that he had been accepted to its graduate program, provided he went to the language school for one semester. The other came from the language school, containing an acceptance letter and a receipt of $5,000 tuition paid for him by his brother.

Five thousand dollars? His brother had paid five thousand dollars for his tuition!

Shan's eyes widened as he stared at the receipt, tears blurring his vision. To him, that was an astronomic figure. If Xiang did not rob a bank, he must have lived an extremely frugal life.

The next day, he applied for a passport. Two weeks later, he flew to Huadu to apply for a visa at the American embassy.

The embassy was a four-story building located in Huadu's east district. To ensure that he had a chance to be interviewed, he left his parents' apartment at five o'clock in the morning. After biking for nearly an hour, he arrived at Anhua Road. From a distance, he spotted a silhouette of a long line on the sidewalk in front of the embassy.

Seriously? It was only six o'clock.

He pedaled faster, parked his bicycle along a curb with many others, and hurried to the end of the line. In the darkness, the light from the embassy's window shone like a beacon.

Two hours later, the door was finally opened, but only a limited number of people were allowed inside, and he waited outside for another hour before entering the building.

What a disappointment.

Rather than the grand hall that he had imagined, the room resembled a little bank in a small town. It had a long wooden counter that stretched from wall to wall, with three officers standing behind it. However, the moment he saw a female officer with a Chinese face, his spirits were lifted.

He felt a sense of connection to her. At the very least, they both had Chinese roots. He had been told that the approval rate for visa applications was quite low, less than fifty percent. It was influenced by the moods of the individual officers. If he were interviewed by her, he was sure his application would be approved.

He went to her line and waited for his turn. It felt more like he was waiting to be warmly welcomed to the United States of America by this woman, not just for his application to be approved.

What a lucky day. She was his Statue of Liberty.

When it was his turn, he approached the counter with a big smile, not only on his face but also deep in his heart.

"May I have your document?" The woman looked at him expressionlessly.

Why did she give him a stone face?

Shan looked into her eye, only to see two black holes. Humbly and respectfully, he handed her a large, light-brown envelope with both hands. She pulled out the materials, flipped them over, and extracted a single sheet of paper to read. A few seconds later, she looked up at him. "Who is going to pay for your living cost? Who is going to financially support your graduate studies?"

"My brother and Professor Maria."

"Who is Professor Maria?"

"She are a friend of I brother."

"She *are*?" The woman frowned and stamped the paper without further question.

"Your application has been denied." She slid all the documents back to him.

"Why?"

"I'm not convinced that she will provide you with full financial support." She tilted her head and waved at the waiting line behind him. "Next."

"Wait a minute. Are you—" Shan tried to protest.

"You may leave now."

He gave her an angry stare and walked away, holding his head high. At the door, he tore all the documents into pieces, threw them into a trashcan, and marched out of the embassy.

He was free. He did not have to go to the US, and he had a plausible justification for his parents. It was the embassy that was to blame, not him. Pursuing a doctorate was not his dream anyway. It was his parents'. He had suffered far too much and for far too long. In such a fast-developing economy, what was the point of studying abroad?

Shan crossed the street to his bike. When he saw two birds flying through the sky to the west, he wondered if his thought of not wanting to go to America was true or just an excuse for his failure. That was hard to tell. Often, when people fail, they look for someone else to blame and distance themselves from the situation. It doesn't matter, he thought to himself. The fact is that I'm as free and joyful as the birds.

Instead of going back home right away, he went to a park to have fun. While there, he hiked the hills, paddled in the lake, and watched shows in a bar until midnight. Upon returning home, he found his parents waiting for him in the living room. After hearing that his visa application had been rejected, his mother walked away.

Glancing at her back, Shan felt bad for having let her down, and as he turned to look at his father, he saw him sigh and shake his head. While he was worrying about whether they could take it, his mother reappeared with a cup of warm milk.

"Don't feel too bad. You are still young, and you will have numerous opportunities in any field you want to pursue." She handed the milk to Shan.

He exhaled a deep breath, thanking the embassy's officer. She provided him with a happy ending to his struggle of applying for graduate studies in the United States.

Chapter 28

Lulu raised her hands, palms out, in front of her. "Please, don't. I'm not attracted to Asians."

Xiang stopped and stared at her, trying to figure out what she meant by not *attractive* to Asians. Although he was confused by the word, he understood her meaning from the way she was holding her body. English language was so confounding. Stepping back, he continued to study her face, questioning if he had ever misunderstood the nature of their relationship. "I thought you were my girlfriend."

"We are friends. We are not dating."

"You have never wanted to be my girlfriend?" He looked into her eyes.

"No, sorry."

Blood rushed to his head, and he could hear his heart pounding as if it were about to burst. He stared at her, his body quaking. "Then, why did you keep inviting me to movies? Why did you invite me to watch the sunrise in the morning and the stars at night? Why did you ask me to come here at midnight to watch the movie when we are the only people in the entire building? Why—"

He ran out of breath.

"I'm sorry." Her tone softened.

Xiang sank into his chair and covered his face with his palms, crying, but the tears only ran into his heart. He heard gunshots in the movie. It sounded like someone had been executed.

"I'm sorry." Her voice was sweet.

In an effort to be as polite as possible, he took a deep breath, stood up, and returned the chair to the table. He thanked her for the invitation and left her room, tumbling down the hallway.

Outside, it was raining. Lightning repeatedly broke the sky, and thunder shook the earth. Without any hesitation, he pushed the door open and dashed into the blackness, letting the water from the sky wash away his humiliation and cool his boiling emotion. Soon, he sneezed and shivered. Afraid of getting sick, he ran back to his room and took a hot shower. He was mad at Lulu, but at the same time, her winsome smile and lovely voice were always there, flickering across his vision, echoing in his ears.

Xiang knew that he should forget about her, but he could not shake off the memories of being with her. They were like treasures, things he could not part with. They were like sweet dreams, luring him back to keep dreaming even after he woke up and realized that they were nothing more than illusions. His fury at her and his love for her collided like cold and hot air masses, creating a savage thunderstorm in his head. His brain was about to explodc.

To survive, he had to do something to erase her from his life and move on. He struggled mentally for a while, then grabbed an umbrella and threw his backpack over his shoulder, and walked out of the building toward his lab. Nothing could keep him from thinking about Lulu except for a potentially dangerous experiment that required his undivided attention.

The laboratory was located on the first floor of the

physics department. Xiang slid his access card through the slot in the door and stepped into the lab's changing room. He donned his cleanroom hood and boots, as well as protective goggles and masks, and then entered the lab through the second door.

A wave of heat welcomed him as if he had entered the sauna in the student exercise center.

Why was it so hot? What was wrong?

He stopped instinctively, wondering whether he should call the emergency contact posted outside of the door. However, he soon rejected the idea because he might be unable to do the experiment for the whole spring break if he reported the situation. He needed research to keep him sane, and also he did not have that much time to waste. Besides, it was two o'clock in the morning, and the emergency staff must have been sound asleep.

He sniffed, attempting to find out whether something was burning. The smell was normal. He scanned the room, thinking about where the heat came from. When his eyes settled on a large diffusion furnace, a piece of high-temperature equipment used to make solar cells, he nodded.

Yes, that should be the source of the problem. Someone must have forgotten to turn it off.

With the air conditioner in the building turned off for the spring break, the running diffusion furnace could raise the temperature in the room to an unbearable level.

He walked up to the equipment and peered inside through a glass window. The bright yellowish, empty interior radiated heat to the window and his face. He took a step back, shut off the machine, and walked across the lab to the change room.

What should he do? Return to work or go home and rest? The room was too hot and stuffy. He'd better leave and come back tomorrow. No, he should stay. A great scientist must be able to endure the challenges that other people could not. Besides, he needed to do research to repel Lulu from his mind.

Xiang removed his sweater, put his lab clothing back on, and returned to the lab. He was going to challenge a harsh condition and fabricate the best solar cells he had ever produced. That was what a scientist should do.

To fabricate solar cells, he needed to clean silicon wafers first. He took out a box of wafers from a closet, carried it to the wet bench, and then reached the chemical cabinet for acid and base, but he stopped when he opened the door.

Do I really need to make solar cells today? It's way too hot. Can I stand in such heat for forty minutes? The chemicals are highly corrosive. If I accidentally spill them on myself, my flesh will be burned, and no one will be here to rescue me.

After a long moment of thinking, he convinced himself that as long as he was careful, nothing could go wrong. Besides, he needed the harsh environment to train his strong will, an essential characteristic of a scientist.

He retrieved the sulfuric acid and potassium hydroxide bottles and carried them to the wet bench, and then returned for the nitric and hydrochloric acid. When he came back to get hydrofluoric acid, he stopped before reaching for the bottle.

This chemical was much more dangerous than all the others. If it spilled on people, it would not cause slight pain or discomfort. It penetrates people's skin and flesh all the way to their bones and dissolves them imperceptibly. By the time a person became aware of the accident, it was too late. He had heard of a tragedy. A graduate student at a university had unknowingly spilled the chemical on his arm and had become permanently disabled.

Xiang squatted in front of the cabinet for a long moment and then decided to proceed. He had used it many times and never had an accident. He pulled the chemical out and brought it to the wet bench. After mixing the chemicals diligently, he dipped a wafer holder with twelve silicon wafers in the liquid. He set the timer and followed the experiment procedure precisely, making sure that he would not make a slight mistake.

As time passed, sweat seeped from every single pore on his forehead, his back, and his chest. He ignored the discomfort and continued the cleaning process.

With each passing minute, more sweat poured out of him as if trying to flee from danger. He thought about stopping the experiment and leaving, but when he looked at the timer on the wet bench, he changed his mind. In thirty seconds, the alarm would go off, and he would move the holder to a deionized water tank to clean the chemicals on the wafers and would not have to deal with the dangerous liquid anymore. In ten minutes, he would finish the whole cleaning process and walk out of the lab with success.

Chapter 29

One evening after returning to the school from Huadu, Shan had dinner with his friend Lei.

"You look depressed. What happened?" Shan asked.

"My company runs into a problem."

"Again?"

"What do you mean *again*? Problems are just a part of our lives as long as we are alive. It's lucky to have them, but this time, I got a tough one."

"What is it?" Shan stopped eating.

"I got a project to build a wall between the Guanghua subdivision and the Yong River, but residents picketed the construction site, denying our access. They said that the wall would block them from the canal."

"I'm not surprised. You make their lives difficult." Shan picked up a piece of chicken with his chopsticks.

"I know, but I didn't choose to do so. It's just a part of the project I got from Jiangkai."

"Have you talked to the residents?"

"Yes, but no use. I don't know what to do next." Lei sighed.

"Don't worry too much. We don't have a class tomorrow morning, so we can go there to check it out. Maybe I can help you find a solution."

The next morning, they went to the Guanghua subdivision and saw a group of more than twenty people in their sixties arguing with young construction workers near piles of red bricks.

"You dare say it again." A burly worker pointed his finger at an elderly woman.

"I have said it." She brushed aside his hand. "Don't point at me."

The young man pushed her. She stumbled backward and fell into a man's arms.

"The young man assaulted people," someone shouted. "Call the police."

Several residents went up to the workers, screaming at them. While they were shouting at each other, more people from each side started to converge on the scene.

Afraid that someone could get injured, Shan rushed in between the two groups, palms facing both sides, and yelled as loudly as he could, "Calm down, calm down."

"Who are you?" The woman who had been pushed by the young man steadied herself.

"I'm Shan, Lei's friend."

"Go away." She ignored him and shouted at the young men again.

Fearing that the situation would spiral out of control, Shan turned to his friend. "Can you get your people out of here? Let me talk to these residents."

Lei and the workers retreated.

Shan turned to the woman. "Ma'am, calm down. Otherwise, you may aggravate your blood pressure."

"Our blood pressure will be fine if you guys go away." A man standing by the woman cut in.

Shan glanced at him for a second and then took out a pack of cigarettes from his pocket, handing one to the man.

"Don't try." The man pushed Shan's hand back.

Shan smiled at the residents and spoke like their

friend. "I understand that building a wall will make your lives inconvenient. If I were you, I wouldn't be happy either. Most of you are retired and have unlimited time to fight against those construction workers and delay the project as long as you want to."

The man nodded. "You have some sense. Tell them to leave. As long as we are alive, they can't build a wall here."

"I hope I can do that, but I don't think they will listen to me."

"Then, there's nothing we can talk about." The woman waved her hand as if trying to brush away a fly.

Shan looked at her. "My friend didn't know about the situation when he signed a contract with Jiangkai. If he had known about it, he would not have taken the project." He then pointed at the workers in the distance. "Look at those young men. They came from the poor countryside to earn money to support their parents and siblings. If you prevent them from doing so, what do you think they will do? Will they give up and quietly walk away with empty pockets or…?"

"You don't threaten us," the woman shouted at him.

"I'm not threatening you. I'm trying to help you understand the situation. If they don't get paid, they will be angry at you, all of you." Shan glanced around at the group. "When emotions run high, the situation can get out of control, and someone may get hurt. Even if the police arrest them, you may live a miserable and painful life for a long, long time."

The residents looked at him in silence.

Good, they're listening to me, and they're thinking.

He handed a cigarette to the man again. The elderly man glanced at it for a second and then took it. Shan lit the cigarette for him and then glanced at the group. "If I were you, I would let them build the wall during the daytime and then take it down at night."

"Why?" The woman glared at Shan.

"By doing so, you will allow them to show the real estate developer that they were capable of building the wall. As for what happens at night, it is beyond their control. Then Jiangkai can't do anything about them. So, it is a win-win situation."

"No, that's not a win-win situation. Don't try to fool us." The woman shook her index finger at Shan.

"Yes, don't try to fool us," several other people echoed.

This woman is a troublemaker, Shan thought to himself. Avoid her and take care of her later.

He turned to the man and asked in the most honest voice, "What do you think?"

The man gazed at Shan for a second and then took a drag from his cigarette. "How about we meet tomorrow? We need to have a meeting tonight to discuss the matter."

"Sounds good." Shan nodded. "Let me check with my friend about the idea."

He left for Lei and came back shortly. "My friend is fine with it. Let's meet tomorrow."

As the residents dispersed, Shan followed the woman to her apartment without her noticing. When she was about to unlock her door, he made a loud sound by clearing his throat. The woman looked at him over her shoulder and immediately turned around, her back against the door and fear on her face. "What are you doing here?"

"I'm here to save your life." Shan stepped forward.

"What do you want to do?" She stared at him. "If

you move forward one more step, I will shout."

"You don't have to. I'm not going to hurt you. I'm trying to help you."

"What do you mean?"

"Everyone can tell that you are the leader of the group. Do you think the construction workers will let you go if they don't get paid because of you? They can easily find where you live, just like me. You're as old as my mother. I don't want to see you get hurt."

Without waiting for her response, he turned and left the building.

When he got back to Lei again, his friend looked at him with a confused expression. "Why did you suggest they tear down our work at night?"

"That's the best way to help you." Shan handed Lei a cigarette. "Does Jiangkai know the situation?"

"Yes, I have told them several times."

"What did they say?"

"They asked me to fix it myself."

Shan lit the cigarette for his friend and himself. "Given the power the company has, it could easily get help from the police, but it hasn't. Apparently, there must be a reason we don't know. So, to solve the problem, we should be tactical. They are retired and have unlimited time. To prevent you from starting the construction, all they need to do is sit around the site and have fun. Time is on their side."

"You're right." Lei nodded. "But I still don't get why you suggest they take down our work at night."

"You have to offer them hope. Otherwise, they will not let you put a single brick there. Letting them demolish your work helps you in two ways. First, you can show Jiangkai that you did the work and how difficult it is. Secondly, you will have an opportunity to complete the project. Taking down the structure will be much more difficult for them than preventing you from working on the project. In the first few days, they may be able to dismantle your construction, but they will soon become exhausted. They are retired, and they just don't have that kind of physical strength."

Lei extended his thumb. "That's a smart idea."

"Listen, here is what you should do. Start slow. Let your construction workers build the wall for three hours a day so that the residents can easily remove your work in the evenings."

"Why is that?"

"That serves two purposes. First, it gives them a sense of accomplishment and convinces them that this method works for them. Second, it minimizes your material loss and labor consumption. I bet that they will wear out in a few days and won't even have any strength to come out of their homes to argue with you. Then, you can accelerate the project."

The next day, Lei and Shan came to the subdivision to meet the residents. The old man said that they would agree with the proposal, and the woman kept looking at Shan throughout the meeting without saying a word.

Throughout the following week, Shan and Lei went to the subdivision to check out the situation from a distance. In the first two evenings, a large group of elderly people came out to dismantle the construction, but starting on the third day, not only did the size of the group keep shrinking, but it also took them longer to finish the task. By the end of the week, no one even came out to touch the wall.

Chapter 30

The alarm clock went off. It was time to take the silicon wafers out of the mixed acids. Xiang extracted the holder from the solution to put it in a deionized water tank, but the holder was empty.

Where were the wafers? He blinked. Had he forgotten to load them?

He remembered a novel in which the protagonist lost his short-term memory due to emotional stress and wandered aimlessly down the street, resulting in an accident.

Oh, my God! Thank you for preventing me from making a huge mistake and keeping me safe and alive.

Although he did not believe in God, there was no one else to thank at that moment. Fear of making another mistake, he soaked the holder in the water to remove the chemicals and started cleaning the area.

No more work. Leave the lab, he told himself as he cleaned off the table. As he reached for the beaker, his eyes widened, almost popping out of his skull. Yellowish-brown fumes were erupting from the container, a thick, billowing cloud-like the highly polluted smoke from a factory chimney.

The liquid was violently boiling inside.

Instinctively, he ducked behind a large piece of equipment a few yards away and peered helplessly at the beaker, waiting for the turbulence to turn explosive. His mind went blank, his heart raced, and he was drenched in sweat. One second. Two seconds. Ten seconds. The fume started to fade, and the turbulence began to calm. As the worst had passed, he felt a rush of relief. He took a deep breath and approached the workspace with caution, trying to figure out what was in the beaker and why there had been so much smoke.

Inside the glass container, a few small irregular pieces of something were jouncing around like popcorn in a pan as the bubbles rose and popped.

What were these? Where did they come from? Xiang had never seen anything like them before. Completely confused, he leaned closer and examined them. They were thin and dark. From them, air bubbles rose, floated to the surface, and were released as brown smoke. He realized that they must be the remains of the silicon wafers that had been dissolved into small pieces during the cleaning process. That would explain why the wafer holder was empty.

He straightened up and sighed.

What a shame. While other students were having a great time on their spring break, he had been working hard in the lab under adverse conditions, only to waste his time and almost cause an accident. He had thought he could endure the high temperature but had forgotten that wafers etched faster at that temperature.

Sweat soaked through his clothes, and dehydration made him dizzy. He quickly cleaned up the workspace, left the cleanroom, and went to the water fountain in the hallway. After drinking a lot of water, he made his way to his dormitory.

In the quiet and empty campus at three o'clock in the morning, the stars in the cloudless sky blinked down at him, as if wondering why he was being so imprudent. He walked along with his shadow cast by the streetlights for twenty minutes before arriving at the building that he and Lulu occupied. When he reached his room, he stopped and stared at the gate that divided the hallway in half, feeling it like an impassable barrier between them. In a state of exhaustion, he opened the door and went straight to bed. By the time he opened his eyes, it was already one o'clock in the afternoon.

He got up, ate a peanut butter and jelly sandwich, and went to the lab. On the first day of spring break, he had failed twice, once in Lulu's room and the other in the lab. He needed success to lift his spirits out of the mud. This time, he chose to do a simple, straightforward experiment so that nothing could go wrong.

He went to a lab located in the new central facility at the school. After changing into cleanroom garb, he entered a well-lit room with a polished floor that reflected his figure and stopped in front of a thin film coating machine. As the only person in the lab, he had the entire space to himself. He transferred his sample box and a diamond scriber from the cabinet to the large table next to the machine, took out all forty samples from the box, and placed them on the desk. He then carefully marked the back of the samples according to their processing parameters to ensure that they could be easily identified later. After spending nearly an hour labeling and documenting the samples, he loaded half of them into the brand-new equipment and pushed the round green button on the front panel.

The process started. It was straightforward, and nothing could go wrong. Success was within his reach.

He sat back and whistled *Today Is a Good Day*, his

favorite Chinese song.

Twenty minutes later, the process would be completed, and he would have his first spring-break achievement and the best samples he had ever made. To fabricate them, he had spent the last two months working meticulously on every step and following the process recipe precisely. The samples would provide him with the most comprehensive and valuable data for his PhD research.

As the victory was coming, he thought about Lulu again and thanked her for having rejected him. Otherwise, he would be having fun with her somewhere else rather than doing his research.

The machine beeped, and the process was complete.

He opened the chamber and examined the samples. Their color looked just right — dark brown. After the final step of the experiment—high annealing, they would become black. To capture all incoming light, the ideal surface of a solar cell should be as black as possible.

Xiang took them out, loaded the other half of the batch into the chamber, and pushed the start button again. Another twenty minutes later, the machine beeped again. He opened the chamber to take the samples out. With the exact parameters as in the last batch, everything should be perfect.

When he looked at them, he was startled, almost fainting.

Oh my God! How is that possible?

All of the samples were not dark brown as he had anticipated, but blue, a color he had never seen before, which meant that all of them were ruined. With half a of his sample batch now destroyed, his entire study became useless.

In the last two months, to fabricate the best solar cells, he had arrived at the lab early in the morning and left after midnight, never having had a single weekend off. He meticulously fabricated the samples and tested them after each major step. They had been the best he had ever produced.

Now they were gone. Once again, his hard work had not only set him back two months but also would humiliate him in front of his professor and the whole group.

With a mood bluer than these samples, he sank into the chair, staring at the ceiling.

Chapter 31

Xiang leaned motionlessly in his chair, his eyes closed. He did not want to open them. He did not want to see anything.

What's the matter with me? Why do I fail at everything I attempt? The two batches of samples have been processed under exactly the same conditions. Why is one batch brown, the other blue?

He let out a long sigh. It did not matter why this had happened. The samples had been destroyed, and two months of hard work had been ruined.

Xiang sat silently for a few minutes before getting up to inspect the equipment, trying to identify the cause of the failure. He checked the parameter settings again and then ran a full test on the machine, checking every aspect of its operation. He watched the display panel without blinking, and two minutes later, he saw that one of the gas flow rates was way down.

How could that be? … Something must be wrong with the gas supply.

He went to the facility room to check the gas tank and discovered that it was nearly empty. Apparently, the engineer in charge of replacing the tanks during the normal school year had not anticipated anyone being stupid enough to work over spring break.

Returning to the lab, he took a piece of paper, intending to tape the failed samples to it. He planned to hang it next to his bed so that he could see it first thing in the morning and last thing at night. It would serve as a reminder for him to be more cautious in his research. He should not only work hard but also be smart.

When he was about to mount the first sample, curiosity struck him. A few days ago, he had read a research paper about fabricating silicon semiconductor devices. It reported that annealing a device at 750°C for twenty seconds could significantly improve its performance. He had been wondering if he could use that technique in his research but had never tried it because his samples were too precious to waste. It was common knowledge that solar cells would die if they were annealed at a temperature higher than 350°C. But at present, he had useless samples, and it was the perfect time to fulfill his curiosity. It would be the most fun part of his spring break, regardless of the results.

Xiang took all the samples to another room and placed the failed samples on a plate in a rapid thermal anneal machine. He adjusted the running program to 750°C for five seconds and then hit the START button. While the machine was running, he felt a kind of eager anticipation. It was like stepping into the wilderness, like setting off on an adventure, with no idea of what awaited him.

A few minutes later, the process was completed. Instead of opening the chamber right away, he sat quietly, preparing himself mentally for the outcome. He reminded himself that he should expect nothing but dead cells. His experience had taught him that assuming the worst could sometimes yield a pleasant surprise.

When he felt ready, he opened the chamber and looked at the samples.

Oh, my! I have broken the machine.

His heart skipped a beat, and he felt dizzy as if blood rushed to his head. For a brief moment, he thought he would faint.

On the grayish device holder, there were many black holes. Apparently, the high temperature had burned the plate.

Breaking such an expensive machine was a major accident, and he would certainly be punished for that. He might even get fired. People say curiosity killed the cat, but his curiosity was going to destroy his career, not the cat. After the initial shock, a thought occurred to him. It was impossible to burn a plate at 750°C because it could withstand nearly 2000 degrees.

He looked at the device holder again, more closely, and then touched one of the tiny holes with the tip of his tweezers. The hole slipped off.

What? How could it move?

He touched it again. It was not a hole, but his sample!

Staring at it, he had difficulty believing that he had developed the best anti-reflection coating better than anything he could have imagined in his wildest dreams. To convert light into electricity, an ideal solar cell should trap every photon shining on it.

His excited heart was pumping so loudly that he could hear it echo in his ears. He took a step back, not wanting to touch the samples because he was afraid his ecstasy would damage them. Once he calmed down a bit, he started to take them out with extreme care and placed them on a piece of clean white paper on the desk. In the large white background, the small samples looked like black holes. After the thrill subsided, he started to worry that although the samples had the best anti-reflection, they might have died. Everyone knew that silicon solar cells broke down at temperatures above 350°C. But he had annealed his at 750°C. That most likely had destroyed them. He took a device to the testing room next door, mounted it on a tester, and launched a testing program.

A moment later, a beautiful curve that existed only in solar cell textbooks appeared on the screen. He stared at it, with his mouth wide open. The new technique not only improved the anti-reflection but also significantly enhanced other properties of the solar cells.

Xiang rushed to the other room and brought all the samples to test them, hoping that what he had just seen was not an outlier. He tested them one by one, and his excitement pumped his heart rate faster and faster. The samples annealed at 750°C performed much better than the ones fabricated by the standard method. After testing, he carefully placed all of the samples in a cleanroom box and carried them to his dorm instead of leaving them in the cabinet as he had usually done. They were too precious to be left in the lab.

For the rest of the week, he did not go to the lab anymore. He had learned his lesson that equipment might not be in the best state during the school vacation.

When spring break was over, he went to see Dr. Rick with a datasheet detailing the results of his experiment. The professor sat between a sizable brown table and a big window, reading a paper. On his right was a large whiteboard with formulas and figures. On his left was a brown bookshelf fully loaded with books and technical journals. Xiang knocked at the open door.

"Come on in." The professor raised his head. "Have

a seat."

Xiang sat in a chair across from Dr. Rick and reported his experiment results. The professor listened quietly, nodding now and then and occasionally frowning. When Xiang finished talking, his advisor continued to stare at the datasheet for a few more seconds and then muttered, "It doesn't make sense."

That reaction did not surprise Xiang. If he had not conducted the experiment, he would not have believed his findings either. To prepare to convince his advisor, he had brought his solar cells with him. "Here are the samples." He opened his sample box and placed it on the table. "See how black they are."

The professor picked up one with tweezers and held it close to his eyes as if inspecting a precious gem.

"Very nice anti-reflection coating." The professor nodded. "But annealing solar cells at such high temperature should have destroyed them." He raised his head, gazing at Xiang. "Did you calibrate the tester?"

The professor's voice was calm, but it sounded like thunder to Xiang.

How could he have forgotten to calibrate the equipment!

Thinking that all of his results could be bogus and that he had made himself a fool before his PhD advisor, he felt his stomach squirm. Ashamed and embarrassed, Xiang wished that he was only dreaming so he could wake up and pretend that none of this had ever happened.

Chapter 32

Dr. Rick placed a sample back in the box and gazed at Xiang. "You might want to go back and check your tester's calibration."

"I will. Sorry for wasting your time." Xiang wiped the sweat from his forehead, his face burning with embarrassment.

Just as he was about to leave, he realized why he had trusted the equipment. He glanced at his advisor again. "The tester should be fine since the results of the samples annealed at 350 were as I expected."

The professor gazed at Xiang for a few long seconds through his thick glasses and nodded. "Would you like to present your findings at our group meeting tomorrow?"

Xiang's eyes widened. Dr. Rick had believed in his discovery! At least to some extent. In excitement, he left the office and rushed to the lab to check the calibration of the tester. After confirming it was in perfect working order, he went to the library to summarize his findings and prepare for his presentation.

The next day, as he walked into the small conference room just down the hall from Dr. Rick's office, his advisor and other students had sat around a large rectangular dark brown table. There was no empty seat anywhere near the professor. He sat quietly at the far end of the table, glancing at his fellow students and imagining their reactions when they heard his report.

A few minutes later, the meeting started, and he was asked to give a presentation to the group. Xiang went up to the overhead projector at the end of the table and placed a slide on the equipment. On the large screen behind him, bright yellow text on a dark blue background said *A New Method of Fabricating Solar Cells*.

"Thank you for giving me the opportunity to present my new findings to you. In my last experiment…" He pointed at the screen with a green laser pointer, speaking with confidence and excitement.

When he got to his fourth slide, Austin, the senior PhD student in the group, interrupted him. "Excuse me. Did you say that you annealed your samples at 750°C?"

"Yes." Xiang nodded at the tall, angular-faced man who sat next to the professor. "As you will—"

"You shouldn't have annealed them at that temperature. You're not supposed to anneal solar cells above 350°C. It destroys the devices."

"I thought so, but my data says otherwise." Xiang placed another slide on the projector. "These data show that the voltage of the solar cells increased after—"

"Hold on." Austin interrupted him again. "Your data doesn't make sense. Are you sure you didn't mess up your samples?"

"Yes, I'm sure." Xiang did not like Austin's tone but answered his question politely.

"Something must be wrong." Austin narrowed his eyes at the screen and spoke in a skeptical tone. "Did you calibrate your tester?"

"The tester worked perfectly." Xiang did not answer the question directly. That would lead to more questions. He threw a look at his advisor, grateful that the professor had asked the same question the previous day.

Austin typed his finger on the table. “Then, you must have tested the wrong devices. Those solar cells should have died.”

An undercurrent of irritation flowed through Xiang's body at Austin's remark. He ignored it and moved on to the next slide. Then, he saw Mark raise his hand.

Mark was a third-year PhD student, a quiet, short, round fellow with a pair of thick horn-rimmed glasses. He usually didn't say much during group meetings, but when he did, his opinions were often insightful.

Xiang nodded at him.

“Do you know why we never anneal solar cells above 350°C?”

Xiang smiled at him without answering. He knew this was a warm-up to a lecture on fundamental physics. That was Mark's style.

Mark adjusted his glasses. “Because above 350, the metal on the surface starts to diffuse into the p-n junction and thereby destroys the device.”

“That's right,” Austin commented. “That's common knowledge. You must have made mistakes somewhere. I'm telling you.”

Xiang had anticipated the challenge from the group and had brought his samples to the meeting. “I have my devices here. I'm passing them around so that you can see them with your own eyes.”

He handed a transparent sample box to the nearest student and continued his presentation. As he pointed to a figure, explaining it, he heard Austin's voice again.

“They look black, but that doesn't mean they're good devices. Charcoal is black, too.”

Xiang turned to look at Austin, who was holding the

box. "I presented the data. You don't believe it. I showed you my devices. You think they're dead. Do you want to go to the lab with me and test the devices?"

Dr. Rick leaned back in his chair with his arms crossed in front of his chest. "Your devices look very decent. However, to convince people, we need to repeat the experiment. Would you like to use this method to make another batch of solar cells and report back to the group later?"

"Sure, I'll do it." Xiang nodded, glad to see that his advisor was more accepting of his results than the other students.

The professor added, "This time, you need to do it more systematically, making sure to characterize your samples throughout the fabrication process. That will give you a deeper understanding of the mechanisms behind this improvement."

Great advice. Apparently, his advisor believed in his data. The professor was a professor, and he could perceive things that students were unable to. The meeting had been a victory. Now it was up to him to prove that his results were repeatable. With his advisor's support, what Austin or any of the other students thought of his new findings was no longer relevant.

After the group meeting, Xiang spent long hours in his lab every day, meticulously fabricating solar cells. Although he wished he could achieve the same exceptional results, he knew it was unlikely. Reproducing exceptional results was extremely difficult. It was just the nature of experimental research. There was nothing he could do other than complete the process without errors. Occasionally he even wished he had never made the discovery. It would most likely do more harm to him than good.

Three weeks later, he finished the fabrication. Instead of testing the devices right away, he spent the night in the library, randomly reading books and newspapers. He was too nervous to know the results.

The next morning, he reluctantly carried his sample box to the testing room. He turned on the tester, placed a sample on the stage, and ran the program. He did not care what he would get, and he would be happy as long as the device was not dead. The fact that his last batch of solar cells survived a 750-degree high-temperature process did not mean this batch would as well. After all, it was common knowledge that silicon solar cells should not be processed at temperatures above 350°C.

On the computer screen, black dots appeared one after another, creating a characteristic curve rising from the lower-left corner to the right. From the shape, Xiang knew that his device was far better than his previous ones.

Too excited to continue testing, he stepped out of the lab and into the parking lot for a short break. The gentle breeze caressed his face, blowing away his past. From now on, he would be admired by his peers.

He strolled for five minutes in the sun before returning to the lab and completing the test, and then hurried to his advisor's office. He couldn't wait an extra minute to share his results.

"You did a great job," Dr. Rick complimented him after hearing his report. "I have been worried about whether you can withstand peer pressure if you fail to reproduce the devices."

If Xiang had been a baby, he would have started to cry. In the last three weeks, he had had so many nightmares, in which his advisor had questioned his ethics and his fellow students had accused him of falsifying his previous data. Now, he realized that even if he had failed, his advisor would not have doubted his integrity and his discovery. He had underestimated how much the professor understood about the nature of solar cell fabrication and how much his advisor cared about him.

Dr. Rick pushed aside a stack of papers and looked at a large calendar on his desk. "There will be an international conference in May. You should present your findings there." The professor paused for a second. "At the conference, people will ask you questions and give you feedback. After returning, you will do another round of the experiment, addressing their questions and polishing your research. Then we will be able to write a journal paper. Maybe more."

How wonderful! After having been stuck in the dark, muddy jungle, with paths winding down through swamps, he had suddenly come out into this sunlit, flowery slope, where the path widened and smoothed all the way to the doctoral regalia lying there in wait for his grasp.

Attending an international conference and publishing journal papers were his dreams. He could not only travel to a different city to see a bigger world but also advance his PhD research significantly. In this group, to get a doctorate, a student had to publish at least two journal papers.

Dr. Rick retrieved a conference flyer from the stack of papers and handed it to Xiang. "The extended abstract submission deadline is this Saturday. Can you do it?"

Tomorrow? That was awfully short notice. There

was no way he could do it.

As Xiang's heart sank at the thought of missing the great opportunity, the professor went on, "I'll be leaving for California on Sunday morning. If you need help, you can come to my office tomorrow. I'll be here the whole day. We —"

The jingling of the telephone interrupted Dr. Rick. He picked it up, listened for a second, and gestured to Xiang that he would like to speak privately.

Xiang left the room and headed to the main library, where he worked on his two-page extended abstract until the building was closed. He hurried back to his dorm and continued to work on it until midnight, during which time he went to the bathroom several times to splash cold water on his face to keep himself awake. After many revisions, he saw Dr. Rick the next morning.

"Overall, it looks good." The professor complimented him after reading the abstract and gave him suggestions on how to improve it.

Xiang revised the abstract several more times throughout the day with the help of his advisor until Dr. Rick left for home in the late afternoon. Xiang submitted the abstract before midnight after working on it for five more hours. When he returned to his dormitory, he fell asleep as soon as his head hit the pillow.

Two months later, he flew to San Antonio, Texas, for the conference, all expenses paid by his professor. Airline tickets, hotel accommodations, and even meals.

The conference was held at a hotel with more than three hundred attendees. His session was in a room with a capacity of forty. Having never before given a presentation to experts from around the world in his field, he sat in the very back row, nervously shaking his legs, as if the motion could somehow calm him.

One speaker finished, then another, and then another. An hour later, a tall, young Chinese student in a dark suit and round horn-rim glasses stepped up to the podium. He shuffled his feet nervously as he spoke, tugging at his ears, and dabbing at his forehead with a handkerchief. The nerves seemed to have found a target and shot across the room at Xiang, exacerbating his own anxiety. His legs shook faster, and his heart raced.

Calm down. You will be fine.. You have good data, and you are well prepared. When you are nervous, you are actually causing yourself harm.

His mind was clear, but his body did not listen to him. He just could not stop his dancing legs. An awful thought came to him. What was he going to do when it was his turn to present?

While he was worrying, his name was called. Concerned, he got up to walk to the podium. Strange. The moment he stood up, his legs quit shaking and all the nerves miraculously disappeared. No wonder people say stand up to challenges, stand up to fear. Standing up did help. At the very least, it steadied his trembling legs.

He went to the overhead projector, placed his transparency on the lectern, and started his presentation. While speaking, he lost himself in the pleasure of describing solar cell fabrication and data interpretation. Although he looked at the audience, he did not see them. He totally lived in his own world.

At the end of his talk, the audience asked him so many questions that the moderator had to step in to keep the session on track. Amid loud applause, he walked off the stage. Instead of returning to his seat, he went to the lobby to get a drink. He walked down the hall and stopped at the refreshment table. While reaching for a glass of water, he felt a hard grip on his shoulder.

"Stop!" An angry and low voice reached his ears from behind. "How dare you steal my work!"

Chapter 33

Two months before graduation, Shan and Lei walked toward their dormitory after playing basketball.

"Congratulations," Lei said.

"For what?" Shan looked at his friend.

"Didn't you hear? There are two job openings in Huadu, one at the Institute of Electrical Engineering and the other at the Electrical Power Research Institute."

"Yes, I've heard."

"According to return-hometown policy, you'll get one of them."

"But I'm thinking about going to Tibet."

"Don't kid me." Lei laughed.

"Don't laugh. I'm serious. The central government is calling on new college graduates to work in Tibet. I'm thinking of going there."

"I want to go too," Lei said with a sarcastic tone. "It's a beautiful and romantic place with a blue sky and green land. It has the highest mountain in the world."

"Don't make fun of me. I'm serious, but I can't make up my mind yet."

"Are you crazy?" Lei glanced at Shan, eyes widening. "Don't be naïve. The real Tibet is not like what you see in the movies, where everyone is dressed beautifully, dancing and singing. It's extremely poor."

"I know."

Lei narrowed his eyes. "Then, what do you want to

get out of it?"

"Help the Tibetans. They live in terrible conditions, far behind the rest of the country. In Tibet, most places don't even have electricity, and some people don't have enough to eat."

"You can't change anything for them but destroy yourself. Tibet is totally a different world, with an average elevation of over 4,000 meters. Unless you were born there, it's difficult to adjust to the environment. Twenty years ago, for the same reason you're considering it, my aunt went to Tibet. In the high mountains, the strong ultraviolet radiation and lack of oxygen ravaged her health. In less than five years, she developed an incurable chronic illness. Now she's living a miserable life.

"I heard that the policy is to encourage new graduates to spend two years there and then return to their hometowns."

"You really believe that? Even if it's true now, anything can happen in two years. If the policy changes, you could be trapped there forever."

Shan slowed his pace, silently gazing at the crimson clouds on the west horizon for a few seconds, and then turned to look at his friend. "Do you know Xiao Hong, a student in the Department of Philosophy?"

"Yes. I believe he's the vice president of the student government at the university. What about him?"

"He's going to Tibet."

"That doesn't surprise me. He's from a farmer's family in the impoverished countryside. He must return to his hometown after graduation. Do you think he's happy about that? No. After studying in the city for four years and seeing the world, going back to the poor countryside is unbearable. So he gambled. Considering the potential gain, working in Tibet is not nearly as bad as returning to his rural countryside. I'm sure he will serve as an example to the government and be assigned to an important position immediately in Tibet. He will have every chance of success there, far more than he would have had back home."

Shan nodded in agreement.

"Don't be stupid. Go back to Huadu, where everyone wants to go but cannot."

As they talked, Shan caught sight of Meng walking out of a building. He turned back to Lei. "I need to talk to Meng. I'll see you later."

"Okay. Be practical. Don't let idealism ruin your life." Lei patted Shan's shoulder and left.

"Meng," Shan called and rushed to his friend. "I've been looking for you. Since we're about to graduate, I thought we could get together."

"I thought about that too. Would you like to take a walk by the lake?"

"Sure."

Together, they headed to the lake, shoulder to shoulder.

Evening scarlet clouds filled the west horizon as if blood had spilled across the sky.

After a few minutes of light conversation, Shan said, "I have had a question for you for a long time but have never found the right time."

"I assume you want to know why the school rejected the department's decision to accept you as a member of the Communist Party. Is that right?"

Shan chuckled. "You know me. So, tell me what happened. Who stabbed me in the back?"

Meng looked around as if to make sure no one else was in earshot and back at Shan. “This is highly confidential information that I should never disclose under any circumstances. I'm telling you this only because we are good friends, and we may not see each other for a long time after graduation.”

“Thank you very much. After the incident, I ran through every roommate in my mind, but I was unable to identify anyone who could have done that to me. Can you tell me who it was?”

“I need you to promise me that you won't tell anyone what I'm going to say.”

“I promise.” Shan raised his hand as if swearing.

“It was not your roommate. It was Qing and Wei.” Meng paused and looked around again. “When the school reviewed your application and the department’s decision, they told the committee that you were anti-revolutionary. They said that you labeled all the Communist Party members as either liars or idiots.”

“What?” Shan gasped. “Are you kidding me?”

“I don't joke about things like this.”

Shan shook his head. “No, that was not possible. Qing is one of my closest friends, and we just had dinner together last night.”

“Friends? It's not uncommon for a friend to stab another friend in the back. Quite often, it is friends who cause the greatest damage to you, because you let your guard down around those you trust, and you are at your most vulnerable. Your friends can hurt you in ways even strangers and enemies cannot. They know you well, and they know how to do that to you. They are the ones who become irritated when you move ahead while they're still stuck in place. It is human nature to be jealous of those they know well. Friendship is a double-edged sword. It can be helpful, but it can also cut you to the quick. You need it, but you also have to be wary of its danger."

Meng's remarks left him speechless, his mouth hanging open.

Perhaps noticing his surprise, his friend added, "My father was betrayed by his closest friends during the Great Cultural Revolution and was beaten to death by them." He stopped talking as if he were having trouble breathing.

"I'm sorry to hear that." Shan tried to console him but could not find the right words.

"I shouldn't talk about that. It's too painful." Meng became silent for a moment. "Now let's get back to you. I have noticed that Qing appears to be your friend and wondered why she did that to you. After giving it a lot of thought, I understand her motives. While she was the vice president of the student government, you were nobody, just an ordinary student. When it came time to elect a new student government, she fought hard to be elected president, but you won without even running for it. That's pretty painful for her. It's hard to take. As she tried to join the Communist Party, you were picked by the department, which made her even angrier. I believe that is why she did it to you."

Shan nodded. "Did the committee really believe that I'm an anti-revolutionary?"

"Of course not. No one believed that. But the committee had to take the accusation seriously after Qing and Wei claimed that you said Communist Party members were either idiots or liars. Mr. Gudong didn't believe either of them, but he couldn't do anything. The charge was too serious."

"Why didn't the committee conduct its own investigation?"

"It did. Qing and Wei said they represented many students who were afraid to speak out and provided some of their names. The committee talked to them and confirmed the allegation."

"Whom did they talk to? Is any of them my roommate?"

"I don't think so."

"Then how did the committee confirm it? The conversation took place in my dorm room, and it wasn't me who said it."

"It doesn't matter how they did it. My guess is that for reasons having nothing to do with you, some members just didn't want you joining the Party, and none of the others was willing to defend you, a person who had no value to them."

Shan remembered what Lei had told him and asked, "I was told that some people used me to attack Mr. Gudong. Is that right?"

"I've heard of that theory. I think you just had bad luck. Here's some good news. During my conversation with Mr. Gudong, I got the impression he would not record this incident in your personnel file. Then, when you return to Huadu, you will have a clean slate to start over."

"Thank you, but I'm thinking about going to Tibet." Shan intended to hear his friend's opinion. As the Chair of the Communist Youth League in the department, Meng might be supportive.

"Seriously?" His friend looked startled. "You must be kidding."

"I'm not, but I have not made a final decision yet."

"Why do you want to go to Tibet? Compared with most students, you're quite lucky. You are from Huadu and have a chance to return and work for a prestigious research institute there. Why do you want to give up such a great opportunity?"

After talking with Meng and Lei, Shan began to wonder if he was being naïve. He wrestled with the decision for several more days until he was convinced that he did belong in Huadu. His best career path lay in academic research at a nationally renowned institute.

Two weeks later, like all the other students in his graduating class, he received a letter from the department about his job assignment. The news was as if thunder had erupted out of nowhere. After reading it, he slammed the paper on his desk and shouted in his head. *Why? Why have they assigned me to the Yellow River Electrical Power Company in Xihe, hundreds of kilometers from Huadu? Why have they taken away my right to return to Huadu and instead throw me a job that no one wants?*

Chapter 34

Xiang flinched and turned. In front of him stood a thin Asian man with sunglasses and a scar about an inch long on his left cheek. He wore a black suit and a scarlet tie and was about a head taller.

Who is he? Xiang took a step back, holding his breath.

"Ha, ha, …. I scared you, didn't I?" The man took off his glasses. "Don't you remember me?"

"Caoyi? You're Caoyi, aren't you?" Xiang cheered.

Caoyi and Xiang had been good friends. They had lived in the same residential building when they were elementary students until Caoyi's mother died in a car accident, and his father committed suicide fifteen years ago.

"Yes." The man extended his hand. "Congratulations! That was a great presentation. Truly amazing."

"Thank you." Xiang shook his hand. "It's so hard to believe that we meet in the United States. How have you been? Are you studying in the United States too?"

"Yes, I'm a PhD student at Berkford."

Berkford? That is one of the top schools in physics.

His friend cast a glance at his watch. "It's almost lunchtime. Would you like to go to lunch?"

"Of course."

They went to a small Chinese restaurant across the

street and were seated in a booth next to a window. While they waited for a waitress to arrive, Xiang leaned forward. “How was your life after you left Huadu? Where did you go?”

“I don't want to talk about it. It was a nightmare.” Caoyi lowered his gaze to his silverware.

Sensing that his friend must have had a difficult life after leaving Huadu, Xiang changed the subject. “What is your research?”

“Bose-Einstein quantum statistics for photons.”

“Can you tell me a little more about it?”

His friend talked about the research, from its history to the present challenges, to potential future applications.

“That sounds very interesting,” Xiang commented.

“Yes, but it's difficult to find a job with that background.” Caoyi sighed. “See, I’m graduating this semester and have been looking for a job for more than two months. There are not enough positions for physics PhDs.”

Xiang had heard that the job market was very tight for non-immigrant PhDs. After China opened to the West, hundreds of Chinese students came to the United States to study physics because it was easier to get an assistantship. Now, there were too many PhDs for too few job openings.

While he was thinking, his friend said again, “You don't know how stressful it is to graduate without a job.”

“I understand, but you don’t have to be so stressed. In the worst-case scenario, you can always return to China. With a PhD, you should easily land an excellent job and establish yourself as a leader in your field.”

“I don’t want to go back to China. The Great Cultural Revolution destroyed my family.” Caoyi’s face turned dismal, and his eyes filled with tears. He blinked several times as if trying to control his tears and then stood up. “Excuse me. I have to go to the bathroom.”

Caoyi had grown up in an intellectual family of four. Both of his parents had been educated in the United States in the 1940s. His father, Jim, earned a PhD in physics, and his mother received her master’s degree in English. Early in the 1950s, shortly after the Communist Party gained control of the country, Jim was invited back to China to lead the national lab where Xiang's father worked. Under his leadership, the national lab advanced defense technology significantly.

However, like many other scientists educated in the West, he was charged with spying and arrested by national lab security guards during the Great Cultural Revolution. He was confined in a small room with nothing but a hard bed and a small table. The food was minimal, mostly grains, and barely any vegetables and meat. In addition, he was not allowed to be visited by his family.

One day, the national lab’s revolutionary committee informed Caoyi’s mother that her husband had become very ill and she was allowed to visit. His mother took him and his older sister to see his father, carrying chicken soup and eggs. When they were crossing the street, a black car owned by the Revolutionary Committee struck her. Soon, her blood flowed out of her clothes and spread over the ground, mixing with the yellow chicken soup and sunny-side-up eggs.

She died.

Caoyi and his sister stood silently before the corpse, their mouths and eyes wide open. After a long pause, his sister burst into hysterical laughter and ran about wildly, hands waving in the air. He continued to stand still like a statue for a long, long time.

After his mother's death, the national lab released his father, who had wounds all over his body and a broken leg. After returning home, he hardly spoke and always stood in front of the living room window, staring into the dark night for hours. Two weeks later, he jumped from his thirteenth-floor apartment at midnight. From his suicide note, people learned that he blamed himself for his wife's death and his daughter's insanity. Caoyi and his sister moved in with Xiang's family and stayed with them for nearly a month before leaving Huadu with their uncle. Since then, Xiang had never heard from him.

His friend came back from the bathroom, eyes swelling as if he had cried.

"Are you okay?" Xiang looked at Caoyi's red eyes.

"I'm fine."

Xiang tried to comfort his friend. "The Chinese government has declared the Great Cultural Revolution a disaster and pledged that nothing like that will ever happen again."

"Do you believe that?" Caoyi sneered.

"Why not?"

"I don't believe it. Even though the current leaders have condemned the Great Cultural Revolution and don't allow it to happen again, there is no guarantee that future leaders will feel the same. The government blames the catastrophe on one leader, but that's wrong. It wasn't one person's fault. It is a result of current politics and culture that has existed for thousands of years. Don't tell me that the Great Cultural Revolution will never happen again. When the time is right, and there is a need for it, it will happen and could be more terrible than before."

Xiang looked at the scar on Caoyi's face, which was caused by a group of Red Guards when he tried to stop them from dragging his father away on a tragic night. Apparently, not only his face but also his heart had been scarred by the Great Cultural Revolution.

To cheer his friend up, Xiang changed the topic. "You are amazing. I just started my PhD program, and you are about to graduate. How could you do that?"

"I've been working extremely hard, and I was lucky. In my first attempt, I found a solution to a very challenging problem." Caoyi paused for a second. "When are you going to graduate?"

"In four years. This is my first year."

"If I were you, I would change my major immediately. There is no future for a Chinese PhD in physics. You can't find a job, and you can't even find a wife. No girl wants to marry a man who has no future. Look at me. I'm still single."

The words reminded Xiang of a breakup letter his ex-girlfriend had written him. He wondered whether studying physics was the reason for Miaomiao to terminate their relationship. She had suggested to him many times that he should change his major to something more practical.

Although Xiang intended to go back to China after graduation, he thought he should get some real-life experience in America first. "I have made a breakthrough in my research. Do you think that will help me land a job?"

"You indeed have remarkable results. But don't get too excited about it. Every PhD student achieves something. My research has exciting outcomes too, and I have published four papers."

"Wow." Xiang glanced at his friend with round eyes.

"Don't look at me like that." His friend smiled but soon became expressionless. Pausing for a second, he rolled his sleeves up. "Look at this." He pointed at a black round spot on his arm, about the size of a ping-pong ball.

Xiang's heart skipped a beat the moment he saw it. "What happened?"

"I don't know. It happened recently."

"Have you seen a doctor?"

"Yes, the doctor didn't know what caused it. I think it was caused by stress. I have been too stressed lately."

Frightened, Xiang started to wonder whether he should change his major. It had never occurred to him that his chosen field was so cutthroat, and that stress could be so harmful. He did not ever want to put himself in such a stressful situation.

Caoyi had a point. The Great Cultural Revolution could not be attributed to a single person. A single match could start a great fire, but it was the dry wood that spread the blaze far and wide, and the vast number of greedy and selfish individuals were the dry wood. They had not changed, and they would turn a flame into a raging wildfire, much worse than the one before.

Xiang turned to look out the window and saw a leaf being whipped about in the wind.

Perhaps I will have to switch my major just in case I have to stay in the United States.

Chapter 35

Outraged, Shan walked out of the dorm and stomped across the street to the administration building, his face flushed and his pulse racing. As a native of Huadu, he was entitled to return to his hometown upon graduation. Something must be very wrong behind the scenes, and he would not accept this injustice without a fight.

As he entered the building, he nearly knocked down his friend Lei.

"Shan!" Lei steadied himself. "Where are you going? You look terrible."

"To see the department head." Shan's voice trembled with fury.

"You can't go to see him like this."

"Why?"

"You want to talk to him about your job allocation, right?"

"Yes, how do you know?" Shan blinked at his friend.

"I heard about their decision yesterday."

"Then, why didn't you tell me?" Shan narrowed his eyes at Lei, unpleased.

"It was for your benefit. If I had told you, you would have lost sleep over it. Also, once the decision has been made, there is nothing you can do to change it."

"I'm not taking it." Shan walked past his friend to the staircase, but stopped suddenly, wheeling toward Lei. "How could you possibly know about it yesterday? They announced their decision today."

"I have my sources. If I were you, I wouldn't argue with them. It will only make things worse for you if you do. When they made the decision, they must have known that they were violating government policy, but they nevertheless did it. Do you know why?"

"I don't, and I don't care. If they don't change their decision, I'm going to fight back all the way to the top."

"Don't be naïve. I'm sure that they have prepared hundreds of justifications for you. I heard that they assigned you a position in Huadu but switched you and Wei a few days later."

"Why?" Shan blinked fast, having difficulty believing what he had heard. "Wei is from here. So, he should get a job here. It's government policy."

"Policy?" Lei shrugged. "Policy is for ordinary people, not for powerful individuals. Wei's uncle-in-law has been promoted to a director in the Department of Education and will be transferred to Huadu in a few months."

"But that doesn't give the school the right to violate government policy."

"Come on, are you kidding? When you have power, you can do anything you want."

"Do you mean that I should just give in without a fight?"

"Of course not, but you need to fight back in a smart way. You need to know what you want and what you can get."

"I want to get what belongs to me."

Lei shook his head. "That's not possible. They have made the decision, and you can do nothing about it. But if you want something else, you may get that."

"Like what?"

"Since they know they're in the wrong, they're most likely to be willing to compromise on something.

"Give me a better job?"

"Not that. The only thing I can think of is that they may be willing to put something nice in your personnel file to help you in your career, such as how good you are."

Shan did not like the idea. But what else could he do? Nothing.

His friend continued, "There is a saying that misfortune is a blessing in disguise. This whole thing seems like a major setback, but if you look at it from a different perspective, it actually benefits you in the long run."

"Oh?"

"If you work for the Chinese Academy of Science in Huadu, you are just one of many talented young scientists. It will be difficult to stand out. But working for the Yellow River Electrical Power Company is a different scenario. You will be one of the few young people with a college education, and you will have a better chance of advancing. The company is a state-owned enterprise under the Department of Energy. If you do well, you can be quickly promoted and transferred to its headquarters in Huadu."

Lei's words had calmed Shan somewhat. He had no choice but to accept his fate and move forward.

****

Two months later, he joined the company along with five other college graduates from three local universities. In an office on the second floor of the administration building, a middle-aged woman from human resources gave them an orientation.

"Welcome to our company. For the next three months, you'll be on probation. Starting next week, you will rotate through different divisions so that you can get to know the company. For now, this will be your office."

The woman talked about the company's history and how important it was in the country. She described the five job openings, one in the Department of Inspection and Quality Control, and the others in manufacturing.

Shan's stomach dropped. He had thought that as a college graduate, he would get a job that required knowledge and skills, not one that was mostly physical. Now, he would have to work on the factory floor since all the other new graduates were from the city. They must have connections that could help them compete for the position in the quality control department. In the corner of his eye, he scanned them, trying to guess who would be the lucky one.

After the meeting, he walked around the campus to get a feel for the company. He wanted to know what the production divisions looked like. When he passed a pile of irregular rusty metal sheets outside a large building that looked like a windowless warehouse, he peered through a partially opened door. Machine tools sat idling, and workers stood around chatting in groups.

Why is no one working? He walked away.

A few minutes later, he reached another big building and looked into it through its open door. The room was filled with machines in various states of disassembly, and workers sat around drinking tea and talking.

Again, no one was working.

That's horrible. Working in such an environment is a waste of time. I am just starting. To survive and succeed in this rapidly changing country, I must learn as much as possible rather than wasting my time as they do.

With these thoughts, he decided to battle against the

odds and get a job in the quality control department, no matter how slim the chance was.

But how? He had no idea.

The next morning, after a quick breakfast, he went to his office. Walking down the long hallway, he was dismayed to see that the floor was dirty, and the windows caked with dust.

Companies did not hire janitors, and employees were expected to clean their own offices, hallways, and bathrooms.

Without much to do early in the morning before everyone arrived, Shan decided to do some cleaning work, starting with his office and then moving on to the hallway. He mopped the floor and then wiped the windows.

As he scrubbed a windowsill at the far end of the corridor, he heard footsteps approaching. Shan turned around and saw a woman walking toward him in a dark blue pantsuit, probably in her fifties.

"Are you one of the new college graduates?" She stopped in front of him.

"Yes." He wondered who she was.

She nodded. "What's your name?"

"Shan Gao."

"Thank you very much." A big smile appeared on her face. "Thank you for cleaning the hallways and windows for us." She took out her keys from her pocket to unlock the door next to him.

Shan glanced at the rectangular nameplate at the top of the doorframe. It read Chairman of the Communist Party Committee.

Wow, how lucky I am! She is the top official at this company, and she could decide my future here.

He remembered his father telling him that the first impression he made on someone could determine how they judge him for the rest of his life. He had gotten off to a good start with her, but he was determined to do more to win her over.

Chapter 36

What should I do after getting my PhD? Return to China or remain in America? China was undergoing an unprecedented economic reform, which provided tremendous opportunities for his generation. In China, he would be one of the few educated in the United States. He would get a good position and advance more quickly than most people. Besides, his parents were getting old, and it was his turn to take care of them. But …

Xiang stood at the large window of his hotel room and looked out at the rainy street below, contemplating his future.

But, what if there was another Great Cultural Revolution? After the Communists took over, many scientists had returned from overseas, full of hope, to help rebuild the country. However, most of them were stripped of their positions and sent to the impoverished countryside for reeducation during the Great Cultural Revolution. Some died from the torture.

The sudden gust of wind sent the rain clattering against the window, bringing back memories of a terrible night from his childhood.

It was a stormy night in June 1968, two years into the Great Cultural Revolution. The trees along the street swayed under the force of the gale, and their branches lashed back and forth like the vicious whips that gangsters were using to beat innocent people. A giant howling wind sounded like starving wolves in the distance, hungry for any flesh they could devour.

From the window of their thirteen-floor apartment, Xiang and his brother watched the dimly lit street below, waiting for their parents to come home from work.

"Brother, are you scared?" Shan turned to look up at Xiang.

"No." Xiang wrapped his arm around Shan's shoulder and held him tightly. He lied to give his younger brother strength. For some reason he could not explain, he felt a cold dread deep in his heart.

Why haven't they come home yet? They always come back home together right after work at around six o'clock. It is already ten now.

As he was thinking, he heard Shan ask the same question.

"They're busy today," Xiang answered, attempting to pacify his brother.

Shan nodded slowly and continued looking out into the darkness. A moment later, he turned back to his brother and pointed to the building across the street. "Is that Jiajia?"

"Where?"

"There. The window on the sixth floor."

Xiang glanced at it and saw a girl looking out at the window in the background of flickering orange illumination, like ghosts in the darkness. Xiang shivered. In the distance, he could not see her clearly, but he knew that it was her, the prettiest girl in the subdivision and his close friend. Her father had returned to China with a doctorate in aerospace from Great Britain soon after the communists took over the country in 1949 and had been a director at the national lab for the past fifteen years.

Two days before, he jumped from that very window, committing suicide. Rumor said that he could not bear the torture of the Red Guards.

The sight of Jiajia made Xiang worry even more about his parents. He gently steered his brother away from the window to the dining table, where they sat down to await their parents' return. Soon, Shan fell asleep. As Xiang was about to doze off himself, he heard familiar heavy footsteps outside the room. He stood up and looked toward the door.

A short moment later, it opened, and their father appeared, his hair mussed and his cheeks swollen as if he had been bitten.

"Dad, you —" Xiang stared at his father. "Your nose is bleeding. What happened to you?"

Father opened his mouth and closed it without a word.

Xiang tilted his head back to look beyond his father, trying to find his mother. However, instead of seeing her, he saw a group of young men and women dressed in green military uniforms and wearing red armbands with golden Chinese characters, the Red Guards.

"Dad, where is Mom?" He then pointed at the guards. "Why are they here?"

Instead of answering his questions, Father glanced at the sleeping Shan and hobbled to Xiang as if injured. He slowly knelt on one leg and put his hands on Xiang's shoulders. "Listen to me carefully. Mom and I will not be home for some time. Tomorrow morning, you take Shan to Ms. Wang's house and stay there until we come back."

"I don't want to stay with her." Xiang twisted his shoulders out of Father's hands.

"Why?"

"Her husband is an antirevolutionary."

Two days earlier, Ms. Wang's husband, the chief editor of the Journal of Astronautics, had been arrested. He was accused of being an American spy because he had studied in the United States and had served as head of the Aerospace Department at Jiangshan University before the Communist Party took power.

Father looked into Xiang's eyes and spoke in a whisper so that only they could hear. "She is a good woman, and her husband is a good man. I do not have time to explain to you what is happening. You are a grown man. When we are not at home, you need to take care of your younger brother. In the top drawer of my desk in the study, there is a brown envelope containing some money. Take it with you and give it to Miss Wang."

Father managed to stand up and turned to leave.

"Dad, I don't want you to go." Xiang grabbed Father's clothes.

"Hurry up!" An angry voice from a red guard shook the room.

Father turned to look at Xiang and said in a weak voice. "I have to go. Listen to me. Wang's family are not bad people. You may not understand what is happening now, but one day, you will." He removed Xiang's hands from his clothes. "Now, go to bed. Everything will be fine. We will be back soon."

Xiang saw tears in Father's eyes.

Father left with the Red Guards, leaving the two young boys behind in a chaotic and frightening world.

Later, Xiang learned that his mother had been detained by the national lab security for refusing to denounce her father, a history professor and a member of the Nationalist Party before the Chinese Communist Party had taken over the country. He also learned that the reason for his father's arrest was that he had rejected the demand from the Red Guards to divorce her.

His train of thought was interrupted by the shrill wail of a siren. A medical emergency vehicle was pulling into the parking lot of the hotel. Its flashing lights and blaring horn reinforced his sense of urgency as he weighed his future.

Should he complete his PhD in Arkansas, and then return to China, or should he change his major and prepare to stay in America in case he had to? He must make a decision right now.

The next morning, on the way flying back to Arkansas, Xiang reflected on Caoyi's advice to switch his majors and on how he had ended up in physics.

In the final year of the Great Cultural Revolution, he had graduated from high school. Like most people of his generation, he was sent to the countryside. The government said the vast land would provide them with a bright future, but few believed it. The Chinese economy had been severely damaged by the decade of the Great Cultural Revolution, and there were barely any jobs in the cities. Therefore, millions of high school graduates were shipped to rural areas to work as farmers against their will.

In the countryside, food was scarce, and he barely ate vegetables or meat. One day, he took a dog to the mountains in search of edibles. He found some elderberries, red and sweet, and brought them home. Shortly after eating them, he vomited, became nauseated and feverish, and was taken to the hospital. Although he survived the poisoning, the lasting damage was done to his stomach.

One year later, Chairman Mao died, bringing an end to the political turmoil. After another year, universities reopened, and the national college entrance examination was reinstated. To escape the poor countryside, he decided to take the examination along with the other five million young people. Xiang took two days off from work to go back to Huadu to discuss his future with his parents.

“Which major should I choose?” he asked them.

“Which fields are you interested in?” his mother asked. “What is your passion?”

“I don’t know, but I know which field I’m not interested in. It’s the cornfield. As for my passion, it’s to get out of the countryside.”

“I suggest physics.” She then turned to his father. “What do you think?”

“I agree with you.” He nodded. “Physics is the foundation. It helps people develop strong logic and analytical skills. If you excel in the field, you can easily move to many others.”

Thus, Xiang chose that major. While he was not particularly fond of physics, he found his interest growing each year. By the time he was a senior in college, he even dreamed to become a famous physicist.

However, that was a daydream.

Now, thinking that the Great Cultural Revolution might happen again, he decided to change his major, just in case he needed to stay in the United States. Upon returning to campus, he went straight to the library to check the prerequisites for the graduate programs in the Department of Electrical and Computer Engineering.

Too bad. He had not taken any of their required courses.

He walked to a window and gazed out, wondering what he should do next. The fluffy clouds looked down at him as if telling him that problems were a normal part of life, just as the white clouds were to a clear sky, adding variety and aesthetic appeal to the blue background.

A moment later, a solution came to him. He should apply to a better graduate school, with more prestigious physics programs. That would increase his chances of getting a job after graduation.

Xiang got a US college catalog and studied it. Once again, he was disappointed. The top universities all required graduate record exam (GRE) scores, and it was too late to take the test. He continued flipping through the pages as if a drowning person who did not know how to swim still hopelessly struggled in the current. Persistence helped. After a few minutes, the University of Georgia in Atlanta caught his eye. Its physics department was one of the best in the nation. Not only did it not require GRE scores, but it also expected its doctoral students to take a number of courses outside the physics, preferably in electrical engineering. And it was in a big city.

He applied immediately.

A month later, when he checked his mailbox at the Student Center, he found a letter from the department. It informed him that he had been admitted to its PhD program and offered him a research assistantship. He shifted his gaze to the large window and saw the courtyard of the Student Center bathed in the golden late afternoon sunlight, with birds swooping around in the foliage. A gigantic water fountain was spewing water jets into the air, creating a mist that glinted and sparkled in the setting sun and produced a stunning rainbow. A little girl, probably five or six years old, was chasing a butterfly while her mother sat in the shade of a spreading oak near the blooming flowers bed, smiling at her.

Suddenly, Xiang felt nostalgic.

Arkansas had been his first stop in the United States. Even though he had been disappointed by the small airport and the rural lifestyle when he first arrived in the state, he had changed. In addition to falling in love with the school, the mountains, and the friendly people, he had made friends and met Lulu. Even though she had turned him down, he still treasured the time they had spent together. It was sad to think that he would leave the place in a few months and might never see it again.

The next morning, he went to see his advisor for a one-on-one weekly meeting.

"Good job." Dr. Rick nodded after Xiang finished his report. "I thought about your research last night. Given the progress you have made, I believe you should be able to graduate in two years."

In two years? He could get his PhD in two more years!

The news excited Xiang and prompted him to consider whether it was worthwhile to transfer to another school. Once he went to a different university, he had to start over, which would take five more years.

No, don't change your mind. What are you going to do after graduation? Going back to China? No, not before the situation of the country became clear.

He took a deep breath. "Dr. Rick." He paused. "Dr. Rick, I … I'll be leaving for the University of Georgia at Atlanta next semester."

The professor blinked a few times. "Why?"

“I’m sorry, Dr. Rick. You brought me to America and trained me for research. If I'd had any choice, I would have stayed here to finish my PhD under your guidance, but I don’t. I must keep my options open in case I have to stay in the United States.”

He then explained why he was worried about returning to China soon. The professor nodded as he listened. When he finished, Dr. Rick leaned back and crossed his hands under his chin. “I understand. Thank you for letting me know.”

Is that all? Why doesn’t he blame me?

Xiang had expected that his advisor would shout at him.

“I’m sorry for disappointing you. Before leaving for the University of Georgia at Atlanta, I will wrap up my research and submit a journal paper about the new research technique. In addition, I will write a detailed fabrication manual so that other students will be able to replicate my process.”

“Thank you.” Dr. Rick nodded again without a smile.

Xiang knew that he had hurt his advisor’s feelings, but he had no choice. He had to have an alternative in case he had to stay in the United States.

Chapter 37

On Monday morning, Lily, the middle-aged woman from the human resources department, took Shan to the assembly factory, the first stop on his rotation.

"Madam Ma," she said to a woman in her fifties. "This is Shan, a new graduate from Xihe University. He will be working under you for a month." Then she turned to Shan. "Madam Ma is the manager here. She has worked for the company for almost forty years. She is the most skilled worker in the division. You can learn a lot from her."

"Overpraised." Madam Ma smiled, the wrinkles on her face deepening. "I only had an elementary school education. All I know is how to solder components."

As the women began their small talk, Shan glanced around. The large, high-ceilinged factory had no windows, sixty long work tables were arranged in six rows with two soldering machines on each table, and all the workers were women. Instead of working, they were gathered in clusters, chatting.

A moment later, Lily left, leaving Shan with Madam Ma.

"This is where you will work." She pointed to a soldering station next to her own. "I'll teach you how to use it." Then she glanced at her watch. "I have a meeting to go to. Make yourself comfortable."

Shan sat down at the empty table and looked at the

group of women near him.

"Do you like my new skirt?" a woman asked the others.

"Yeah," a woman responded. "Where did you get it?"

"In the new clothes outlet downtown."

"I like the design and the color."

...

Shan found their conversations uninteresting and wished he could do something useful, but there was nothing he could do. All of the tables were empty. He considered going back to his office to get some books, but he declined the idea. He had to mingle with them and be part of the group. Otherwise, they might think he did not respect them. Reading alone would give the impression that he did not want to be with them. He was on probation, and he needed their kind words for his three-month evaluation.

Shan forced himself to engage in the conversations, or at least appeared to be listening, but the subject was so boring that his head began to bob and his eyelids drooped. He yawned to keep himself awake.

That was not good. It would hurt their feelings, and worse, create resentment. What should he do?

He struggled to find a solution and eventually came up with one. He would listen carefully to their talking, not just to the words but to the nuances of their tone. He would observe their facial expressions, the movement of their eyes, and their body language. He was going to process all of this information to predict their personalities, character traits, and backgrounds. It would be fun and challenging, and it would help him develop his sixth sense of humanity. Most importantly, it would keep him awake.

He listened to them tentatively and occasionally asked questions. A few minutes later, a woman sitting near him moved her chair closer to him. “What university did you graduate from?”

“Xihe University.” To improve their interaction, he added a few more details. “I studied electrical engineering.”

“My son also graduated from Xihe University,” the woman said with a delighted laugh as if she had reconnected with an old friend.

Shan spent all day with the workers, and by late afternoon, he had developed a basic impression of most of them.

A man came with a box of motherboards about an hour before the factory closed. “Manager Ma.” He set the box down on the table in front of her and said in an unhappy voice. “These parts were rejected by the inspection department. The rejection rate is far too high.”

The women at nearby tables stopped talking. They looked at him for a second and then went on with their conversation as if it were none of their business.

The manager smiled at him and whispered. “Calm down, Bi. You know how the company is doing. When rumors about the future of the company circulate, who would take their work seriously?”

Bi looked into her eyes quietly for a moment and lowered his voice too. “Can you have them fixed by the end of tomorrow?”

“I'll try.”

Their conversation alerted Shan.

What rumors? What was going on with the company?

He looked around and realized that the workers had not done any work for the whole day. Even though he had noticed that, he had not really given it much thought until now. He wanted to ask Madman Ma why the factory had idled all day but changed his mind before opening his mouth. It might not be the best time or place to raise such a sensitive subject. He would wait and find the right time.

After the man had left, manager Ma held up two rejected boards high enough for everyone to see. “We've got rejections. Who'd like to fix them?”

No one responded. No one even glanced at her.

With an embarrassed smile, she looked at Shan. “Would you like to learn how to fix the problems?”

“Yes.” He had been waiting all day to do something useful.

She turned on her soldering station and pointed at the black crosses on the back of a board. “These marks tell us which components are not connected well with the board. Usually, you can tell which soldering is bad and which is good just by looking at their shapes.” She moved her finger to a tiny, perfectly spherical silver dot. “This is a good one. It looks smooth and pretty.” She then pointed to an uneven dot. “This one is bad.”

Manager Ma took her hot soldering iron, scraped its tip against a wet sponge on the soldering stand a few times to clean it, and then touched rosin. It produced a little streak of white smoke and a quick-burning sound. “Rosin cleans the metal. It allows the component to bond better to the board.”

She pressed the tip against a solder bump next to a mark and waited. The irregular grayish metal was melted down to a tiny round dot. She stopped and turned to

Shan. "When soldering a component, you need to be careful. Don't overheat it. Overheating can damage the component." She set her tools down on her ironing station and handed the board to Shan. "Would you like to try?"

Shan did, but his soldering did not look nearly as good as hers. "It doesn't look very good," he said, flushing with embarrassment.

"Don't worry. It requires practice."

A bell jangled. Time to go home. Shan walked out of the factory along with the women and headed for the employee cafeteria for a quick dinner. Then he returned to the factory floor, working on the motherboards for hours until he finished both of them.

As he walked out of the building, he was glad that he had not only learned the new skills but also had gotten to know the workers. He sensed that they took a liking to him, especially the three young women. Although he had no intention of dating any of them, he liked the way they looked at him. However, the feeling vanished the moment he remembered the conversation between the man and Madam Ma.

What were the rumors that she referred to? What did she mean by the current situation and the future of the company?

Chapter 38

Xiang arrived in Atlanta a few days before his first semester of school was to begin. After settling into his dorm at the University of Georgia at Atlanta, he took the subway into Chinatown.

The Chinatown looked like a strip mall, with Chinese characters on the shop signs and a large entrance at the center of the complex. He walked straight into a small bookstore crammed with bookshelves lining all the walls and a long table in the center of the room. Many of the books appeared to have been banned in China. He pulled out a volume called *The True Story of the Great Cultural Revolution* and read it. Half an hour later, he put it back. The book was too depressing. It revealed the dark secret behind the political turmoil. On the first day of his new life, he did not want to let any sadness spoil it.

He walked out of the store and entered the mall through the main entrance. As he walked down the main corridor, he peered through the windows of a hair salon and browsed the gift shops. As he proceeded down the hall, a delicious aroma filled his nostrils. It was so familiar, so nostalgic, and so sentimental. It was the smell he had missed for so long since coming to the United States, and it was the one he associated with good times. He followed the scent to the food court.

Wow, Chinese food court!

He walked clockwise around the food counters,

trying to decide what to eat. With a limited stomach capacity, he had to choose wisely. Looking at the delicious cuisine, he wished he had four stomachs like a cow.

A few minutes later, he stopped at the counter where a young Chinese cashier was reading a book. She was so focused that she did not realize that he was standing right in front of her. He glanced at the large menu board on the wall behind her without disturbing her. Dumplings. The specialty of the house was dumplings, his favorite food.

He looked back at her for a moment and finally asked, “Excuse me. What are the most popular dumplings?”

Startled, she looked up at him in embarrassment. “I’m sorry. I didn’t know you were here.” She turned to view the poster. “Many people like the number five.”

“Then, I would like to have the number five.”

As she was filling out his order, Xiang studied her. She was a few inches shorter than him. Her black hair brushed against the shoulders of a light pink T-shirt.

“Are you from Huadu too?” he asked.

“Yes. How did you know?” She looked up at him.

“From your accent. I’m from Huadu.”

“Really?!” A broad grin spread across her face. “How long have you been in the United States?”

“I came to the United States a year ago but just transferred to the University of Georgia at Atlanta.”

Her eyes grew wider. “I study at the University of Georgia at Atlanta as well.”

“Are you an undergraduate?”

“Yes, I'm a junior in biology.”

With the order in hand, she walked into a small door behind her and soon returned, continuing to talk with him. He learned that her name was Tanjing, and, like him, she had been born and raised in Huadu. She had studied at Huadu University for two years before coming to the United States with her father, who was a visiting professor at University of Georgia at Atlanta.

A man in his forties came out of the kitchen behind her with a bowl and set it on the counter. "Here are your dumplings."

Xiang thanked him and turned to Tanjing, intending to continue their conversation. Just then, a family of three came.

Disappointed, he picked up his food and walked over to a table nearby. He ate slowly, hoping to have a chance to talk to the pretty girl again, but the family took forever to order. By the time they finished, a line had already formed behind them. Reluctantly, he finished his dinner quickly and left Chinatown for his dormitory.

Two days later, he attended a new student welcome party sponsored by the Chinese Student and Scholar Association at the University of Georgia at Atlanta. When he entered the ballroom, the dance had already started. He leaned back against the wall next to the door, watching people dance. Soon, he noticed a girl dressed in a crimson knee-length chiffon cocktail dress in the crowd.

Tanjing? His eyes widened, and he stepped aside a little to get a better view of her. Yes, it's her! Lucky me.

He watched her dance until the music stopped and approached her as soon as she returned to her seat. "May I dance with you next?"

"It's you!" she exclaimed, smiling broadly. "Sure." She then turned to look at the man who had danced with her, as if seeking permission. He nodded without expression.

Who was he? Why did she need his approval? Were they dating or just friends?

The music started. He offered her his hand and led her onto the floor. They moved into the rhythm together. He held her smooth, soft hand in his left and wrapped his right arm around her waist. They danced the Huadu University Waltz in harmony as if they had learned it together. With her so close to him, he could smell the faint perfume she wore and feel the warmth of her body. He had not been so close to a woman since he had left China. At times, he closed his eyes to enjoy the sensation of holding her in his arms.

All night long, she danced with him, swaying and twirling to every song, fast or slow, and gliding across the floor. In the dim ballroom, lit only by the flashes of colored lights reflected from the ball in the ceiling, her large eyes, glowing skin, and the way she flung her arms out to the side made him want to hold her tight to his chest and never let go.

When the party was over, thinking about walking her home so that he could spend more time with her, he asked, “Which dorm do you live in?”

She turned to look at him. “I live with my parents off-campus.” She paused for a moment. “Could you give me a ride?”

Off-campus? A ride?

His heart sank. “I don’t have a car yet.”

“It’s all right.” She glanced at the young man standing by the door with whom she had been dancing before Xiang arrived. “He can give me a ride. He lives not too far from my home.”

With that, she waved goodbye to Xiang and went to

the man. Together, they disappeared into the crowd.

Xiang left the building alone. Alone in the crowd. Walking down the dark street, he felt like he had just awoken from a sweet dream. The music, the dancing, and Tanjing were all gone. A convertible passed him, and two girls in the back waved and shouted something he could not make out.

Gazing at the vanishing vehicle and the girls, he thought about purchasing a car.

But what about his brother? He was counting on Xiang's financial support to come to America.

That night, he had a dream. In it, he bought a car with the money he had saved to help his brother. As he and Tanjing drove across the country, they hit and seriously injured a pedestrian. To his surprise, it was his brother.

Awakened in fear, he sat up in bed, sweating.

It's just a dream, he kept telling himself. It's just a dream.

He rested at the edge of his bed, waiting for his heartbeat to return to normal and blaming himself for even thinking about purchasing a vehicle so he could date a girl.

The sun rose, pouring its light into the room through the window as if to remind him that it was time to get up and study. He had a quick breakfast and left for the library.

The building was much bigger than the one at the University of Northwest Arkansas. Curiously, he wandered from floor to floor and finally stopped on the fourth one.

Near the southeast corner of the room, behind a row of bookshelves, was a table by a large window. From there, he could look out over the expanse of green lawn and the large trees. He retrieved a book about American history from the shelf and sat down at the table. Reading it not only helped him learn more about the United States but also improved his English. After a while, he heard footsteps. He raised his head and saw a girl dressed in an orange T-shirt and dark blue shorts emerge from behind the bookshelves.

Tanjing! He blinked fast, wondering if he was dreaming.

She stopped and glanced at the empty chair across the table, as if hesitating over something. From her facial expression and body language, it seemed that she came here to study but was surprised by his presence.

What a coincidence.

Smiling, he waved at her. “Hi, Tanjing.”

“Hi.” She waved back, casting another look at the vacant chair across the table.

Xiang moved his books on the desk to make room for her. “Would you like to join me?”

Nodding, she walked over to the table and set her backpack on it. “I didn’t know you were here.”

He looked out the window at two squirrels running in the grass, then back at her. “I like it here. It’s quiet, and the scenery is beautiful.”

Without further conversation, she took out a thick textbook on chemistry and started to read it. At first, he glanced at her from time to time, hoping for an opportunity to speak with her. However, after seeing her completely absorbed in her study, he quit trying and concentrated on his reading. Each of them spent the next three hours in their own worlds as if the other did not exist.

By noon, his stomach growled. He glanced at his wristwatch, then at her. "Lunchtime. Would you like to go to lunch together?"

She shook her head. "Sorry. My mother is waiting for me." She put her book into her backpack.

Her mother? Where was her mother? What did she do?

Thinking that Tanjing had the whole family here, he sensed that it would be difficult to get her on a date. Mothers were usually very protective and picky about whom their daughters dated. He stood up and headed out of the building along with her. At the door, he stopped and looked at her. "Will you come back to study this afternoon?"

"No." she shook her head. "I have to work in Chinatown." Her tone was monotonic.

They bid each other farewell and headed off in opposite directions. On the way to the student cafeteria, he kept thinking about her.

Why was she so different from the night before? She had been warm then, but now she looked cold. Why?

He thought hard as he walked.

She probably just wanted to keep her distance from him. Given the ratio of Chinese men to women in the camp, she must have been surrounded by many young men.

The next morning, he went back to the fourth floor, not expecting to see her. However, as he made a turn at the bookshelf near the corner, he nearly tripped her over as she tiptoed, trying to reach for a book on the upper shelf.

"He reached out and caught her arm as she stumbled. She looked up at him and laughed. He let go of her arm and glanced at the table, noticing books had taken up half the space and her backpack stood next to the chair she had sat in yesterday.

Apparently, she has been waiting for me, he thought.

He handed her the book from the bookshelf and walked to the table with her. They studied together until lunchtime, occasionally exchanging a few words, then separated for the remainder of the day.

For the next few days, they repeated the same routine, except that they talked more and more. On Friday morning, Xiang went up to the fourth floor as usual, but she was not there. He read casually and waited for her. After quite a while, he gave up, believing that she would not come. The school year would start the next Monday, and she probably had a lot to do before the semester began.

Throughout the day, he sat alone in a corner, studying. An hour before the library closed, he sensed someone sitting across the table from him. When he looked up, he was surprised to see Tanjìng smiling at him. He quickly gathered his scattered books and papers to make room for her. “I thought you worked in the afternoon.”

“Not today. This morning, my restaurant's owner asked me to fill in for someone.” She set her backpack on the table without taking out a book. “Today is the last day of the summer break.”

“Yes, it is.”

“How many classes are you going to take next semester?”

“Four. Three in physics and one in electrical engineering.”

“Why do you want to come to the United States?”

She raised one hand and ran it through her hair.

Xiang wondered why she did not seem as hurried to study as she usually had been.

"Everybody wants to come to America. In modern Chinese history, many famous and important people were educated in the West."

They continued the conversation until the library closed. When they exited the building, they stood at the stairs, quietly looking into each other's eyes. Xiang considered asking her for dinner but instantly dismissed the idea. He did not have a vehicle and would not be able to give her a ride her home afterward.

After a moment of silence, she spoke, "I wish you had a car so we could go somewhere tonight."

Their gazes locked. They were just a few feet apart, but without a car, the distance was insurmountable.

Chapter 39

Celebration. A big celebration for the 65th anniversary of the Chinese Communist Youth League was going to take place in the employee cafeteria at eight o'clock that morning.

Shan entered the building a few minutes before the event started and noticed that the room had been packed with about 200 young employees. He glanced at the dining hall to see how they were going to celebrate but found no decorations at all. It did not look like they had planned to hold a meeting or a party inside the building. Probably they just gathered there for a short time before going somewhere else.

Still a few minutes earlier, he walked to a large window and looked out, thinking about how the company would mark this special occasion.

Were they going to have a picnic at Three Moon Lake or in the Phoenix Mountain?

Two butterflies caught his attention. They were fluttering over a clump of red Chinese roses on the roadside, flitting from flower to flower, from bush to bush, chasing and being chased. As he watched the carefree and happy creatures, one butterfly stopped in midair between two shrubs. It twisted its body and flipped its wings, fluttering and flapping, but it remained in the same spot.

What happened to it? He stepped closer to the glass

and gazed at the butterfly. Oh my, it must be caught by an invisible spider web.

As he felt sorry for its misfortune, he heard *attention*, *attention*, and turned to see what was happening.

The chairman of the company's Communist Youth League was waving his hand to the crowd. "Today is the 65th anniversary of the Chinese Communist Youth League. The best way to celebrate it is to demonstrate that we still remember that we are part of the working class. We will spend our morning cleaning the cafeteria. When other employees come to have lunch, they'll see a new and fresh environment."

After the announcement, he turned to a young woman who was standing nearby and smiled at her with his full-blown grin. She appeared in her early twenties, dressed in a red skirt and white blouse, with shiny black hair pulled back in a bun. Her heart-shaped face, dainty nose, and rosebud lips made Shan's heart lurch.

Who was she? He had never seen such a beautiful girl in the company.

A minute later, the chairman left the room, and the girl disappeared into the crowd of people. Shan moved away from the window, ready to work, but the others stayed where they were, talking and laughing. A minute went by, then five, then ten. Still, no one worked.

What a waste of time. The sooner they finished cleaning, the sooner they could get back to work. Why didn't they understand that?

Then it dawned on him that no one wanted to work. According to rumors, the company was in very bad financial shape and on the verge of bankruptcy. Considering that, he felt he could not afford to waste any time. He had to learn as many new skills as possible before the company went out of business so he could find a decent job. He picked up a mop, intending to work.

Suddenly, he remembered a conversation he had had seven years earlier.

After graduating high school, he had been forced to move to the countryside along with millions of other young people. He worked hard without realizing it. Somehow, he did not fit in with the other young men in the village.

One day, when he was resting with Anlin in the field, his friend asked him, “Do you know why so many people don't like you?”

“No. I always work hard and never cause trouble for anyone.”

“That's the problem. While everyone else drifts from day to day without doing a damn thing, you work harder. You make them look bad. That's why they hate you.”

The flashback prompted Shan to lay the mop down. He did not want to repeat the mistake. Walking over to the window, he leaned against the wall, waiting for someone to start working. However, after a long while, no one had taken action. Watching the precious time slip away, he could not stand it any longer. He did not care if they liked him anymore. If the company went bankrupt, he might never see them again. He walked over to a group of chatting young men and women nearby without thinking about what he was doing.

“Excuse me.” He smiled at a short girl with a sweet round face who was talking to several guys, thinking that she might be a leader. “Could you get your people together to clean the windows over there?” He pointed to the one next to the entrance.

She looked at him for a second, and without questioning his authority, turned to the others. “Let’s get to work.”

Shan then went to other groups and directed them to clean the tables, mop the floor, and wash the sinks. All of them followed his instructions without question. When he reached the last group, he saw the red-skirted girl laughing with five men. He hesitated for a second and then said to them, “Excuse me, could you wipe the dining tables over there?”

Everyone else went to work, but the girl gave him a who-do-you-think-you-are look and walked off in the opposite direction.

Shan stood still and looked at her back for a moment. Well, he said to himself. I don't care what you think, and I don’t give a damn if you're pleased.

He then picked up a mop and joined the cleaning army. Within an hour, the cafeteria was spick-and-span, and everyone started to leave. Rather than walking out of the building with the others, he sat on a bench and looked around at the dining hall, enjoying the feeling of achievement. A thought occurred to him.

Why did these people follow his instruction? He was a newcomer, nobody. There was no reason for them to listen to him. Yet they did. Why?

He pondered hard for a while and concluded that since none of them had seen him before, they must have mistakenly thought that he was a new leader of the Youth Communist League Committee.

Smiling, he stood up and walked out of the building. At the door, he saw the red-skirted woman squatting by the red roses. He subconsciously surveyed the surroundings and the far end of the path. No one else was in sight. His heart thumping hard against his chest, he felt a burning desire to know her, the most beautiful girl he had seen in the company. However, when he remembered the condescending look that she had given him, he abandoned the idea and kept walking with his head held high.

Perhaps hearing his footsteps, she turned to look at him over her shoulder with a sweet smile. "Hi."

"Hi." His face flushed.

She stood and walked alongside him on the narrow path. "Are you a recent college graduate?"

"Yes. How do you know?"

"I have never seen you before. What school did you attend?"

"Xihe University."

"Really?" She sounded excited as if she had met an old friend. "I graduated from Xihe University too. What was your major?"

"Electrical engineering."

"I majored in the precise instrument. Our dorm is across the street from yours."

"Oh, yes. I remember." Shan pretended to be indifferent.

She stopped, facing Shan. "My name is Mei. What's yours?"

"Shan." He glanced at her, wondering why she had suddenly become so friendly. It was not quite common for a woman to give her name to a man the first time they met. They resumed walking. After a few seconds of silence, she raised the flower to her nose. "The flowers smell sweet."

She then held it out to him as a gesture for him to smell it. When he reached for it, she extended it toward his nose, rather than giving it to him.

He sniffed. "It's really good."

She chuckled.

He could not understand why she laughed. What was so funny?

"Do you like music?" She smiled at him.

"Yes, I do." He pondered why she switched the topic from flowers to music.

"I have some new tapes at home. If you want, I can bring them to you tomorrow."

What is she up to? Shan was confused.

The two walked and talked, and he learned that she was associate chair of the Communist Youth League Committee and worked for the R&D department. When they reached an intersection, she stopped and glanced at him. "Which way are you going?"

"This." He pointed to the left.

"Oh." She nodded slowly. "I have to go this way." She gestured to the right. "I'll see you tomorrow."

Shan waved her goodbye and turned. Instantly, the wind blew in his face and whistled in his ears. Walking against the wind, he looked up at the sky. Massive dark grey clouds swirled and rolled toward him, indicating a thunderstorm was coming. He picked up his pace and headed back to the assembly factory.

For the rest of the day, he kept thinking about her and questioning why she had suddenly changed her attitude. That night, he had a hard time falling asleep. He kept seeing her vivid hourglass figure, her beautiful eyes, and her smile. Her sweet voice always echoed in his head. After rolling over on his bed for nearly an hour, he warned himself to forget about her.

She's a rising star in the company, but you are a new

graduate on probation. A beautiful girl like her must have many admirers. Don't fall into unrequited love.

But his warnings had no use. For the first time in his life, he lost sleep.

Chapter 40

On his way back to the assembly factory from the cafeteria, Shan saw Mei standing at the intersection where they had parted earlier that day. She was holding a fashionable red purse and was looking his way. The setting sun shone behind her, outlining her slender figure.

He hurried toward her. “How are you today?”

“Pretty good.” She pulled out three cassettes from her purse and handed them to him. “I have the tapes for you.”

He took them and read the labels. “They are my favorite.”

“I have more. Once you finish these, I'll bring the others to you.” She gazed at him with a sweet smile.

“That's great. Have you eaten yet?”

“No.” She shook her head.

“Would you like to have dinner with me?”

“I thought you had already eaten.”

“Me?” Shan's face reddened slightly. “How did you know?”

“You just came back from the cafeteria. You didn't go there to clean windows.” She finger-combed her hair. “I have to go home. My parents are waiting for me.”

He walked her to the bus stop right outside the company. As they stood at the curb to wait, she looked into his eyes. “Are you going to the Desert Mountains?”

"Desert Mountains?"

"Next week, the company will start a one-month campaign to improve the environment. Everyone will go to the mountain to plant trees for a week."

"Oh, yes, I remember it. I just didn't know it would be in the Desert Mountains. I have signed up for it."

"Which week are you going?"

"Next week."

She lowered her head for a second and then looked up at him. "I've signed up for the week after next, but I'll see if I can change it to next week."

The words echoed in his mind. While feeling joy and confusion at the same time, he asked himself what was on her mind. Why did she change her schedule for him?

A bus pulled up in front of them.

"I must go," she said softly and stepped into it.

Through the window, she waved at him and rode away on the bus, leaving him standing alone in the busy street.

The next day, he went to the intersection after dinner, expecting to see her again, but she was not there. Not wishing to draw attention to himself by standing alone, he wandered around but always kept an eye on the crossroads to see if she would come. She did not. For the next two evenings, he returned to the same place after dinner in hopes that she would appear, but she never did. She had vanished. A pang of anxiety passed through him.

What was going on? Was she sick?

He considered going to her office the next day but quickly dismissed the idea.

Maybe I have misjudged her kindness and overreacted to her interest in me.

He gave up hope of running into her at work. However, he still wished that she would join him for the company's tree planting event the next week as she promised.

Monday arrived, and he arose before dawn in good spirits.

After breakfast, he sat at the table and read the Chinese classic novel *Three Kingdoms*. When he looked out the window an hour later, thick fog obscured his view. In the gray whiteness, he could only make out an overhanging branch just near the building. Concerned that the trip might be canceled completely, he hurried to the entrance of the company complex to check. As he got closer, he saw the silhouettes of two buses without anyone around. He approached one of them and saw the driver inside.

"Good morning," he said loudly. "Are we still going to the Desert Mountains today?"

The driver rolled the glass down. "Yes, we are, but we have to wait until the fog disappears. It may take an hour."

Shan thanked him and headed back to his room. Lying down on his bed, he closed his eyes to rest. Slowly, he drifted off into a dream, in which he and Mei walked hand in hand down a foggy mountain. All of a sudden, she vanished into thin air. He jerked awake and looked out of the window. The fog was gone, and the sun was shining brightly.

Oh, my! What have I done!

He sprang from his bed and dashed out of the dorm, running down the street toward the gate with his suitcase. When he rounded the corner of the office building, he saw that one of the buses had left, and the other one was slowly pulling away from the curb.

"Stop, stop." He ran toward it, shouting and waving. The vehicle continued to move but stopped a moment later. With one hand on the open door, he glanced at the driver, breathing heavily. "Thank you so much. I'm sorry for causing you trouble."

He rested for a second before boarding the vehicle. On the way to the back, he glanced at each side of the aisle to see if Mei was here. No, she was not. He sighed and sat down in the last row, closing his eyes. In a few minutes, the combination of the vibration from the vehicle and his lack of rest for the last few days lulled him to sleep. When he opened his eyes again, they had arrived at their destination.

Shan stepped off the bus, thinking that perhaps Mei was in the other vehicle. He looked around, trying to find her, but she was not there.

The area appeared parched and desolate. It was said that the site had been a prison before the communists took over the country and had been then converted into an education camp. After the country began its economic reforms, the camp was dissolved, and the place was deserted. Recently, in response to a central government campaign to plant trees, the local authorities had renovated the area to accommodate the volunteers.

Under the scorching sun, he carried his suitcase along a dirt road to a compound of one-story grayish buildings. As he walked, he kept looking around for her.

Minutes later, he saw her in a red dress near the corner of a building a hundred meters away.

"Mei, Mei," he called out, waving his hand high.

Instead of looking back, she kept going and vanished behind the building. He sprinted over to it.

When he reached the corner, he realized it was not Mei, but someone he had never seen before.

Dropping his luggage to the ground, he breathed heavily, resting his hands on his knees.

Where was Mei? Was she there or had she changed her mind and decided not to come at all?

Shan did not see Mei anywhere, not in the dining hall, not in the residential area. Without her, the Desert Mountains looked even more deserted. Dejectedly, he walked toward the courtyard where the members of the Communist Youth League were to meet. As he approached it, he saw her speaking to a group of people.

He picked up his steps and waved to her, wanting to call her out aloud but was afraid of attracting too much unwanted attention from the others. She glanced up and caught his eye, but she immediately averted her gaze.

Why? Why did she act that way?

Shan stopped for a second, his hand frozen in mid-air, then continued walking toward them.

"Attention, everyone." Mei waved at the crowd. "We will be planting trees in teams over the next few days, two people per team. You may now choose your partner. We will leave in five minutes."

While Shan was pondering whether he should team up with her, a tall, muscular man approached her. "Mei, can we be a team?"

She glanced over at Shan and then nodded yes to the man.

His stomach churned. He had screwed up. He had just wasted a chance to be alone with Mei for the whole week. Glaring at the muscular man, Shan cursed himself for being so slow in making a decision. He and Mei planned to meet up on this mountain so they could be together, but she ended up with that handsome, strong man.

Damn, why was I so indecisive! Don't you remember that aggressiveness wins?

As he turned to find a partner, he heard her voice. "Shan, would you like to join us?"

He swung around to look at her, wondering whether she had changed her mind.

She added, "We are an odd number today."

Wow, how lucky he was.

He joined them with a renewed spirit. Even though he could not be alone with her, it was better than not spending any time with her at all.

"Shan, this is Gu." She motioned to the man beside her. "He joined the company last year." She then gestured to Shan. "This is Shan, a recent graduate."

Gu had not only an athletic body but also, as Shan discovered later, rich life experiences.

"I love Geneva," Gu said to Mei as they walked to the working site. "The day we arrived in the city, I immediately fell in love with its unique streets, snowy mountains, and famous lakes. They are so beautiful."

"When did you go there?" Shan asked.

He hesitated for a second. "I went there when I was five. My father was an ambassador to Switzerland at that time."

Shan glanced at him, remembering his childhood. When he was five years old, the Great Famine had swept the country, and he had barely had enough food to eat.

Gu continued. "I love Moscow even better. It was a city that combined beauty and power. The moment I walked onto the Red Square, I had that feeling."

"You went to the Soviet Union too?" Mei sounded

surprised.

"Yes, my father was transferred there three years later as the ambassador to the Soviet Union."

Shan looked at the man from the corner of his eyes, wondering whether Gu was telling the truth. A person with such a family history should work for the Ministry of Foreign Affairs in Huadu or another important government institution, not a company that was about to go bankrupt.

Not only was Gu talkative, but he also seemed to enjoy flexing his muscles and showing off his physical strength. During the first two days of planting trees, he removed his shirt, revealing his startlingly muscular chest and abdomen. Under the scorching sun, he dug holes, carried young trees from trucks, and wrestled them into position without a moment of rest. Beads of sweat glittered on his chest and dripped from his face under the burning desert sky.

On the third day, in the morning, Gu did not appear in the courtyard.

"Where is Gu?" Shan asked Mei.

"He's going back home today."

"Why?"

"I think he got heatstroke. Several other people did too. The company has decided to take them back to the city."

Shan smiled in his mind. He was pleased to be rid of the muscular Gu, but he felt guilty for not having sympathy. He wondered if he was being too selfish.

Maybe, maybe not. No one is unselfish when it comes to fighting for a girlfriend.

From that morning on, he worked tirelessly to prove he was as good as Gu, and he drank lots of water to avoid heatstroke. The last thing he wanted was to be sent home like Gu and not be able to be with Mei. Time passed fast. Before he had realized it, it was already Friday, the final day of the trip.

In the late afternoon, after the last trees had been planted, Shan and Mei sat on a rock to rest.

"When do you think we'll be leaving tomorrow?" he asked.

"Eight," she replied without looking at him. A moment later, she turned slightly toward him. "When will your probation end?"

"Next month."

Shifting her weight to face him fully, she smiled. "Great! Next month, the Communist Youth League will hold an election."

He nodded, wondering why she looked so happy and why she talked about the Communist Youth League

"You should run."

"What?" He could not believe what he had heard.

"You should run."

The words echoed in his mind. It sounded like an order but felt more like a gentle kiss on the cheek.

She cares about me, about my future.

There could be only one explanation for that. With the feeling of being loved taking over his whole body, he decided to do it, for himself and for her, but backed off right away. There was no way a new graduate could get elected. He blinked at her, unsure of what to say.

She leaned forward slightly. "Being a committee officer can advance your career."

"But, but, I just joined the company. I don't think people will vote for me."

"If you put down your ego, you'll win."

"My ego?" He was confused about where that came from.

"Here at the company, people with high education barely talk to the workers who did not go to college. They believe they are better and consider mingling with the workers will lower them."

"I have noticed that." He nodded.

"So, if you're willing to make friends with the workers, you will get their vote. They outnumber the college graduates."

Shan's eyes widened in surprise. Looking into her eyes, he said to himself that she was the right girl for him. She was beautiful and also sophisticated. He felt like pulling her toward him and holding her tight in his arms but refrained from doing so. Such behavior would be inappropriate and dangerous in the early stages of the relationship. He remembered hearing that a young couple had been arrested for kissing each other at work during the absurd Great Cultural Revolution. Although that political disaster had ended, any intimate behavior in a public place was still considered improper by many people and would generate gossip and scandal.

After managing to control his emotions, he grabbed a sharp rock near him, got up, and went to the nearby tree. He turned to look at her. "Come here."

"Why? What are you doing?"

"Just come." He waved at her.

She got to the tree.

"This is the last one we planted." He carved on it. "I wrote my name here. Would you like to write your name next to mine?"

He grinned as she wrote her name with the same rock, thinking that someday they could come here to visit it with their children. It would be a witness to their love.

In the golden light of sunset, they stood quietly, looking into each other's eyes. And then, without a word, he took her in his arms and kissed her.

Chapter 41

After parting with Tanjing, Xiang returned to his dorm room and studied until midnight. Exhausted, he went to bed. As he was about to drift off to sleep, his phone jangled.

Who was calling at this hour?

He grabbed it from his desk without getting out of bed. “Hello?” he said in a sleepy voice.

“Xiang, it’s me.” A soft female voice.

“Tanjing?” He instantly sat up, wide awake, and all the tiredness was gone.

“Yes. Are you sleeping?”

“No, not at all. How was your night?” Xiang put on his slippers and went to the window, looking out at the moon.

“Very good. I went to a church with Fei.”

“Who is Fei?”

“That guy who danced with me at the new student welcome party before you came in.”

“Oh, yes. I remember him. He looked so lascivious when he ogled you.”

“Don’t say that. He was very nice. A gentleman.” She paused for a second. “I wish you had a car so we could go out tonight.”

Xiang's heart hurt like it were being torn apart. He wanted to buy a car so he could date the lovely girl, but he also had to save money for his brother to study in the

United States.

While he was struggling, she asked in a soft voice, “What did you do tonight?”

“I studied.” He went back to his bed with the phone.

They chatted, laughed, and yawned for the next few hours, even when their voices lowered, and their words slowed. Eventually, neither of them spoke, and Xiang fell asleep with the phone next to his pillow.

The next Monday, he went to their corner in the library between his classes, hoping to see her there. She never came. And she completely disappeared the whole week. At midnight on Friday, he called her from his dorm after returning from the physics department. It took a long time for her to respond, and when she did, she sounded happy for a second, and then seemed distant and absent-minded.

“I'm sorry to disturb you,” he said after unsuccessfully initiating conversations several times. “It’s too late now. I’ll talk to you later.”

“Wait, don’t hang up.” The panic was evident in her voice.

“It's almost midnight, and you must have been ready for bed.” He sounded as if he planned to hang up, but he really wished to stay talking to her, and he wondered why she spoke like that.

“I’m not. I have a lot of homework to do.”

“A lot of homework? School just started.”

“Yes, I'm taking twenty credit hours, and I have to work too.”

“Twenty credits?” He paused. “That’s a lot of hours.”

“Yes, it is. So, I can’t talk to you, but I want you to be on the phone.”

"Why?" He blinked.

"I just want you to be with me."

Her words traveled from his ear to his heart and diffused into every single cell in his body. The sound came out of the speaker and gradually formed a hologram image of her right in front of him. It was so vivid that he could even see her eyelashes and so real that he could feel her warm body and smell her perfume. He immersed himself in such a world for a few seconds, then set the phone down on his desk with its speaker facing him, and opened his books to study along with her.

The room was quiet, and the only sound was from his flipping pages.

An hour later, he seemed to hear something from the speaker. He picked up the phone. "Did you say something?"

"Yes. What are you doing?"

"I'm studying thermodynamics."

No more comments, no more questions, nothing, but the weak sound, like a pencil scratching on paper at the other end. In the next few hours and days after, they studied in different rooms, miles away from each other, with a thin telephone line connecting their hearts.

Christmas was approaching. As usual, Xiang called her after returning from his lab at midnight, but she did not answer.

That's strange. Where was she? Why hadn't she picked it up?

He attempted a few more times before giving up, then took a shower and retired to bed. As he was drifting off, a loud, piercing sound jolted him awake. For a brief moment, he thought the fire alarm had gone off, but then realized it was his phone ringing.

It must be Tanjing.

He quickly grabbed the phone on the desk next to his bed. “Hello?”

No one answered.

“Hello?” he repeated.

Still no response.

It must be a prank. He hung up.

The phone rang again.

“Who is this?” He raised his voice, irritated.

Once again, the line was silent, but he heard a sound, very weak, a faint signal like that from the far end of the universe. He pressed the phone against his ear hard, trying to capture it. A few seconds later, he detected a rhythm. It was the sound of a familiar breathing.

“Tanjing, I know it's you,” He laughed, thinking that she was playing with him. “Don’t try to scare me. You know I'm afraid of nothing.”

The breathing turned into a soft whimper.

“Are you crying?” He jumped up from his bed. “What happened?”

No response.

“Tell me what happened?”

“My mom . . . she . . . she . . .” Her voice broke into a heartbroken sob.

“What happened to your mother? Is she okay?” He held his breath, hoping it was not a car accident or some kind of tragedy.

“She’s fine.”

“Then what is it?” He let out his breath.

“My mom told me that Fei talked to them today.” She paused. “He wants to marry me.”

“He has the nerve to approach your parents about marrying you. It is time to let him know your feelings.

Tell your mother to turn him down." He guffawed. "By the way, I have to admit that this guy is quite brave."

Xiang had noticed that Fei had been trying to date Tanjing, but he was unconcerned since, in his opinion, Fei's love for her was unrequited.

"Xiang, I'm afraid." She whimpered again.

"Afraid of what?"

"My mom."

"Do you mean your mom wants you to marry him?" Xiang felt like being teased.

"She talked to me for hours tonight, trying to persuade me to marry him. She said it was best for me."

Her weak voice sounded like thunder. In China, parents' attitudes were often a deciding factor in their children's marriages.

After a second of silence, he said, "You don't have to marry him. You don't have to listen to your mother. It's your marriage, not your mother's."

"I have to. It doesn't matter whether I agree or not. I can't let her down," she said, sobbing.

"Why?"

"To help me study in the United States, she resigned from her position as a senior scientist at the Chinese Academy of Science. For the last two years, she has worked as a janitor at the Civil Engineering Department and as a housekeeper for several families. I can't let her down."

What a huge sacrifice. No wonder she looked sorrowful whenever she mentioned her mother. In China, janitors and housekeepers lived at the bottom of the social ladder, but scientists were highly respected.

Sensing that losing her was almost inevitable, he struggled to seize the last straw. "Do you love him? If you don't, then you shouldn't marry him. Otherwise, you will not have a happy marriage."

A long silence. A deadly silence.

He clenched the phone tightly as if to hold on to her. A surge of panic went through him.

"He loves me." Her voice trembled. "He said that he would quit his job and move to North Carolina with me when I go to medical school next year. He'll look for a job there or go to law school."

"Do you love him?" Xiang could think of nothing else to say.

"He loves me more than you do. He's willing to do anything for me. Are you willing to quit your PhD program for me?" She paused and spoke with a firm tone. "You won't. I know that."

Tanjing was right. Besides the required courses, Xiang had been taking extra classes in electrical engineering. If everything went well, he would have his master's degree in electrical engineering in one year and his doctorate in physics in three years. He could not simply drop everything and accompany her to North Carolina.

"I can't quit now, but I will try to find a job near you after I get my PhD." He paused. "Don't marry him. You can't marry someone you don't love."

"Don't tell me that… Love is not everything. More than half of American marriages end in divorce. I'm sure that they were in love when they got married. I want a family that can last forever and someone who will never leave me alone. He loves me, and he is willing to do anything for me."

"Tell me, do you love him?"

Another long silence.

"I will." She paused. "Without you in the way, I will love him." She paused for seconds. "Eventually."

Xiang heard a click. Apparently, she hung up. He called back immediately, but she did not answer. He called her several more times but only received busy tones. Finally, he collapsed into his chair, with the phone falling to the floor.

With no strength and no desire to move, he sat like a half-dead animal and drifted off into sleep. When he woke up, it was already the next afternoon. Unlike any other day, rather than leaping out of bed to get started on his studies, he lazed in bed, letting time float past like water in a creek. He did not need time. He just wanted to lie there, doing nothing.

A half an hour later, he heard Merry Christmas and Happy New Year greetings in the hallway and realized that winter break was coming, and the dormitory would be closed. He sprang to his feet and grabbed a yellow book from his bookshelf, searching for an apartment. He had to find a place to stay for the winter break. In the last few days, he had contacted several landlords, but none of them was willing to take him for two weeks.

He flipped through the book and dialed the numbers, one by one. He was rejected, rejected, and rejected. When he had exhausted the listings, he sat back in his chair, thinking of nothing, feeling helpless. A few minutes later, a thought occurred to him.

Maybe I should try the housing department. They may make exceptions for international students who can't go home during the holiday.

He called them. The phone beeped for a few seconds before a woman with a sweet voice answered. "Housing department. May I help you?"

"Yes, I'm an international PhD student living in Anderson Hall. Since I can't go back to China during the winter break, I am wondering whether I can stay in my room for the next two weeks."

"Sorry, you can't. Residence halls will be closed over the winter break and reopen on January 4."

"But I have no place to go."

"Have you tried apartment rentals?"

"I did, but none of them were willing to rent an apartment to me for only two weeks. Do you know anyone who can help me?"

"Oh, yes. I know some." Her voice was pleasant. "Hold on a second. Let me find them for you."

What a relief. He did not have to worry about his winter break anymore.

Xiang went to the window, glancing at the snow and the students in the parking lot, feeling the spirit of Christmas.

How stupid I was. Why didn't I call the housing department in the first place? I have made a simple matter so stressful and difficult.

A moment later, he heard the woman say again. "Hello, are you there?"

"Yes, I'm here."

"I found several for you. Do you have a pen and paper?"

"Yes." He sat down at his desk and grabbed a pen.

"Here are their phone numbers. The first one is …."

He jotted it down.

"That is the Matio Hotel number."

What? He blinked. He didn't need a hotel number.

He waited for the next, believing she would have valuable information.

"Here is another one."

He wrote it down.

"That is for Dobatte Hotel."

Is she kidding me? I'm a poor international student. How is it possible for me to stay in a luxurious hotel for two weeks?

"This is —"

"Madam," he cut her off. "I'm a poor international student, and I don't have the money to stay in a fancy hotel for the whole winter break."

"Oh, I'm sorry." The woman sounded surprised. "But I don't have any other information for you."

"Thank you for your time." He hung up the phone and slumped in his chair, drained.

Outside, snowflakes drifted down from the overcast sky and piled up on the snow-covered roofs of the buildings across the street, reminding him of the funeral parades he had seen in Chinese movies, in which everyone wore white and held white banners and flowers.

He leaned back in his chair, trying to think what to do. After a long silence, he rose and went to the window. A few miles away, on the other side of the downtown skyscrapers, was a homeless shelter. Last month, a female Indian graduate student had moved into it after her parents had cut her off because she had rejected an arranged marriage.

Maybe I should...

He was frightened to continue thinking.

Chapter 42

One late night after returning from the mountains, Shan studied the design of a power system in his office with the door half-closed. All the lights in the building had been turned off except for his office and that of the Chinese Communist Party Committee. The top management of the company was having a long meeting at the other end of the corridor.

In his quiet and peaceful room, Shan was completely immersed in his reading, losing track of time. Suddenly, loud noises broke the tranquility and startled him.

"Quick!" a man thundered.

"Hurry!" another man yelled.

Shan looked at the doorway and heard footsteps pounding toward his office. The door swung open, and the president of the company, a retired Army officer in his sixties, appeared at the door. "Young man," he puffed, "we need your help."

Shan sprang up, jaw-dropping. Never before had he seen the president pant with his mouth wide open like a dog in the heat of summer.

"Hurry." The man waved at him. "Chairman Zhu has a heart attack. We need to send her to the hospital immediately. Quick, help us carry her downstairs."

Shan rushed into Zhu's office. There she lay, stretched out on a couch, her eyes closed as if she were sleeping peacefully. Three other men in their sixties stood, looking down at her silently. Heavy footsteps sounded in the hallway, and soon a young company security guard charged in with a wooden board.

Shan and the security guard gently lifted her onto the board and carried her down the stairs.

"Gentle, gentle," someone said behind Shan.

They slowed their pace and walked with extreme caution, as if she were a precious and fragile treasure. After they loaded her onto the company's large van, everyone boarded the vehicle and headed toward Xihe General Hospital.

Thirty minutes later, the van pulled up in front of the emergency entrance near several medical staff standing at the curb holding a gurney.

A tall man in a white coat approached the president as he stepped out of the vehicle from the passenger side. "Are you with Yellow River Electrical Power?"

"Yes."

"I'm Doctor Liu." The man extended his hand. "Is her husband Lieutenant Governor Yan?"

"Yes." They shook hands.

Doctor Liu turned to his staff. "Take her to the west wing emergency room. *West wing*."

The medical staff transported Chairman Zhu from the vehicle to the stretcher and rushed her into the west wing emergency room through a solid and elegant double-door across the hallway.

In the hallway just outside the doors, the president exhaled a long breath. He looked down at his wristwatch before turning his gaze back toward the group. "It's past midnight. I think we can go home now. But before we do that, we should make sure one of us will be here tonight just in case. Her husband is on a business trip in the

United States, and her son is studying there." He paused for a second. "Who would like to stay?"

No one spoke.

After a moment of silence, he glanced at Shan. "How about you?"

"Sure." Shan was glad to have such an opportunity.

He knew it was going to be a long, boring night and that staying there all night might be too much for these older company leaders, especially for those who might have this or that kind of health issue. But for him, a young man, it would not be so bad. Besides, if Chairman Zhu knew he was there for her when everyone went home, she might be grateful. That would be helpful when it came time to evaluate his probationary period.

The president nodded. "Thank you. What's your name? I have seen you many times, but have never had a chance to talk to you."

"Shan Gao."

"Thank you, Shan." The man nodded again and wrote something on a piece of paper. "This is my phone number. Call me if there is an urgent need."

After everyone had gone, Shan went to the soft, red bench across the hallway and sat down to rest. He took out a cigarette, inhaled deeply, and blew a fat ring. As it lazily drifted away, it grew bigger and bigger. His eyes followed it, and through it, he saw many people sitting on rows of blue plastic chairs at the other end of the corridor. Near them was a big rectangular red sign, Emergency Room.

That must be for the general public, and this one, he looked at the double doors in front of him, was for high officials.

After a while, Doctor Liu and three young, beautiful

nurses came out of the emergency room with Chairman Zhu on a gurney.

Shan approached Doctor Liu. “How is she doing?”

“She is fine. For her safety, she should remain in the hospital for the next few days for further observation.” The doctor turned to the nurses. “You may take her to the high-official ward.”

Shan followed them to the double doors on the third floor. As he was about to walk in behind them, one of the nurses stopped him. “You are not allowed inside. There is a waiting area on the second floor.” She went through the entrance and shut the doors behind her.

Instead of going to the resting area, Shan gently pushed the doors, intending to see what the inside looked like, but the doors were locked. He stepped back against the wall across from the doors, waiting for a chance to sneak in. He had heard that the high-official ward was very luxurious but had never seen it.

A few minutes later, the doors opened, and three young, pretty nurses walked out, heading toward the elevator. Shan dashed to the doors and slipped inside just as they were closing.

The moment he entered the ward, he felt as if he had wandered into a five-star hotel. The floor was polished marble. An expansive corridor was flanked by a glass wall and expensive-looking reddish-brown wood doors. He walked down the hall, trying to see as much as he could before someone stopped him. When he reached an open door, he stopped and looked inside.

The room was lit by fluorescent ceiling lamps. The large window was draped with white transparent curtains, and nearby a polished tea table was surrounded by three leather couches, all in matching reddish brown.

A large screen TV sat on the left and a door leading into the adjacent room was on the right. It opened to reveal a large bed with a hardwood frame and an upholstered headboard and base.

As he was looking, he heard a woman's stern voice bark. "Hi, you. Who are you? What are you doing here? How did you get in?"

Shan looked over his shoulder and saw another young nurse standing behind him. Glancing at her, he wondered why all the nurses in the high-official ward were so pretty. Before he was able to answer her question, she continued. "You're not allowed in here. You should wait outside."

She escorted him out and closed the doors behind him, shutting him out of the world that belonged only to the powerful. Standing in the hallway, he stared at the door and remembered his uncle Ling.

A year before, because of a severe heart attack on Chinese New Year's Eve, Ling had been sent to the emergency room of a hospital and kept there for observation. The place was crowded, and some of the paint on the walls had peeled off. Eight people shared one room, and the air smelled like something rotten. Shan tried to stay in the ward to take care of his uncle, but a short nurse in her fifties expelled him. Several hours later, Ling died.

The sound of clacking heels and low laughter broke Shan's recollection. Two young nurses dressed in starched white uniforms came around the corner. As a courtesy, he stepped back against the wall to make room for them. Without a glance at him, they walked right past him and into the ward, leaving a whiff of their perfume in the air, the scent of the feminine and natural flower.

He glanced at the solid double doors and said to them in his mind. Power. Only power can open you. I'm going to open you, for me and for my parents.

Shan took out a crumpled pack of cigarettes and lit the last one. Crushing the empty pack in his fist, he dropped it into the garbage can. He was sick of these cheap cigarettes. He deserved better. He wanted to climb to the top so that he and his family could benefit from the finest services that were available, and he would not be pushed around anymore.

But how?

He paced up and down the corridor, thinking and smoking. As a nameless nobody from an ordinary family, he could go nowhere unless he forged connections with the powerful. Looking at the doors that separated him from the elite, he thought about Chairman Zhu, hoping she would recover soon. She was the top official in the company, and her husband was a lieutenant governor. They could drastically change his life if they were willing to help him. She liked him already. As her son and husband were in the United States, she was alone and ill with no one to care for her. That was the perfect opportunity for him to gain her trust. All he had to do was let her know he was always there for her and show how loyal he was.

Yes, that was it. He tossed the cigarette in the trash.

That same instant, the doors flew open, and Doctor Liu rushed over to him. "Chairman Zhu is in critical condition. Can you call your company's president?"

Chapter 43

Chairman Zhu survived her heart attack due to the excellent care she received as a high-ranking official. Soon after she recovered, she left the company and became Deputy Director of the Development and Economic Reform Commission, a prestigious position with few actual responsibilities. Shan was happy that she had survived the heart attack but was sad that their relationship had ended so abruptly after two months of careful nurturing. Luckily, he was assigned to the quality control and inspection department when he completed his probation. No one had told him why, but he suspected that it had something to do with her. She must have done him some kind of favor before leaving the company.

The department was responsible for inspecting all products before they were shipped and providing technical support to customers. His job allowed him to visit all divisions to observe their operations and how products were made. He made a rigorous study plan, deciding to be an expert on all the products before the company was possibly bankrupt. He spent all his time studying the product's design and manufacturing, never sleeping before midnight and never taking a weekend off.

Initially, he had been concerned that his hard work might make people resent him, but he soon realized that he had made everyone happy. His colleagues constantly sought his help or even threw their responsibilities on him, and when a new task arose, instead of looking for someone else to do it, the director, Hua, turned to him.

Three months later, Director Hua came to him. "Shan, would you be comfortable going to 83793?"

He looked at the director, questioning whether he had heard it right. 83793 was a military installation in the deep mountains of Sichuan. It had been moved there from a big city in the 1950s to avoid possible Soviet or American attacks.

"Today, we got an urgent call from 83793," Hua continued. "They requested we send someone to the factory immediately to fix their equipment. Ms. Zhao is the point of contact, but she is ill. She recommended you, saying that you understand the product better than others."

Shan knew that could be true. Since 83793 was a major customer of the company, he had spent much time on its products and helped her. However, he was a little concerned about going there alone.

"I'd love to go there, but I'm not sure that I can solve their issues."

"I believe in you. Also, you can call me anytime."

Although Shan still had some reservations, he was glad to have the opportunity. It would be his first time representing the company independently to its major customer. Once he succeeded, it would open more doors for him.

He spent the rest of the day reviewing the documents and going over details of the product and the trip with the director and left for the company the next morning.

His travel to 83793 was more difficult than he had anticipated. It took him two days by train to reach

Chengdu, one of China's largest cities, and then seven hours by crowded, old bus to get to a small town. A company car picked him up at the bus station and drove him another two hours to the factory in the mountains. Along the way, he wondered whether Ms. Zhao was actually ill or if she had simply decided not to put up with the discomforts of travel. After all, people did not like to work very much in those days.

By the time he arrived at the guesthouse of the complex, it was already late evening, and all his muscles had soured.

Following dinner, he strolled around to relax and explore the environment. He arrived at the school zone, where several elementary school students were jumping ropes, and teenagers were playing basketball and soccer. He watched them for a while and then kept going. After passing a hospital and a shopping center, he stopped at a gate guarded by two soldiers, beyond which was the restricted area where he would be working for the next few days. Then he went back to the guesthouse and studied the product documentation that he had brought with him until well past midnight.

The next morning, he went to the gate. A sentry checked his ID, read the letter from Yellow River Electrical Power Company, and then made a phone call. Ten minutes later, a tall, middle-aged man appeared. He saluted the soldier, passed Shan, and looked around. Seconds later, he turned to the guard. “Where is the engineer from Yellow River Electrical Power?”

“It’s him.”

The man looked at Shan. “You…?”

“Yes.” Shan nodded and extended his hand. “I’m Shan.”

"I'm Guo from the maintenance department." He shook hands with Shan. "I thought Ms. Zhou would be here." He paused for a second. "You look so young. Are you a new graduate?"

"Yes, I am. Ms. Zhou is sick, but she will be here in a few days. My company sent me here to begin the business, so when she arrives, we can fix the problem immediately." Shan lied, fearing Liu would be offended by a junior engineer being sent to fix the problems. He believed that once he repaired the equipment in a day or two, nobody would care about what he had said.

"That's very kind of you." Guo smiled. He then pointed to a mountain behind him. "Let's go to the factory. The equipment is there."

As they walked along a wide gravel road shaded by tall evergreens, Shan commented, "This place is beautiful. It's like a forest."

"That's why we have moved here. Nobody can see us from the sky. Neither airplanes nor satellites."

A few minutes later, they arrived at the entrance of a large tunnel. After passing through the security, Shan found himself in a long hallway about three adults tall and five people wide. The engineer led him to a big, gray machine in a facility room.

"It stopped working last week." Guo pointed at the equipment.

Shan stared at it, wondering if it was made by someone else. He had never seen anything like it before. He stepped closer to it to read the Chinese characters printed on its front panel. Dragon Fire II.

His heart sank.

This must be a very old power system. It was impossible to fix it within a day or two. He regretted telling a white lie a moment ago. If he could not fix it in time, his company would have to send Ms. Zhao here. Then his lie would be exposed, and he would be perceived as dishonest.

While he was thinking, he heard the engineer say, “I have to go to a meeting. Come see me if you need anything. I'm in room 317.”

After Guo left, Shan sat down and stared at the unit, feeling stupid for not having asked which power system was giving them problems before coming over. It was too late, and there was no use in regretting it. The only thing he could do was to solve the problems.

As his reputation was on the line, he studied the manuals all morning, had a quick lunch, and then returned to the station for more diagnostics until the evening. He returned after dinner, intending to continue troubleshooting, but he felt exhausted.

Instead of systematically diagnosing the instrument as he had done before, he played with it without a plan. Curious about the workmanship from many years ago, he removed the back panel, pulled out the motherboard, and looked at the thousands of tiny dots that connected the transistors and resistors to the board.

That’s amazing. They did a much better job back then.

As he admired the soldering, a small, discolored bump caught his attention. He touched it with a pair of tweezers, and it moved.

Aha, this could be the cause of the problem.

As his heart pounded from the excitement of possibly winning the lottery, he turned on the soldering iron, heated the tip, and soldered the component into place. He then installed the motherboard, turned on the equipment, and stared at it.

Please, please, please. His fingers typed wildly on his lap as the machine booted.

Within a minute, the equipment started running, and it worked properly.

He jumped up and rushed toward the door to tell the engineer the great news but stopped a second later.

Wait! Wait! Don't tell them. Don't you remember the story Lei told you?

Two engineers had assigned to solve a product problem. The younger one worked day and night trying to crack the issue. He even thought about it when he walked, ate, or went to bed. In two days, the problem was solved. His boss and coworkers praised him, but quickly forgot about him. The elder one, however, had taken his time. He reported his progress to his manager every day. Some engineers suspected that he deliberately made the situation sound extremely challenging, but his manager was pleased with his effort. The longer the process dragged on, the more impressive he and his manager looked in the eyes of the company leaders who lacked technical expertise. In the end of it, he and his manager were both hailed as heroes in the company.

After recalling that, Shan sat back down and disassembled the equipment so that he could learn about it from the inside out. For the next two days, he kept himself busy in the facility room, giving the impression that he was completely focused on his tasks. In reality, he was learning the equipment and attempting to become an expert on it. He communicated with Guo and his director twice a day to discuss its design, operation, and past technical issues. On the third day, he told them that the problem had been resolved.

"Thank you so much for your hard work!" The engineer shook his hand firmly. "We're all very grateful for your efforts and dedication."

His director said to him over the phone, "Excellent! I know you can do it. Come back quickly. I need your help on several other tasks."

Chapter 44

After looking down at the downtown area for a long time, Xiang grabbed his backpack, slung it over his shoulder, and hurried out of the building. He walked past the highway bridge south of the campus and stopped at an intersection. Instead of crossing the street and proceeding straight toward the homeless shelter, he took a right turn, heading toward a grocery store. After purchasing a full backpack of Instant noodles, hot dogs, apples, and bananas, he rushed back to the dorm.

He locked the door behind him, flipped off the lights, and walked over to the window, ducking behind the blinds so he could look down at the parking lot without being seen. He was going to hide out in his dorm room over the winter break.

The next few hours would be critical. A janitor might come to clean the room, or the residential manager could inspect each room to ensure everyone had departed.

What should he do if they came? His heart pounded so fast that he was afraid he was going to have a heart attack. Calm down, calm down, he told himself.

He glanced under his bed and then at the closet, estimating the spaces to see if they were large enough for him to hide if he needed to hide. Time passed minute by minute, like a turtle. Even after the parking lot had become empty, he still stood still and looked down at the entrance to the building.

The sun disappeared behind the western ridge, and orange streetlights illuminated otherwise dark streets.

It was safe now. The building was closed, and the whole dorm was his.

He turned on the light, pulled his purchase out of his backpack, and walked down the corridor to the bathroom, carrying a ceramic bowl. A minute later, he came back with a bowl of water, set it on his table, and dropped a pack of Instant noodles into it. He sliced a hot dog onto the noodles, heated them in the microwave in the corner of his room, and went to the bathroom again to wash an apple. Soon, he got the dinner ready — an apple and a bowl of noodles garnished with red hot dogs and golden oil spots. Sitting down at the table, he started to enjoy his first winter break dinner.

Suddenly, he realized something was wrong.

The well-lit room was like a beacon in the night, sending out signals to the whole world, telling everyone that he was hiding in the dorm. He jumped up and dashed across the room to flick the switch off. Then, he ran back to the window and looked down at the parking lot to see if anyone was coming. His heart pounded so loudly that he could feel each beat in his ears.

Outside was quiet and empty, and no one was in sight. After continuing to watch for two more minutes, he closed the window shades completely and opened it slightly, allowing the light from the hallway to come in. He then resumed his delicious dinner.

After the meal, he went to the hallway with his backpack, sat against the wall, and studied for his qualifying exam that had been scheduled to take place at the beginning of the following semester. It was the most important test for the students who pursued PhDs.

Several hours later, feeling sore in his muscles, he rose to stretch and then walked back to his room to check the time. It was almost eleven o'clock. Not wanting to continue to study, he decided to go to sleep early.

As he lay in bed after his shower down the hallway, he remembered a cassette that his ex-girlfriend had given him. He got up, dug it out of the drawer, and put it in the cassette player. Then he lay back down and let the soothing melody of *Colorful Clouds to the Moon* wash over him.

The next morning, after waking up refreshed from a good night's sleep, he had Instant noodles and hot dogs for breakfast. Then, he read *the Theory of Mechanics* until noon.

Noon came. He ate Instant noodles and hot dogs.

Dinner came. He ate Instant noodles and hot dogs.

For the next few days, each day was identical to the previous one, as if it were created by a copy machine. On the fifth morning, as he reached for a pack of noodles, his hand froze in midair. The monotony of the food was beginning to affect his stomach, and he could not take it any longer. He stood silently for a moment, then decided to skip breakfast, hoping that hunger would make the food taste better. When lunchtime rolled around, he skipped it again. By dinnertime, he had become so hungry that his survival instinct overcame his pickiness. He prepared the food and pinched his nose while feeding himself the noodles and hot dogs.

He followed the strategy the following week.

On New Year's Eve, he cooked the noodles and hot dogs in the microwave. When he opened the door, he ducked back. The hot air wafted the sickly odor of the food into his nostrils, making him feel queasy. After staring at the bowl for some time, he carried it to the bathroom, dumped the food into the toilet, and flushed it. He then took his textbooks to the corridor and sat against the wall to study.

A few hours later, he felt a stabbing pain in his stomach. Knowing that it was caused by hunger, he got up to prepare some food, but the pain made him difficult to move. He sat back down, one hand pressing against his stomach. Instead of lessening, his agony only intensified, and he began to fear that his stomach issue had resurfaced and that he was in serious trouble. He managed to get back to his room and reached for a yellow book on the windowsill. He needed to call for a medical emergency before it was too late.

When he touched the book, his hand bounced back as if it had been shocked by electricity. He could not contact them. If he did, he would never be able to return. Furthermore, he could be disciplined for hiding in the dorm.

Slowly, he made his way to his bed and lay face down, continuing to press his hand against his stomach, hoping the time would help him recover. Within a minute, sweat poured down his forehead and he panted for breath. Lightheaded and dizzy, he began to shiver.

Having never felt pain like this before, Xiang became alarmed and tried to reach for the phone book again.

Chapter 45

Xiang could not call an ambulance. If he did, he would be taken to the hospital and not be able to return to the dormitory. He decided to stay in his room, taking a risk in hoping that his mind would heal him. He remembered a story his father had told him when he was a child. A very old man was about to die at any moment. His only wish was to see his grandchildren one last time before leaving the world. But they were far away, and it took them six months to reach him. The grandfather miraculously held on until he saw them. If the human mind could extend its lifespan, why could it not also assist people in recovering from ailments?

He closed his eyes and focused his mind on his stomach, trying to fight against the pain with the power of his will. However, the ache refused to subside. He sweated and shivered, but he did not give up. Not because he was strong, but because there was nothing else he could do.

Ten minutes later, the pain subsided and eventually disappeared. Xiang was not sure if that was nature taking its course or if it was because he had willed it to go away. It did not matter. He did not have time to think about it. The urgency was that he had to eat, otherwise, the trouble would return, and it would only be worse. He glanced at the Instant noodles and hot dogs, but just the sight of them made him feel nauseous.

What should he do?

He walked over to the window and gazed out at the snowy landscape. Not too far away on Main Street, there was a Chinese restaurant. It would be ideal to have dinner there.

That's not going to happen. He shook his head. I don't have a key. If I leave the dorm, I won't be able to come back in… Wait a minute. Don't give up so easily. There must be a solution, and you just have to be creative.

He glanced in the direction of the restaurant, thinking hard. A moment later, he turned around, grabbed his backpack and stapler from his desk, and stepped out of the room.

To avoid being seen as he exited the building, he decided to use the rear entrance, which opened onto a small garden surrounded by trees and shrubbery. From there, he could slip unnoticed out of the dorm and return.

He descended the stairs to the door and peered through the small glass pane to see if anyone was around. No one. Pushing the door open, he placed the stapler at the corner of the door frame to prevent it from closing. As he stepped through the doorway into the garden, a blast of cold, fresh air filled his lungs and invigorated him.

Xiang had been in the garden many times, even just a few days before, but he had never given much thought to it. Now, it was so much more than just a garden. It was a paradise of freedom. In the past, freedom had just been a word, a concept, but now it was something that he could touch, smell, and taste. After two weeks in a one-person room with nothing to do but study, eat, and sleep, he now had a whole world. The trees, the sky, and, most of all, the Chinese food that awaited him.

Two birds flew up from the thicket and perched on a high branch of a tree. He looked up and imitated their chirping. Suddenly, a loud sound startled the little creatures and sent them into the air. Xiang jerked his head around, realizing that the building's alarm had gone off because he had left the door ajar too long. He ran back into the entrance, snatched up the stapler, and shut the door.

Heart pounding, he glanced around the garden and out into the street beyond it to see if anyone had noticed the alarm. No one was in sight except for a homeless man shuffling along the sidewalk, his head down, seemingly lost in his own thoughts. Xiang then darted back into his room and peered out through the window at the parking lot to check whether the campus police had arrived.

The parking lot was covered in pristine white snow, with no footprints or tire tracks. As he was about to relax, he noticed two police cars in the distance headed his way, lights flashing.

He froze, not knowing what to do.

What if they found me? Are they going to arrest me?

His heart again pounded, his stomach tightened, and his mind went blank.

The vehicles moved closer and closer. A moment later, they passed the entrance to the parking lot and continued down the road. Xiang exhaled his stress and turned to walk away from the window, giving up the idea of going out to dinner. However, the moment he saw the packs of Instant noodles and hotdogs on the bookshelf, he felt stomach sick again.

What was he going to do? He could not eat these for another week.

He paced in the room, thinking about how to leave the building and return back inside safely. Ten minutes later, he reached for his desk, took a two-inch-wide roll of clear tape from his drawer, and headed down the stairs with his backpack on his shoulder. When he arrived at the rear door, he pushed it open, taped the latch bolt so that it would not protrude, and then let the door close to test his idea. He had his hand on the doorknob just in case the alarm went off. If it did, he could quickly remove the tape and shut the door, minimizing the chance of alerting anyone.

This was his last hope. He stood silently like an inmate awaiting his freedom. The time dragged, second by second. Then, after what seemed an infinitely long wait in his life, he yelled, "Yes!"

His method worked.

He pushed the door open, walked out of the building, and headed to the Chinese restaurant.

In the snow, to avoid sliding and falling, he leaned forward and walked flat-footed with his toes slightly pointing out like a penguin. A moment later, he stopped to shift the backpack straps from one shoulder to both to balance his weight and then continued. Due to road conditions, he alternated between sidewalks and the roadway, going against the flow of traffic and keeping an eye out for any vehicles.

Do I really want to go to the restaurant? What if the tap failed and the door was locked itself?

He kept asking himself the same questions as he walked. Though he thought about returning to his dorm so many times, his stomach kept him going. Thirty minutes later, he arrived at the destination. Grabbing the icy handrails, he climbed the steps at the entrance. As he entered the building, a middle-aged woman behind a stand smiled at him. "How many do you have?"

"One."

"Table or booth?"

"Booth."

Xiang followed her to a window. After sitting down, he looked around. The small restaurant had four booths and five tables, and six Asian students were eating at a table filled with many dishes as if they were having a party.

He ordered a big meal - shrimp with snow peas, gong bao chicken, and spicy tofu - intending to eat his fill and take the rest back to the dorm. After so many days of Instant noodles and hotdogs, he needed something different.

The food arrived quickly, along with a delicious aroma that made his stomach growl. In front of the enticing dishes, he wanted to eat as much as he could, but he had to restrain himself to avoid another stomachache. He ate a small portion and packed the remainder to take back to his dormitory.

From that day on, the tape became his best friend and his key to freedom. For the rest of the winter break, he was able to go out to eat and exercise whenever he wanted. His healthy lifestyle and high spirits enabled him to prepare for the qualifying exam more effectively. When school started again, he easily passed both qualify exams from Electrical Engineering and Physics.

After searching for his PhD advisor in both departments, he chose Dr. Smith, a world-renowned expert in optical sensors, in the Electrical Engineering Department.

On the first day of his joining the group, Dr. Smith

introduce him to a man in his forties, about six feet four, with a walnut-colored complexion and big teeth that protruded like a wolf's.

The professor motioned to the man. "This is Larry, my process engineer. He will teach you how to fabricate optical sensors. He is very meticulous and can fabricate the devices with consistent quality."

Glad that he was going to get the best possible training, Xiang extended his hand to the engineer. "Nice to meet you."

"Nice to meet you too," Larry said in some kind of strong accent, offering his hand.

When Xiang tried to shake Larry's hand, the engineer thrust his wrist back such that Xiang could only grip his four fingers and shake them unilaterally. In a surprise, he blinked at Larry, feeling insulted but quickly reasoning that this must be a different way of shaking hands, a cultural difference. At first, he wanted to ask Larry where he was from but decided not to because it might not be an appropriate question at the time.

The phone on the desk jingled, and the professor placed his hand on the receiver, looking at the engineer. "Larry, could you take him to the department office to get some student supplies?" He then picked up the phone and spoke into it.

Larry led Xiang out of the office and said to Xiang, "I need to make an urgent call. I'm sure you can go and get your supplies by yourself."

Xiang looked at the engineer's eyes and saw his own images reflected in Larry's pupils. They were so small and so vulnerable that they vanished the instant the engineer blinked.

"Thank you. I'll do that," he said humbly.

They parted ways, heading in opposite directions.

About thirty minutes later, Xiang returned to see Larry to schedule a training time. He wanted to show the engineer that he was a diligent student who had added value to the group. When he arrived at the office, he found the big man sitting behind a dark brown desk, giggling at the computer monitor.

He hesitated for a second and then knocked on the open door.

The engineer lifted his head and frowned. "Yes?"

"Sorry for disturbing you. I just want to check with you about the training. I'm available at any time."

Larry scowled. "I'll be very busy over the next two weeks. Dr. Smith asked me to fabricate some devices for him."

Two weeks? That was like infinity. As a new incoming graduate student, Xiang did not have so much time to waste. He took a step forward. "Can we perhaps —"

"I'm busy now." Larry stood up, escorted Xiang out of his office, and shut the door.

Since arriving in the United States, Xiang had never encountered such boorish behavior. He could not understand why the engineer was being so rude to him.

After waiting two weeks, he went to see Larry again, attempting to schedule the training sessions.

"Sorry, I can't do this right now." The engineer leaned back in his chair, rotating a pencil between his fingers. "My work has taken longer than I expected. I need a few more days."

Though frustrated, Xiang asked politely, "Then, when can you train me?"

"I don't know." Larry frowned again.

Not wanting to appear too pushy, Xiang swallowed his frustration, thanked the engineer, and left. On the way back to the student office, he ran into his advisor.

"How is your training going?" Dr. Smith asked.

"It hasn't started yet. Larry says he is too busy fabricating devices for you."

The professor stared at him silently for a moment. "He is always busy. To learn from him, you need to be aggressive. I hope you will complete the training in two weeks."

After his advisor left, Xiang returned to Larry's office. On the way, he kept thinking about the best way to broach the subject with the engineer so that he could get trained.

When he reached the office, Larry was leaning back in his chair, eyes closed, earphones over his head. Xiang stood quietly in the doorway for a few seconds and then knocked.

The engineer opened his eyes and glared at Xiang. "What?"

"Sorry to interrupt you. Dr. Smith just asked me about the training."

Larry instantly took off his headphones and sat up straight. "What did you tell him?"

"I said that we haven't started yet because you've been very busy fabricating devices for him."

The engineer bit his lip, stared into Xiang's eyes for a moment, and then took a deep breath. "Well, if you want, I can start the training tomorrow."

"Sure." Xiang was taken aback by Larry's abrupt shift and almost imperceptible fear. "What time?"

"Ten o'clock."

"Thank you."

After leaving Larry's office, Xiang wondered why the engineer had lied to him about fabricating devices for Dr. Smith for the past two weeks.

Chapter 46

The election had finally arrived.

Shan headed to the cafeteria, confident that he would be elected to the committee. Over the past two months, instead of publicly campaigning for the election and appearing power-hungry, he had played basketball with the workers and had become their friends. Their support should give him enough votes.

On his way, he ran into Lan, one of the new college graduates who had joined the company at the same time as him. He did not like her very much because she always acted as if she was superior to everyone else, but he nevertheless greeted her. “Good morning! How are you?”

“You look very happy.” Her tone seemed sarcastic.

“Why do you say that?”

“You know why.” She sneered. “You have been working hard over the past few weeks.”

“What do you mean?” He scowled, regretting having spoken to her.

“Don't act like you don't understand me.” Her lips twisted. “You've been playing basketball every day.”

“I love playing basketball.” In his mind, he told her it was none of her business. “Exercising makes me feel good.”

“Really? Becoming a committee member will make you feel even better.” She raised her eyebrows. “Don’t think we can't see through your scheming. You suddenly mingled with the workers and played sports with them. Why? Because you want their votes. You didn't play basketball with them. You played them."

Now he understood why she was mad at him. They were competitors for the same position, and she knew that she would lose.

Sorry, but it's too late for you to change anything.

"I heard you want to be elected to the committee. Good luck," he said sarcastically and walked away before she could say anything.

On his way to the dining hall, he reflected on how she had found out about his plan and concluded that she must have read a lot of books. No wonder monarchs despised the educated elite throughout history. It was difficult to hide anything from educated people. Shan also felt sorry for the intellectuals. Even if they saw something wrong, they did not have the courage or even bother to speak up, let alone take action to change the situation.

At the dining hall, he was greeted warmly by the workers, and they told him that they would support him. With their backing, he was decisively voted into office.

One evening a few days after the election, the five-member committee held its first meeting in the spacious office of the Communist Youth League Committee chairman. It was a long one, largely talking about how to align young employees' thoughts with central government policies to prevent the inculcation of Western ideas. Toward the end, the chairman said, "Morale among young people is very low these days. What can we do to lift it?"

"There isn't much we can do," a member replied.

"It's not their fault. People won't work hard if they think the company has no future."

"I think we need to help the young workers," Shan said. "They don't have much education. Rumor says the company may go bankrupt. If that happens, it will be difficult for them to find new jobs. I can tell that many of them want to get a high education too. We should help them."

"How?" Another member asked. "Only less than one percent of young people can go to college. These workers are just not competitive enough. They either didn't study hard or didn't want to study hard when they were in high school."

The discussion dragged on and on until Mei came forward to support Shan's position. "I agree with Shan. We should help the workers. Our government has launched a remote higher education program through which people can earn their college degrees by taking government-sponsored television courses. Once they complete the required classes, the government will issue college diplomas to them. These diplomas won't be as good as a normal college degree, but they are better than high school ones."

Her support changed the dynamics in the room. After further discussion, the committee decided to launch a night school program to help the workers. Shan and Mei were assigned to run it.

By the time the meeting ended, it was already 9 o'clock. For the first time, he could walk her to the bus stop outside the company compound late at night without fear of being seen. From now on, they would have a legitimate reason to meet every evening without causing suspicion and rumor. He was so glad that he had joined the committee.

As they strolled along, he wondered why she had backed him up in the meeting. Was it because she believed in the course, or simply wanted to show her support for him?

While he was thinking, he heard her say, “I like your idea. Do you have a detailed plan?”

“Yes. I have given this a lot of thought. I think the night school should aim to prepare workers for the national remote education entrance test.”

Mei nodded. “I agree.”

He continued, “The first thing we should do is to prepare study materials for the workers. Their salaries are much lower than ours. If we require them to purchase books, they may hesitate to come to the night school. However, if we make the classes free, they may be interested in attending. I still have the books I used to prepare for the national college entrance exams. We can select relevant content from these books and prepare teaching materials for them.”

“That sounds like a lot of work.” She stopped to look at him.

“We should be able to do it if we work on it every night.” He paused for a second. “We can talk to the company to get you a temporary dorm room.”

She locked eyes with him for a second, as if trying to peer into his thoughts, then nodded. “I’ll talk to the company tomorrow.”

Shan looked at her with a blank face, hiding his exultation. He thanked the young workers in his mind for bringing him such good fortune. Having played basketball with them, he had gained their trust, and they had elected him to the committee. This gave him an excuse to be around Mei. By helping them prepare for the entrance exam for the national higher education programs, he was able to spend every night with Mei for many weeks to come. No wonder so many rulers loved the working class—it was simpleminded and could be easily manipulated. Shan hated the fact he had taken advantage of them. He would now assist them in passing the exams in whatever way he could.

The next day, Mei moved into the dorm, and they began preparing the night school handouts. They sat side by side at a table in a small conference room, paging through physics books and choosing relevant material. After working until midnight, they left for the dorm, parting ways on the second floor in opposite directions. The national entrance exam for remote education was only three months away, so they worked together every night, even on weekends.

In the absence of copying machines at the time, they used wax-resist copying to produce their handouts after selecting contents from physics, history, mathematics, and Chinese language books.

She used a stylus pen with a steel needle to write the content onto wax paper by removing the wax to expose the fiber pores. He attached the carved paper to the screen frame, placed it on top of a sheet of paper, and inked the screen with a paintbrush. Then he rolled a roller back and forth across the wax paper to squeeze the ink through and transfer the text to the paper.

The process was tedious and time-consuming, but they accomplished a great deal in a second, at least Shan felt like it. During those days, the earth rotated much faster, and time flew by, especially at nights when he was with Mei. Before he knew it, the second week was over.

On Sunday, Mei wanted to go home to see her parents. It had been two weeks since she had seen them. After finishing the math handouts at night, they walked to the bus stop together.

"How many people have signed up for night school?" she asked, brushing her windblown hair with her fingers.

"About fifty."

She nodded. "If we keep the speed, we will have all the materials done in two weeks. Next week, we should start recruiting volunteer teachers."

They arrived at the bus station. As they waited, Shan lifted his arm, trying to wrap it around her, but let it fall before his hand touched her back. The wind grew powerful and blew a large cloud toward the bright half-moon. He felt a strong desire to reach out, grab her, and cling to her, but he feared that it would make him look like a bad guy.

Maybe it's okay. Maybe she was waiting for his move. When they were alone in the conference room, their shoulders often touched, and she never moved away.

With those thoughts, he raised his arm, but then dropped it again, still concerned that it would jeopardize their relationship. From the side, he saw her gazing ahead motionless, letting her hair blow in the wind. He attempted to think of something to say but could not find a word. After a long struggle, he was unable to resist himself any longer and put his arm around her waist.

"Don't. People will see." Gently, she pushed his arm.

Instead of letting her go, he lightly pulled her closer and kissed her cheek.

"Don't. People will see." She looked into his eyes with a smile on her face.

He wanted to kiss her again, but a bus pulled over in front of them.

She kissed his lips and then stepped onto the bus. Waving through the window at him, she was taken away by the powerful vehicle, farther and farther away. Turning around, he walked in the opposite direction to his dorm. The wind howled and massive clouds engulfed the moon.

That night, he had a dream about her, in which they took their children to the mountains to see the trees they had planted.

When he was awakened by thunder booms in the early morning, he saw the wind whipping the heavy rain against the windowpanes. Rather than going to the cafeteria, he ate a bowl of instant noodles and left the building for his office with his umbrella. As soon as he stepped outside, his legs and shoes were soaked.

After two hours, the storm died, but a steady drizzle continued throughout the day. In the evening, he went to the Communist Youth League office as usual and waited for her. But she did not show up.

What happened to her?

A strange concern stirred within him, but he kept telling himself not to worry. She might not have come to work due to inclement weather. Without her, he did not feel like doing anything and went back to his dorm. The following evening, he waited in the office for her again, but she did not appear.

Worried about her, he went to her office the next day, only to discover that she had suddenly left the company.

Chapter 47

Shan walked along the sidewalk of the busy downtown district, painfully reflecting on Mei's abrupt departure.

Maybe I've been completely wrong all along. Maybe I'm in love with her, but she doesn't feel the same way. Maybe my intimacy with her last Sunday night was the reason for her leaving the company.

As he was lost in these thoughts, a black car pulled up beside him. With the window rolling down, the driver shouted, "Shan!"

He bent over to look inside. "Lei! Long time no see. What are you doing here?"

"I'm just passing by. Want to go to dinner?"

"Sure."

"Come on in. I'll take you to Jinxuan Restaurant. It's all on me."

Shan opened the door and got in. A few minutes later, his friend pulled into the parking lot in front of what appeared to be a three-story building made of large white grayish stones. They got out of the car and walked up to the entrance that was flanked by two large rock lion statues. As they approached the double glass doors, two young women dressed in red silk cheongsams—a mandarin gown—opened the doors for them. Stepping into the doorway, Shan saw red lanterns hanging from the high arched ceilings and a red carpet running down the hall. On either side of the entrance, stood four beautiful young women dressed in pink silk cheongsams, their graceful slender necks rising from mandarin collars and a tantalizing glimpse of flesh visible through the split skirts.

"Welcome to Jinxuan Restaurant," they said as they bowed almost ninety degrees with their hands crossed in front of them.

Shan's first instinct was to bow back, but when he saw his friend walking straight ahead as if the girls did not exist, he responded with a friendly smile and nod. A girl led them to a table at the back of the high-ceilinged dining hall, where they could see the large stage down at the far end.

Lei pulled out a cigarette pack from his pocket, set it down on the table, and pointed to the stage. "How do you like it here? They have a show here every night at seven."

Shan looked around, realizing it was not a three-story building at all but rather a magnificent restaurant. The dining tables were spaced well apart, and each was covered in red linen cloth. White cambric napkins were folded into fat triangles and tucked into crystal goblets. Silverware gleamed in the light of the restaurant's large chandeliers. "This place is incredible."

Lei handed him a cigarette. "Are you still working for the same company?"

"Yes." He looked at the leather-bound menu in front of him, wondering how expensive the restaurant was.

"Your company is in financial trouble."

Shan raised his head, facing his friend. "How do you know that?"

"I work for the governor's office." Lei lit a cigarette

for Shan and then for himself. “As the largest enterprise in the province, your company is always on our radar.”

A young waitress came. “What would you like to order?”

Without looking at the menu, Lei ordered food for both of them. “Chicken cutlets in chili sauce, sweet and sour spareribs, beef with mushroom and bamboo shoots, braised fish, shrimp tofu soup, and a bottle of red wine.”

“Anything to drink?” she asked.

“Green tea.”

She left, and Lei turned back to Shan. “Your company may have to go bankrupt, but it’s hard to say at this point. The government may not afford to let it fall. It’s too important for the country.” Lei took a drag on the cigarette and leaned forward. “By the way, do you know a girl named —” He paused as if he could not remember her name. “Mei, yes, Mei.”

The word pierced Shan's heart. He looked into Lei’s eyes, wondering why he had asked such a question.

His friend burst into laughter. “Look at you. Why are you staring at me like that?”

Shan forced a smile. “How do you know her?”

“I don’t know her. She just transferred to our Bureau of Science and Technology from your company.” Lei paused, gazing at Shan for a moment. “Buddy, don’t tell me you're dating her.”

Shan sighed and then told his friend about his relationship with Mei.

“Forget about her, buddy.”

“Why?” Shan’s eyes widened.

“Do you know why she left your company?”

“No.”

“A few days ago, she turned down the son of the

vice chairman of the provincial Political and Legal Committee. She told her parents that she wanted to marry an engineer in your company. I assume that's you. Furious, they immediately transferred her to the Bureau of Science and Technology. They don't want their daughter to marry a nameless minor engineer who works for a company that's on the brink of bankruptcy."

Feeling both insulted by her parents and loved by her, Shan said in a firm tone, "I'm nobody now, but one day I'll be somebody. I'm doing very well in the company and have also just been elected to the Youth Communist League committee. In ten to twenty years, no matter what happens to this company, I will be someone people admire and look up to."

"You wish. You have no idea how this society works. You can work hard to become a low-level official, but you won't get anywhere unless you have the right family connections. It's not the one who works hard that gets ahead, but the one with the best connections. Look, without a powerful father, you won't even get the girl you like."

"I'll go to see her tomorrow," Shan said with full confidence.

"Don't be stupid. You're looking for trouble."

"Why?"

"You're competing against the son of the chairman of the Political and Legal Committee."

"I don't care who he is. I have the right to date her, and that doesn't violate any laws."

"How naive you are. You don't have to break any laws to get into big trouble. That guy is evil. He will do anything to get what he wants. One of his previous relationships involved an actress. As soon as he saw her, he wanted her, but she refused. When he learned she had a boyfriend, he had thugs beat the man so badly that they broke his nose and tore his face. If you don't let go of Mei, you will become the second one. Listen to me. Forget about her." Lei took a deep breath. "He's a real son of a bitch. We have a problem with him too, but we can't do anything about it."

"Oh?" He furrowed his brow. "What is it?"

"I assisted Jiangkai in obtaining authorization to turn the Phoenix Mountain District into the province's greatest tourist attraction. But, the owner of the illegal building on top of the mountain refuses to relocate. Now, the project is on hold. Worse yet, we may be forced to abort it."

"What does it have to do with him?"

"He is the owner of the building."

"Why don't take the matter to court?"

"To court?" Lei looked at Shan as if he were a child. "You have no idea how powerful his father is. The provincial Supreme Court, the Police Bureau, and the Attorney General all report to his father. Two years ago, he hired some goons to beat up a developer in a real-estate dispute. The developer sued him but was arrested for prostitution, which he didn't commit."

"How do you know?"

"That developer is gay and is not interested in women."

"That's ridiculous!" Shan pressed his cigarette against the ashcan forcefully. "He can't put himself above the law."

"You wish. His family is too powerful. No one can do anything to him."

"I don't believe that. There must be some way to

teach him a lesson." After a brief moment of silence, Shan continued. "Are you sure that building is illegal?"

"Absolutely."

"Then maybe I can help you."

Lei stared at him for a moment. "I believe in you. You always come up with unexpected ways to do things. Tell me how."

Shan took a deep breath. "But I'm not sure if I should get involved. He has taken Mei from me, and his family flouts the law and uses their power to bully others. I do want to give them a taste of their own medicine, but that risk is too high."

His friend leaned forward and whispered, "Tell me. If it works, Chief Wang will be extremely happy. That would be a great opportunity for you to meet with him and build a relationship."

Shan watched his friend silently, pondering his options. He was right. This could be a once-in-a-lifetime opportunity. To succeed in life, he needed such connections with the powerful.

Chapter 48

The next morning, Xiang arrived at the lab at 9:45, fifteen minutes early for his training. Upon entering the cleanroom, he found his friend Johnson seated at a workstation, testing samples. Johnson was a tall Chinese student who was about to graduate with his doctorate.

"Good morning," Xiang greeted.

"Good morning," Johnson said as he turned to look up at him through his protective eyeglasses. "You look very happy today."

"Yes, I am. Larry is going to train me today."

Johnson shrugged and rolled his eyes. "Good luck."

Xiang could tell Johnson was being sarcastic. He did not know why. After a brief conversation, Johnson returned to his work, while Xiang sat on a bench, reading an equipment manual and waiting for Larry to arrive.

At ten o'clock, Larry had not arrived.

By ten-thirty, Larry still had not arrived.

Xiang had grown impatient. Feeling that the engineer had stood him up, he exited the lab and went to Larry's office.

The door was closed. Through its glass window, he saw that the room was dark and that the engineer was not there.

Has he forgotten about the training or is he playing games with me again? Or maybe he went to the lab while I'm looking for him.

Xiang dashed back to the cleanroom, but Larry was nowhere to be seen.

"Did Larry come in?" he asked Johnson who was still testing his samples.

"No." Johnson turned and shook his head. "He is not in his office, is he?"

"No. How did you know I went to see him?"

"It's obvious. You waited for him to train you, and you looked anxious when you left the lab. When you returned, your first question was whether he was here. So, where could you possibly go? The only explanation is that you went to his office to check on him and found out that he wasn't there."

"You should become a detective." Xiang was impressed by Johnson's analysis.

"He will not come. His baby is sick today." His friend shrugged.

"How do you know? Did he call in a moment ago?"

Rather than answer the question, Johnsona added. "Or his car broke down, or his house caught on fire. You'll see."

Not believing Larry could be so mean, Xiang decided to stay in the lab and wait for the engineer in case he came. He never came. By lunchtime, Xiang left the lab and stopped by Larry's office on his way out of the building.

The door was open, and the engineer was sitting behind his computer.

Xiang tapped on the door. "Hi, Larry. I was in the lab the whole morning, waiting for you."

"Sorry." The engineer looked at Xiang over the edge of his monitor. "My baby was sick. I had to take her to the doctor."

Xiang had no idea if Larry was telling the truth, but it didn't matter to him. For him, the most important thing was to be trained so that he could start his research.

"Can you teach me tomorrow?" Xiang asked.

"I'm busy tomorrow."

"How about the next day?"

"Let me check." The engineer vanished behind the computer screen for a moment, then reappeared. "I can do it at ten o'clock."

It turned out that Larry failed to show up again, and his excuse was that his vehicle had broken down.

Why has he been doing this to me? ... Have I unknowingly offended him? ... I don't think so. I have always been respectful and humble toward him.

After reflecting on this for a while, Xiang decided to help Larry in any way he could. The key to having a good working relationship with coworkers was to give and take.

He paid Larry a visit the next morning. "I apologize for the inconvenience I caused you. I understand that you are very busy. If there is anything I can do to help you, I would be glad to do it."

"No, nothing." The engineer shrugged.

"Are you going to be able to teach me tomorrow?" Xiang asked humbly.

"I don't know. Come back and check with me in the morning."

Afraid that Larry would play another game with him, he asked, "What time?"

Larry frowned. "I don't know. Just drop by whenever you have time."

The next day, Xiang visited Larry many times, but he was never in his office. At around noon Xiang ran into

Dr. Zhang, a postdoctoral fellow in the group, in the hallway.

"Hi, Xiang. I have been looking for you. We're going to have a dinner party at my apartment for Johnson's birthday tonight. This will be his last birthday with us. Would you like to come?"

"Sure." Xiang needed something to relax him. Larry had been giving him too much anxiety in the recent weeks.

Dr. Zhang lived in a one-bedroom apartment off-campus. He had joined Dr. Smith's group after earning his PhD from a university in Texas one year before, leaving his wife at the school to finish her doctorate in chemistry. Unlike Johnson who was the information hub of the group, Dr. Zhang was a dedicated researcher.

At the party, the postdoc and three Chinese PhD students gathered around the dining table, making dumplings.

"How is your training?" Dr. Zhang asked Xiang.

"Frustrating."

"What happened?" The postdoc looked at Xiang through his thick glasses.

Xiang sighed and told them what had happened.

"That's no surprise." Johnsona shrugged.

"Why did he do this to me? Since day one, I have respected him."

"Your gratitude means nothing to him." Johnson sneered. "Don't you see that he has been trying to provoke you?"

"No. Why did he do that? I did nothing wrong." Xiang glanced at his friend, stopping making dumplings.

"You did."

"What? What did I do?" Xiang's eyes grew wide.

“Your fault was joining the group at the wrong time.” Johnsona shrugged again.

“What do you mean by that?” Xiang blinked in confusion.

“Larry is applying for a green card, so he needs job security. His primary responsibilities are fabricating optical sensors for Dr. Smith and training students. If everyone can make the devices as good as him, what’s the point of him being here?” Johnsona paused for a second. “So, he has to do anything he can to prevent us from learning the skills.”

Xiang exhaled a sigh of relief. At the very least, he had not done anything wrong, and the hostility was not personal. However, he grew even more concerned when he realized the root cause of the conflict ran deeper and could not be resolved no matter how hard he tried.

“Then, what should I do?”

“Control your emotions,” Johnson advised. “No matter what he does to you, don't fight him. You will lose if you do it. He is Dr. Smith’s right-hand man. Think about it. In Dr. Smith's eyes, who is more important, you or Larry? Whom does Dr. Smith trust more, you or Larry? He has been in this group for five years, but you are brand new.”

“Johnson is right.” The postdoc commented. “Avoiding confrontation with Larry is the key. Training new students is his job. As long as you don’t make an excuse for him not teaching you, he eventually has to train you how to fabricate the optical sensors, regardless of how reluctant he is.”

Johnson added. “That’s right. Just avoid arguing with him. If you do, he will take advantage of it. That was how Holden left the group.”

"Who is Holden?" Alerted, Xiang's gaze darted to Johnson.

"He was a PhD student. Larry tricked him into a fight and then managed to kick him out of the group."

"Does Dr. Smith know what Larry has been doing?"

"No, of course not." Johnson continued. "To him, Larry is the most reliable and trustworthy person in the group."

"Yes, Dr. Smith told me that Larry works very hard." Xiang nodded in agreement.

"Works hard?" Johnson sneered. "How often do you guys ever see him in the lab?"

"Not very often," Dr. Zhang answered. "But I did notice one thing. He reserved a lot of equipment time every week."

"That's true," Xiang added. "I've never seen him in the lab. I—."

Xiang stopped. How could Larry possibly work hard without actually being in the lab? What was going on between him and Dr. Smith?

The more he thought about it, the more confused he became.

"Think about this." Johnson scanned the group who were still making dumplings. "Larry hardly ever goes into the lab, yet Dr. Smith keeps saying that he is a hard-working engineer who is able to fabricate optical sensors with consistency and high quality. Why?"

"Why?" Dr. Zhang stopped wrapping his dumpling and looked at Johnson.

"Because Larry works the system." Johnson continued. "Dr. Smith doesn't go into the lab to check on who is working. He looks at the logbook. Larry knows that, so he reserves a lot of equipment time to make it look like he puts in the hours."

"That's quite shrewd," Jimmy said. "But it doesn't make much sense. Dr. Smith is a results-oriented person. Larry had to deliver, otherwise, he would have been caught."

"Apparently, he hasn't been caught. That tells you how crafty he is." Johnson adjusted his glasses. "When Dr. Smith asked him to fabricate some sensors, instead of using one silicon wafer to make the devices, he used twelve, the maximum capacity of a wafer holder. So he can produce twelve times more devices with almost the same amount of work."

"I see." Dr. Zhang nodded. "He always goes the extra mile and gives the best sensors to Dr. Smith. No wonder Dr. Smith likes him."

"You wish." Johnson sneered. "After fabricating them, he only gave a few to Dr. Smith and kept most of them for himself. Next time, when Dr. Smith asked him to fabricate more devices, he did not have to do any work. He simply signed up for many equipment hours as if he worked hard. Two weeks later, he retrieved a few more sensors from his drawer and gave them to Dr. Smith."

"No wonder Dr. Smith always says that Larry is the most reliable engineer and is capable of producing optical sensors with consistent quality," Dr. Zhang said. "Being fabricated in the same batch, the devices naturally had comparable performance."

"That is cheating," Xiang exclaimed. "How did you find out all of these?"

"I have known him for five years. That is long enough to discover his tricks."

"Booking equipment and not using it creates trouble

for others. That's very mean." Jimmy shook his head.

"Others? Other people mean nothing to him." Johnson shrugged. "He did much worse than just book the equipment. To make it look like he was using the machines, he turned them on, pretending that he was using them."

"Why don't you tell Dr. Smith about it?" Jimmy asked.

"Why should I do that? It's like when a husband has an affair, and no one wants to tell his wife. He is Dr. Smith's right-hand man. I don't want to get into trouble." Johnson then turned to Xiang. "Do you know why Larry always gave you ridiculous excuses for not teaching you? When people lie, they usually try to avoid getting caught, but when he lied to you, he always made sure that you knew it."

"Why?" Xiang's eyes widened.

"He tried to make you so enraged that you would fight with him."

Xiang blinked, confused. "Why did he want to do that?"

"Because it would give him a reason to report you to Dr. Smith, so he can get rid of you."

"Are you serious?" Xiang felt a chill down his back. "I almost fell into his trap."

"Of course I'm serious."

The information disturbed Xiang so much that he decided to take precautions. Starting the next Monday, he began writing down every interaction he had with Larry in a spiral notebook. It would serve as a record in case he needed it.

In a one-on-one meeting with Dr. Smith a week later, his advisor asked him how his training was going.

"It hasn't started yet," he replied.

The professor frowned. "What is the reason? You have been in my group for more than one month."

"I have been trying to learn from Larry, but he always found excuses to avoid teaching me." Xiang opened his notebook and handed it to the professor. "Look at this. I have recorded what happened." He pointed to the page where he had written:

March 24, Larry did not show up in the lab. His daughter was sick, so he took her to the doctor.

March 26, Larry did not show up. His car broke down on the way to the school.

March 27, Larry did not show up. His wife fell and badly hurt herself.

…

Dr. Smith looked at the paper for a moment, then leaned back, raising an eyebrow and staring directly into Xiang's eyes.

"I don't know what's going on between you and Larry, but you need to work this out." The professor took out a piece of paper from his drawer and handed it to Xiang. "Here's what Larry gave me."

Xiang read it.

March 24, Xiang did not show up for training. Reason unknown.

What? That's ridiculous! Liuer boiled up in Xiang's chest. He glanced at his advisor and continued to read.

March 26, Xiang did not follow instructions, resulting in a chemical spill.

Liar! A liar, a shameful liar! Xiang shouted in his mind.

Trembling, he read further.

March 27, Xiang did not show up. He apologized for

forgetting about the appointment.

Enough. There was no point in going any further. He wanted to tear the paper into pieces as if it were the engineer. He bit his lip and clenched his fists, using all his willpower to restrain the anger boiling up inside.

He took a few deep breaths, then looked at his advisor. "Dr. Smith, he is lying."

A professor furrowed his brows. "I don't know what's going on between you two. One of you is not telling the truth. You say one thing, and Larry says the opposite. I don't want any of this in my group. You need to work with him and finish your training in two weeks. Larry is the most trustworthy person. If you are unable to work with him, I don't know who else you can work with."

The shock of the accusation made Xiang's head spin. For a brief moment, he saw Larry floating behind Dr. Smith, maniacally laughing at him. He took another deep breath and opened his mouth, trying to defend himself, but decided not to speak.

It was pointless. It would be only his words against Larry's, the professor's right-hand man.

Chapter 49

Shan lit another cigarette and took a few drags, staring into Lei's eyes. "To help you, I must ask you one more time. Are you sure the building was illegal?"

"Yes."

"How big is it?"

"It's a three-story office building."

"In that case, just take it down. It shouldn't be that difficult."

"Are you kidding?" Lei's eyes widened. "No one would dare to do that."

"I will do it if I must."

"You are crazy. You can go to jail for that."

"On what grounds? Demolition of that illegal building? They can't even launch a formal investigation." Shan took a few more drags before tapping his cigarette into the ashtray. "Let me ask you another question. How important is this case to Chief Wang?"

"Very important. This is a battle between two political factions. He can't afford to lose."

Shan thought for a moment. "Well, we can pay construction workers out of town to demolish the building over a weekend. They come in, do the job, and then leave. With enough bulldozers and manpower, it should go pretty fast." He paused for a second. "But before we do anything, we need to check out the building. Do you want to go have a look after dinner?"

"Sure, but I'm still concerned about the consequence. What if—"

"Don't worry. I won't do anything without thoroughly assessing the situation and careful planning."

They started their dinner, watched the show until nine o'clock, and drove to Phoenix Mountain.

As they neared the bottom of the hill, Shan pointed to the parking lot of a nightclub. "Let's leave the car there and walk up the hill."

"Why?" Lei slowed down the car.

"If we drive up the main road, we may run into someone. It can draw their attention, and they may remember your license plate number. You don't want that to happen."

"You're right." Lei pulled the car into the parking lot. "But we have to act like customers first. Otherwise, the bouncers will break my car window after we leave."

They got out of the car, entered the building, and stayed inside briefly before heading up the mountain. After hiking through the woods for nearly an hour, they reached its peak. In the dark, a building stared down at the Three Moon Lake kilometers below. A big window on the second floor cast a bright yellowish glow into the night as if to show off the owner's power to the world. In the full moonlight, they saw a car parked at the front entrance.

"Let's hide over there." Shan pointed to a big pine across the parking lot. "People may come out of that building at any time. We don't want anyone to see us."

They went behind the tree and waited for people to leave so they could investigate the area. A moment later, an older man in his sixties and a young woman in her early thirties appeared at the window with glasses in their hands, gazing out. The man took a drink, wrapped his arm around the woman's waist, and said something to her ear. They laughed. The young woman poked his cheek with her finger, and he grabbed her hand, stuck out his tongue, and licked her fingers.

"Who is that sick man?" Shan asked.

"He is Han, the vice chairman of the Political and Legal Committee."

"And she?"

"She works for the provincial prosecutor's office. Her husband works for Han."

"Oh my! Does her husband know about this?"

"I don't know. Maybe, maybe not. It could be possible that her husband arranged it so that he could advance quickly."

The man set the glass on the windowsill and kissed the woman on her lips, both hands cupping her face. She dropped her glass and put her arms around his neck. They clung to each other for a moment and then walked away. Soon, the lights went out, and the window vanished into the night.

"I hope they won't stay here all night," Shan said. "If they do, they can stay here on any other night, making it more difficult for us to schedule the demolition."

"I doubt it. Both of them are married. They can find some excuse to stay out late, but they will eventually have to go home."

Shan nodded. "They should be busy for some time. Let's check out the building."

They walked around the structure, inspecting it. After they returned to the tree, Shan stated, "This structure is not complicated. It appears to me that they installed the electricity and telephone lines themselves, rather than through the utility companies. Also, I noticed a water pipe. They probably stole water from a nearby water tower."

"I agree with you. Since it's an illegal building, they obviously want to make it as simple as possible, so it won't attract too much attention."

"Do you still have Zhuzi's contact information?" Shan asked.

"No, but I can find it. I've heard he has a construction company down in Yanyi. That's about 200 kilometers from here."

"Perfect. They can come in on a weekend night to demolish the building and disappear immediately. Once you give me his information, I'll contact him. All you have to do is to get the money ready."

The yellow light appeared briefly from the window and went out. A few minutes later, the young woman and the old man appeared and descended the front steps of the building, arms around each other's waists. After they drove away, Shan and his friend emerged from behind the tree and headed down the hill.

"Do you think Zhuzi will take the job?" Shan asked.

"As long as you don't tell him the details, I think he will."

"What if he asks?"

"No, he won't." Lei shook his head." There are many small companies out there, and the competition is fierce. Most of them will do anything you ask without question."

****

The next morning, Lei called Shan at work. "I have good news for you. Zhuzi will be in town tonight to meet with someone at the Ocean Bathhouse."

"How do you know that?"

"I work for the governor. If I need to find someone, I have all of the resources at my disposal."

Shan was taken aback by the words. It also meant that Han could easily discover who was responsible for destroying the building.

The information changed everything. Following the phone call, he walked to the window and looked out. The wind blew over the cloudy sky, making it difficult to tell what would happen next, sunshine or storm.

What should he do? Should he continue helping Lei or back down? The whole situation was more dangerous than he had anticipated, yet the opportunity was still too good to pass up. By demolishing that building, he would be able to make connections with Chief Wang, which would be very useful in the long run, but at the same time he would expose himself to great risk. The associate head of the Political and Legal Committee was way too powerful. He could launch an investigation and found Shan in no time.

Shan pulled out a cigarette and lit it. He took a long drag and slowly exhaled, pacing the room and continuing to debate with himself.

If you want something, you have to pay for it. Nothing comes for free. Also, I have already told Lei that I will help him. It would be rather embarrassing to retract now. Besides, the higher the risk, the greater the reward.

He walked back to the window and gazed out at the clouds again, continuing thinking.

As someone in such a high position, Han must be cautious and calculating. This was his fatal flaw. He could not afford to launch an investigation into the taking down of his illegal building. Quite likely, he would assume that his political enemies were behind the matter, and that they were using it to try to publicize his corruption and bring him down.

As Shan thought about these, he ground his cigarette into the ashtray and decided to carry on the task. All he needed to do was play well to minimize his risks.

In the evening, he took a taxi to the Ocean Bathhouse.

The building looked like a six-story hotel, with white lights along its edges and a large red neon-lit Ocean Bathhouse sign on its roof. He walked in through a revolving door.

"Welcome to Ocean Bathhouse." Six tall, beautiful young women standing on either side of the entrance bowed at him in unison.

Shan responded with a smile and walked over to the check-in counter at the far end of the large high-ceilinged lobby that was adorned with eight grand chandeliers.

"May I help you?" a young woman asked.

"Yes, is there a room available for tonight?"

She looked at the reservation book on the desk. "Yes, we do. Would you like to buy a Super Pass? It includes a one-night room on the sixth floor, unlimited use of the bathing facilities on the second floor, and a free all-day buffet in our newly renovated dining hall."

"I'll take that."

Shan went to his room and sat on his bed, pondering the best place to approach Zhuzi. He needed to get a sense of what kind of person the young man had become. Thinking that almost everyone who came to the bathhouse would enjoy the expensive meal, he carried a book to the dining hall and sat near the door, from where he could see everyone entering the cafeteria. An hour later, Zhuzi came in with a small group of young men and women. They went to a booth, set their belongings on the table, and then headed to the food counters.

Shan got up and walked over to the seafood section where Zhuzi was piling a plate with lobsters.

"Hi, Zhuzi!" he exclaimed as if he had just noticed the young man.

Zhuzi turned to look at him. A second later, he broke into a wide grin. "Shan! It's good to see you."

"Long time no see. I'm sitting over there. Why don't you join me?"

"I came with my friends, but I can sit with you for a moment."

Shan got some fish and then led the way to his table.

"How's life?" Shan asked after they sat down.

"I'm doing well. I have my own construction company now."

"Really? Congratulations!" Shan widened his eyes, pretending to be surprised.

"I have to thank you."

"Me? Why?" Shan tilted his head to the side, blinking.

"Remember the night we met at the East Temple?"

"Yes?"

"At that time, I was at my lowest point. I considered quitting my job and returning to the countryside. You told me to stay on. You even bought me food the first time we met. At that time, I was a poor construction worker. No one respected me. You did. I promised myself I would repay you someday."

"You don't have to do that."

"I'm not joking. If you ever need help, let me know."

Shan leaned back in his chair. "Regarding that, I am looking for someone who can demolish a building."

"We can help you with that. How big is it?"

"A three-story office building, about thirty meters long and twenty meters wide."

"How soon do you need it gone?"

Shan thought for a second. "Ideally, within the next two to three weeks."

"No problem. We can do it."

Shan had intended to keep vital information from Zhuzi, but he felt it would be dishonorable not to reveal it now. He bent forward. "You haven't even asked why I want to demolish that building."

"Don't tell me. I learned something during those years. Don't ask, don't talk, just do your work. People do things for many reasons. I keep my mouth shut and do the work that people give me. It's safe for everyone. That's how my company grows."

After a brief conversation, Zhuzi left to join his friends. Shan was struck by how unpredictable the world was as he watched the young man's back. It seemed strange that the boy he had accidentally helped three years earlier would become crucial to his fate.

Was the young man able to deliver what he promised? Shan was not certain. After all, he had only met Zhuizi once and had not seen him for more than two years.

Chapter 50

Xiang walked out of Dr. Smith's office, regretting that he had joined the group. With Larry in his way, it was impossible to complete the training within two weeks. He knew that the engineer would ensure his failure. Then he would have to leave the group, lose his student status, and go back to China empty-handed.

He could not allow that to happen. It would be a disgrace to him and his family. His parents were proud of him for coming to America to pursue a PhD, and his relatives and friends admired him.

He had done nothing wrong yet faced termination. He did not deserve such treatment. But what could he do? Nothing. He was an ant, and Larry was an elephant.

To avoid being fired and forced to return to China, he had to find a new advisor and leave the group in two weeks. He had taken several courses from other professors and had developed good relationships with several of them, particularly Professor West. So, he decided to talk to the professor to see if he could join his group.

He changed his course and went to Professor West's office. When he got there, the door was open, and the professor was sitting at his desk, reading. Xiang knocked.

The professor raised his head to look at him, then smiled. "Come on in. So nice to see you."

Xiang sat across the table from Dr. West. After some small talk, he asked, "Do you have any openings for graduate students?"

"Yes, I do. I just received some funding for my optical fiber research."

"I want to join your group."

"Welcome." The professor's voice was happy. Then he paused. "I thought you are working for Dr. Smith."

"Yes, I'm."

"Then, why do you want to quit?"

Xiang told him what he had gone through. When he was finished, the professor said, "I sympathize with your situation, but I don't want to get involved in the politics of Dr. Smith's group. We have been good friends for many years. It would be best if you could work things out with him."

Xiang thanked Dr. West for his time and left. Standing in the hallway, he did not know where to go. The world was big, but he had no place in it. He roamed the campus for a while, then went downtown, and wandered into a place he did not know. He heard a dog bark and turned to look in its direction. It was a toy dog barking at him from the sidewalk.

He had heard dogs bark before, but he was taken aback by the small creature's audacity this time. Despite being small, it did not hesitate to make a loud noise to protect its territory.

What's the matter with you? You don't even have the guts of a dog. When someone tries to destroy you, you don't dare to fight back. Go on, get even with him.

It was easier to say than to do. How could an ant fight an elephant, and win?

The rumbling thunder shook the earth, and dark

clouds rolled across the sky. It was like a giant monster was trying to devour him. A severe storm was brewing, not just in the sky but in his mind as well, a storm that would change everything.

He gazed up at the monster and said through his teeth, "Larry, you are forcing me into a corner, and you are destroying my future. I have no choice but to fight back, and fight hard."

The following morning, he studied the logbook and purposely selected two specific time slots for training. After that, he went to Larry's office, banged the door open, and strode straight across the room to the engineer. He looked down at Larry, waved a sheet of paper in his face, and spoke in a firm and bossy voice. "You, listen up. I have reserved these hours for our training. Look at them, see what times are good for you." He slammed the paper on the desk and tapped it with his middle finger. "If you are busy during these hours, we can go talk to Dr. Smith. I'm sure he can help you reset your priorities."

While he was talking, the engineer stared up at him with frightened eyes and a gaping mouth. After he was finished, he held his breath, trying not to shake, which would reveal his nervousness. He remembered his friends telling him not to fight with Larry and was prepared to apologize for his behavior as soon as he saw any signs of anger from the engineer. He could not afford to have a direct confrontation with Larry.

The engineer stared blankly into his eyes for a moment before leaning forward and pointing to two time slots on the paper. "I can train you during these times."

"Very good. I'll see you then." Xiang nodded slowly and spoke like a boss. To infuriate Larry to the utmost, he said *thank you* to the engineer, deliberately enunciating the words in a thick accent that sounded like fuck you. Without giving the engineer a chance to speak, he walked away, holding his head high.

On Wednesday morning, Xiang went to the lab fifteen minutes early for his appointment. As he had anticipated, Dr. Zhang and Jimmy were testing their samples.

"Good morning." He greeted them.

"Good morning," they responded together.

He chatted with them for a few minutes and glanced at the clock on the wall. "Sorry, I can't talk to you. I must get ready for Larry. He is coming soon to train me."

To make it look like he was eager to get started, he transferred chemicals from their storage cabinets to the wet bench, turned on a hotplate to heat them up, and moved around the lab, cleaning the tables. Even though he was busy preparing for the training, he knew it was all a ruse because Larry would not show up. He knew it.

Thirty minutes later, he walked over to his friends, feigning frustration. "I don't know why Larry hasn't come yet. I need to use the restroom. If he comes in the meantime, please tell him that I'll be right back."

He left the cleanroom for the parking lot outside the building, enjoying the sunlight for the first time in days, and returned fifteen minutes later.

"Did Larry come?" he asked his friends, who were still characterizing their samples.

"I don't think so." Dr. Zhang shook his head.

Once more, Xiang made himself appear angry. "We scheduled training at ten o'clock. Now, it is ten forty, and he still hasn't shown up."

He sat with his friends, watching them test the samples until lunchtime. When they walked out of the lab together, Jimmy said to him, "You may need to talk to Dr. Smith about this. You can't let Larry keep doing this to you."

Xiang did not need to talk to anyone. He had his plan.

The next afternoon, he went to the lab again. As he had expected, Johnson was in the cleanroom, operating the deep etching machine.

"Hi Johnson, how are you doing?"

"Good. You?"

"Pretty good. Larry is going to teach me how to fabricate optical sensors in a few minutes."

Johnsona shrugged. "Good luck." His tone was sarcastic.

Xiang chatted with his friend for a few minutes, then left him to set up the training equipment. After making him appear busy for forty minutes, he went to Johnson. "Larry was supposed to be here thirty minutes ago, but he is still not here. I need to go to the bathroom. When he comes, please let him know I will be right back."

Once again, he went to enjoy the sunlight in the parking lot. When he returned to the lab, he asked Johnson if Larry had been here.

"No." Johnson shook his head. "You should tell Dr. Smith what happened today."

"Thanks. I think I may have to."

By now, Xiang believed that he had gotten everything ready for the showdown and would resolve the problem with Larry once and for all.

Chapter 51

Zhuzi led a fleet of bulldozers and construction workers to the summit of Phoenix Mountain at midnight on a Saturday. In his direction, they disconnected the electricity, water pipes, and phone lines. Then the bulldozers pounced on the building from all sides, ripping off the ceilings and knocking down the walls. The massive sounds of destruction reverberated in the mountains, but none of that din could be heard on the other side of the city, where the vice chairman and his son slept soundly in the subdivision of the provincial government.

As the workers demolished the office building, Shan watched from a safe distance. He imagined the chairman jumping up and down on the following Monday and cursing and threatening to throttle anyone who dared to tear it down.

At five o'clock in the morning, the building was gone, and the area had been covered in bricks, glass, and metal, leaving behind the once a powerful symbol in ruins. As Zhuzi directed his crew to begin cleaning the site, Shan stopped him. “Leave it alone.”

The young man opened his mouth twice as if trying to ask questions but said nothing.

“The situation is a little complicated,” Shan said. “Besides, the large number of fully loaded trucks moving through the city will attract unwanted attention. Get your men out of here as soon as possible and never mention what happened here to anyone."

Zhuzi nodded and walked over to talk with the workers. When he returned, he led Shan to his car and left the mountain with the rest of his crew. As they descended, Shan looked back at the mountain, finding it difficult to believe that he, a nobody, had orchestrated the demolition of a building owned by one of the most powerful men in the province. He wished that he could be there the following Monday to see Han's reaction when he discovered that his luxurious office building had been reduced to rubble.

Monday came. Lei called Shan in the morning. "How was the thing going?"

"It went well as planned," he replied.

"Did anyone see you?"

"I don't think so. I had spotters on every street and intersection near Phoenix Mountain while we were taking down the building. They didn't see any police or something unusual."

"Thank you very much! I'll keep an eye on Han and keep you updated"

Later that evening, while studying in his office, Shan received a call from Lei. "Shan, I think that you should leave the city for a few days. Han is furious and vows to throw whoever did it into jail."

"On what charge?" Shan scoffed. "Taking down his illegal construction? Don't worry. He doesn't even dare conduct a formal investigation. That will open a can of worms."

"Theoretically, you're right, but I'm still worried about you."

"I'll be fine. He has no choice but to swallow the

pain. I guess the building is only the tip of the iceberg of his corruption. If he launches an investigation, he will be shooting himself in the foot. Besides, he probably believes that the whole thing is a set-up to bring him down."

"That makes sense. Let's see what happens next."

A few days later, Lei called Shan again. "Good news for you."

"Han has given up seeking revenge, hasn't he?" Shan guessed.

"More than that. Chief Wang would like to invite you to the Chinese New Year dinner tomorrow at Jinxuan Restaurant."

"Invite me?" Shan was not sure he heard it correctly.

"Yes. He wants to thank you for clearing up the obstacle for him and get to know you."

Shan did not respond immediately. This was too good to be true. He knew he had cleared a major hurdle for the chief, but he had not expected to be invited to such dinner and had thought that it would take much longer than that to build a connection with Chief Wang.

While he was thinking, Lei continued. "You have value to him. These people are smart. They think twenty, thirty years ahead. When they are in power, they promote a younger generation who will look out for their interests after they retire."

After hanging up the phone, Shan looked out the window at the swaying tree branches and told himself that, from now on, his life would change. He would be on the right side of the wind.

The next afternoon, Lei picked him up at the company and drove him to the restaurant. It was the same restaurant where they had planned to dismantle Han's office building. Instead of dining in the public area, they passed two terra-cotta warriors at the entrance to a staircase, ascended to the next level, and walked through a hallway lined with marble sculptures to the Presidential Dining Room. At the far end of the room, a big round table was covered with a dark red tablecloth and set with crystal glasses and fine utensils. A tall vase of flowers stood in the center of a spinning glass tray. Rich oil paintings of famous landscapes and a three-tier classic crystal chandelier hanging down from the high ceiling added grace to the room. On the far right, several people were chatting, beers in their hands.

An overweight man in his fifties came to shake Lei's hand. "It's great to see you."

"Glad to see you too, Judge Bai."

"How is your father? I haven't seen him for a while." The man continued shaking Lei's hand.

"He'll be back from Huadu in a few days."

"Say hello to him for me. After he comes back, we should get together to celebrate his promotion."

A tall, slender man with glasses joined them in their conversation. "Congratulations, Lei. I heard your father has been promoted to Lieutenant Governor of the Sujiang province."

"Yes, thank you." Lei shook hands with the man and then introduced him to Shan. "This is Chief Zhao from the City Bureau of Transportation."

While they were talking, a balding, paunchy man in his late fifties, dressed in a dark blue business suit, walked in. Like needles to a magnet, people flocked to him and shook his hand. After that, with a big smile, Judge Bai led him to a chair to the north of the table.

"No, no." The chief laughed, waving his hands.

"Today is a gathering of friends. Don't be too formal."

Judge Bai pulled out a chair for him and laughed. "You must sit in the north. According to our tradition, the highest-ranking person sits in the north. If you don't take this seat, no one else will dare to sit here." He then signaled to the others. "Let's take a seat.

People took their places according to their rank, with Shan, the least important person at the dinner, seated across the table from the chief. Not knowing anyone, he stared down at the table and thought of nothing. Soon, his eyes were caught by the off-white bowl in front of him. At first glance, it appeared simple, but looking more closely, he noticed intricately engraved designs.

"Nice dinnerware," he murmured.

"Yes, it is." Lei leaned toward him. "Although it is a line of high-end products made in Great Britain, it looks simple and doesn't attract much attention. It suits Chief Wang's taste. He likes to keep things low-key."

Two waitresses brought dishes and set them on the rotating serving tray. Walnut shrimp, roast chicken, pepper salt spareribs, and many others. Looking at the large bowl of chicken soup at the center, Shan's mind wandered back to his childhood in the countryside.

In 1967, a year into the Great Cultural Revolution, the political situation in Huadu deteriorated. As more and more scientists who had been educated in the United States were arrested and accused of being spies, Shan's parents sent him to live with his aunt and grandparents in their village in the mountains of Shaxi, far from the political center.

Initially, life there was peaceful. He played in the fields with his friends, hunted rabbits and small animals with his grandpa's dogs on the hilly land, or tended the vegetable patch with his grandpa. However, the idyll was short-lived. A few months later, a revolutionary committee of the people's commune was formed. Every day, from before sunrise to after sunset, speakers atop trees blared revolutionary songs, denounced anti-revolutionaries, and chanted slogans of the Great Cultural Revolution.

On Shan's first Chinese New Year's Eve in the village, his grandpa killed the only chicken they had and made soup to celebrate the traditional holiday and his aunt's impending birth. When dinner was ready, the family sat outside in the yard around a wooden table that had fissures and cracks on its surface, like a broken spider web.

Just as they were about to eat, a loud bang shook the yard, and the gate flew open. A troop of Red Guards wearing green army uniforms with red armbands burst in. They wielded clubs and shouted, "Down with feudalism!"

As they approached the table, a tall red guard pointed at Shan's grandpa. "It was reported you're celebrating the Chinese New Year."

The old man got up and spoke humbly, "Yes, we're celebrating the holiday."

"You're not allowed to do it. Chinesc New Year is a feudal tradition. We are the new China."

The red guards charged at the family, smashing the table and the pot of soup with their mighty clubs. Splashes of liquid, chicken, and broken pieces of china flew through the air and fell on the ground, mixing with the dirt.

"No!" Shan's aunt attempted to stop the person near her, but he kicked her. She tumbled a few steps back and fell like a rock into the mud.

As Shan was recalling the past, a waitress placed a small bowl of fish soup in front of him, bringing him back to the present.

"This is pufferfish," Lei said. "Have you had it before?"

"No."

"It's very delicious. Pufferfish is the most expensive and extremely poisonous fish. It can be lethal if not properly prepared."

"Oh." Shan withdrew his spoon from the soup.

Perhaps noticing Shan's alarmed look, Lei added. "Don't worry. The chefs have removed the toxic part. Eating pufferfish is a lot like in real-world situations. You have to take risks to get the best things in life."

"What are you trying to say?"

"My point is that the risk you took in destructing that office building got you connected to Chief Wang."

Shan leaned toward Lei and whispered, "He is only the CEO of a real estate company. Why are all these high-level officials trying to please him?"

Chapter 52

The next day, Xiang went to the main cafeteria for breakfast. He sat at a table by a large glass wall that overlooked the campus. The warm sunlight cast a glow over the grassy fields, where birds flitted and chirped in the trees, and squirrels ran around. He ate scrambled eggs and oatmeal with almonds and dried cranberries, taking his time and savoring the moment. When he was finished, he went to the food counter and returned with a full plate of fresh fruit and a glass of orange juice.

There was no rush. He needed to wait until Dr. Zhang, Johnson, and Jimmy were all in the lab, and Larry was in his office.

Two weeks before, his advisor had told him that the deadline for him to complete the training was today. If he could not complete it, he would have to leave the group. So far, he had not even started.

At 9 a.m., believing that they should all be in school, Xiang walked out of the dining hall and headed for Dr. Smith's office. When he arrived, he saw the door open and the professor sitting at his desk, reading. Xiang feigned anger before lightly knocking on the door frame. His advisor raised his head, his eyes widening and his lips parting as if surprised. A second later, Dr. Smith said, "Are you all right? You look angry. What happened?"

"Larry . . ." Xiang deliberately paused as if he was

too furious to speak. “Larry and I had two training sessions scheduled, but he stood me up again. He has done this to me since I joined the group.”

Dr. Smith shook his head and sighed, then dialed his phone. After several beeps, he said, “Larry, could you come to my office for a moment?”

A minute later, Larry walked into the office, smiling. “Good morning, Dr. Smith.”

“Good morning, Larry. Xiang told me that you scheduled two training sessions with him. Is that true?”

Larry threw a quick glance at Xiang and answered, “Yes, one was on last Wednesday, and the other was on last Thursday.”

“Xiang also says that on both occasions you were not there. Is that true?”

Larry's face flushed and his voice rose in anger. “He's a liar! I was there both days. He didn’t show up at all.”

When Xiang heard Larry's response, he knew that everything was proceeding exactly as he had planned. The engineer had just shot himself in the foot, and the game would soon be over. To push Larry closer to the edge of the cliff, he looked into the engineer’s eyes and spoke in a calm but firm voice. “You are lying. You did not come to the lab as we agreed. This is not the first time you have been doing this all along since I joined the group.”

“You don’t talk to me like that! I waited for you in the lab both Wednesday and Thursday, but you never showed up!” Larry then turned to the professor. “I’m fed up. I can’t train him anymore.”

Here you go. I know you are going to do this. That is exactly what Johnson told me you would do.

Xiang remembered Johnson's advice of not confronting Larry. Anyone who fought the engineer would lose.

That could be true in most situations, but not today. Today, Xiang needed a confrontation with Larry to win his advisor's trust, to teach the engineer a lesson, and most importantly to survive. The more severe the fight, the better his chances. He purposely raised his voice just a little, but kept it calm, allowing the professor to see that, although he was angry, he was still being professional. "You're lying again. You never taught me anything, either making excuses or just not showing up."

They talked back and forth for several minutes until Dr. Smith cut in. "Stop. I'm tired of this. One of you is not telling the truth." The professor paused for a second, taking rough breaths and looking at both of them. "I'll give you one last chance to tell the truth."

"Dr. Smith, he is a liar." The engineer stepped forward. "I have worked for you for five years. Have I ever lied to you? I always gave my best effort to everything you assigned me."

The professor nodded before looking at Xiang.

To add oil to the emotional fire in the room, Xiang said furiously, "He is lying. He has been lying to you all the time."

For a moment, he thought about revealing how Larry had cheated Dr. Smith by signing up equipment logs and turning them on to pretend he was working when he was not at all. But he decided not to. That would be too much information for his advisor, and no one knew whether it could backfire.

Dr. Smith looked down at his desk for a moment and then back at them. "I can't take this anymore. One of you must go."

The room went quiet. Neither Xiang nor Larry spoke.

A few seconds later, Dr. Smith asked, "Was anyone else in the lab during those hours?"

Xiang glanced at Larry, waiting to see how he would respond. The engineer shuffled his feet before standing still, his face expressionless.

With a smile for the final victory rising in his mind, Xiang answered, "Yes, Dr. Zhang and Jimmy were in the lab on Wednesday, and Johnson was in the lab on Thursday."

The professor picked up his phone and dialed. A few seconds later, he said into it, "Dr. Zhang, could you find Jimmy and Johnson and bring them to my office? … Yes, right now."

Within a few minutes, all three people arrived.

Dr. Smith looked at Dr. Zhang. "Were you in the lab at ten o'clock last Wednesday morning?"

"Yes, Jimmy and I were collecting data for our conference paper."

"Who else was there at that time?"

"Xiang."

"Was Larry in the lab?"

Dr. Zhang blinked rapidly, turned to look at Larry, and then back at Dr. Smith, mouth half-open as if not knowing what to say.

Xiang's confidence in winning the battle was shaken by Dr. Zhang's hesitation. It felt as if he were perched on the edge of a bottomless abyss, about to fall. If Dr. Zhang was afraid of telling the truth, that would set a precedent for Jimmy and Johnson. The consequences were unimaginable. Not only would his plan for revenge be foiled, but he would be expelled from the group as well.

Holding his breath, Xiang gazed at the postdoc and waited.

After a long deadly silence, Dr. Zhang said with a blank expression, "No, I didn't see Larry. Jimmy and I spent the whole morning in the lab."

Xiang exhaled. He knew that the darkest moment of his life had passed. He wanted to tell Dr. Zhang how much he appreciated his courage to stand up to Larry, but this was not the right time.

The professor turned to Johnson. "Were you in the lab at three o'clock on Thursday afternoon?"

"Yes, I was."

"Did you see Xiang in the lab?"

"Yes, I saw him. He waited for Larry to teach him the fabrication process." Johnson answered without looking at the engineer.

"Did Larry teach him?"

"No, he did not show up that day," Johnson answered right away, giving Xiang the impression that he had been waiting for this moment for years and was eager to take the offensive against Larry.

Dr. Smith turned to Larry, red-faced. "What do you have to say?"

Larry shrugged, expressionlessly. He did not seem fazed at all.

"You have been working for me for five years, and I always believed you were honest. Why did you do that?"

Seeing the professor become angry, Xiang was glad that a storm was brewing. He stood motionless, not looking at anyone while waiting for the incident to unfold.

The room fell silent, and the air seemed to freeze. Larry did not speak, nor apologized nor explained himself.

That was so strange. Why hadn’t he apologized to Dr. Smith? If he had, the professor might have given him another chance.

Xiang noticed the engineer staring at the window with his head held high as if he did not care. Perhaps provoked by Larry's demeanor, the professor burst out, “You’re fired!”

The engineer turned and walked out of the office without saying a word.

That was the oddest thing. Xiang turned to look at his advisor and saw him staring blankly at the back of Larry.

What was Dr. Smith thinking? Was he regretting what he had said? Would he change his mind once he calmed down?

Xiang began to wonder whether the relationship between the professor and the engineer was stronger than he had thought. Like a father and son, they fought, but reconciled in the end. In that case, this victory would turn into a nightmare. Larry's retaliation would be far more insidious and devious.

Chapter 53

After the New Year dinner, Chief Wang regularly invited Shan to various events, from dining in upscale restaurants to playing card games in high-end hotels, even sending him to a prestigious driving school with all expenses paid.

One morning, around two o'clock, Shan was awoken by a call from the chief. “Can you pick someone up for me?”

“Sure, Where?” He got up and put on his clothes.

He had been used to picking up people for Chief Wang at midnight, sometimes at airports and sometimes at train stations. He saw it as a sign of trust.

“In Shangji.”

“When would you like me to fly there?”

“You don’t fly there. You drive there.”

What? Driving there?

For a moment, Shan thought that he was dreaming. Shangji was about two thousand kilometers away.

Chief Wang continued. “Now take a taxi to Hailong Subdivision. You will see a black car in front of Building Three. The key is located on the inner side of the right front wheel.”

“Okay, I’m leaving right now and will be there in forty minutes.” Although he was concerned with the strange request, he did not let that show in his voice. He could not afford to sound hesitant.

After hanging up the phone, he grabbed a twelve-pack of drink and hurried out of his dorm.

The sky was dark, no stars, no moon, only dense clouds, and the air was cool and damp. In the far distance, a thunderbolt frequently broke the darkness.

A sensation of unease lodged in his chest, growing stronger and more urgent with each step he took forward, but he kept pushing it away and continued walking. He should not think about why he had to drive to Shangji or cast doubt on anything relating to Chief Wang. He had to demonstrate total loyalty to the man.

The street was empty at two o'clock in the morning except for the occasional taxi driving by with its lone passenger. Shan shivered under a streetlight, hands buried in his pockets. As he waited for the taxi, he wondered why he couldn't fly to Shangji and who the person was. Once again, he warned himself not to ask questions.

With nothing else to offer, his only value to Chief Wang was his complete loyalty. If he wanted to maintain and further this trust, he would have to do whatever was asked and take risks that he would otherwise never consider.

A taxi pulled up alongside him and whisked him away to the Hailong Subdivision. Forty minutes later, the cab dropped him at the gate. He walked past the entrance and looked around as he walked down the dark street toward Building Three. All the lights in the apartment buildings had gone out, and the whole neighborhood was asleep. After he arrived at the building, he retrieved the key from under the car and drove away to Shangji.

Two hours later, he ran into a storm. The rain poured on the window, thunder rumbled, and lightning flashed.

He switched on the windshield wipers at their highest setting, but still found it difficult to see. Afraid of causing an accident, he pulled over onto the shoulder of the highway and waited for the storm to subside. He could not afford to have an accident, not out of any concern for his safety, but because it would prevent him from picking up the chief's guest in time. That person had to be extremely important to Chief Wang.

The sound of the rain splashing on the car quickly lulled him into a fitful sleep. When he awoke in horror from a nightmare, in which he had transferred a drug dealer from Shangji to Xihe, the storm had passed. He pulled back onto the highway and drove well over the speed limit to make up for the lost time. After another ten hours of driving, during which he kept drinking to stay awake and rested three times at the highway curb, he arrived at the city in the afternoon.

He called Chief Wang on the phone provided in the car, asking for detailed instructions.

"Go to the east entrance of Central Park. Under an ancient pine tree to the left of the gate, you will find a young woman with a red umbrella. Her name is Yan. When you return, be careful. Make sure no one else sees her."

A girl? Who was she? Why did the chief want to keep her existence a secret?

He purchased a map from a newspaper vendor and used it to navigate his way across town to the park. From a distance, he saw a young woman, probably in her early twenties, standing under the tree with a red parasol in her hand. She wore a white boxy top with high-waisted blue jeans, her long black hair falling just below her shoulders. Beside her stood a black suitcase.

Everything makes sense now, he thought. I have been wondering why the chief doesn't have a lover. Nowadays, many rich or powerful person has at least one.

Shan stopped the car in front of her, got out, walked around to the passenger side, and opened the door for her. “I'm Shan. I'm here to take you to Xihe.”

“Thank you. I prefer to sit in the back.” She smiled slightly, opened the back door, and slid in.

On the way to Xihe, Shan glanced into the rearview mirror several times to check on her, but only found her sitting quietly, gazing out the window as if lost in thought. During the entire trip, they barely spoke, not even at meal breaks. At first, he felt uneasy but quickly got used to it and became comfortable. He realized that not talking made his life easier. He did not have to please her and did not have to worry about accidentally saying something wrong.

By the time they arrived at the Hailong Subdivision, it was almost midnight. Shan called Chief Wang, “We have arrived. What do you want me to do?”

“Bring her to my apartment. Room 302.”

The building had no elevator, so Shan carried the suitcase and led her up the narrow cement stairs. When they arrived on the third floor, the chief was already waiting for them by the open door.

With a big smile, Chief Wang reached for her hand. “I'm so glad you came. How was your trip?”

“Good.” She nodded gently and stepped into the room.

Shan did not follow them. “If there’s nothing else I should do, I’m going home now.”

“No, no, no. Come on in. You must be hungry now.

I have ordered food for everyone."

It had been five hours since Shan had last eaten, and it had been a small meal. The word of food and the delicious aroma wafting from inside pulled him through the doorway.

The apartment had three bedrooms. Near the large window in the living room stood a traditional Chinese red hardwood table and chairs with intricate designs. Across the room sat a long red leather couch facing a new television. Despite its small size, the apartment must have been quite expensive because of its location.

As Shan was looking at the room, he heard the girl ask, "Where is the bathroom?"

"Here." The chief led her to the bathroom.

When Chief Wang returned to the living room, he motioned Shan towards a couch. "Let's sit." He sat down himself. "I appreciate your getting her here. She didn't want to come. It took me a year to convince her. Hopefully, she'll like it here."

"Thank you for giving me this opportunity." Shan sat on the edge of the sofa, leaning slightly forward with his hands crossed in his lap in a posture of humility and respect.

The chief poured tea into two small cups, handed one to Shan, and took a drink himself. "How is your company? I heard chairman Zhu has left."

"Yes, she got a government position after having a heart attack. How did you know?"

"Your company's president is a friend of mine. He told me about it." Wang leaned back in his seat. "We'll have dinner next month. I'll introduce him to you then."

"Thank you." Shan's heart leaped, but he kept a porky expression to conceal his excitement. How fortunate he was. He had already made a favorable impression on the president. His relationship with Chief Wang would impress the president, further advancing his career.

As they were chatting, Shan heard a toilet flush, then another, and another.

Chief Wang glanced at the bathroom door. "Are you all right in there?"

A moment later, the door opened. "I'm fine, but the toilet… the toilet is clogged."

The chief got up to the bathroom. "Oh, my."

Shan sat on the couch, contemplating what he should do. Offering them help might embarrass them, but remaining seated would appear callous. As he debated what to do, the stench of feces and urine reached his nostrils. Something must be seriously wrong. No longer able to ignore the situation, he went to the bathroom to help. When he reached the door, he saw the yellowish wastewater mixed with dark brown had overflowed from the toilet onto the floor.

"Do you have a toilet auger?" Shan asked the chief.

"No, I've never anticipated this. Who built such a poor toilet?"

"Then, I guess I'll have to buy one."

"It's past midnight," the chief said. "All stores are closed."

Shan looked around the bathroom, thinking of options. When he saw the pretty girl was about to cry, he was determined to do whatever it took to take care of the situation. They would be grateful for that.

He rolled up his sleeves, took a deep breath, and knelt on the wet floor. His bare hand delved into the toilet hole and pulled out a wad of toilet paper and a chunk of something soft. Not wanting to look at what he had fished out of the toilet, he set them aside, turned his head away to take a deep breath, and then thrust his arm back into the hole again. He kept this up for some time until he successfully unclogged the toilet.

Chapter 54

After Larry was fired, Johnson was assigned to teach Xiang how to fabricate optical sensors. One day, while they waited for the equipment to reach the vacuum, Johnson asked, "Have you heard Larry is going to International Optical Sensor?"

"No." Xiang's mouth dropped open. "How is it possible for a person with his qualifications to find such a good job in two weeks? I would be surprised if he could find any job."

"Dr. Smith helped him."

"Why? It was Dr. Smith who fired him."

"That was impulse anger. Larry has worked for Dr. Smith for five years. They went through good and bad times together."

"What a nice professor." A pang of relief swept over Xiang. Although he had plotted revenge, the firing surprised him and left him feeling guilty. He had not intended to go that far.

With the engineer no longer in his way, Xiang could devote his full attention to his research, which advanced rapidly. He completed his PhD research in three years. By the time he was about to graduate, he ran into difficulty deciding which direction to go. Return to China or stay in the US.

After studying in the U.S. for five years, he had fallen in love with the country. Here, as long as he got his job done, he did not have to go out of his way to please anyone. He was free to express his technical or political views without fear of punishment. If he chose to remain in the United States, he would have access to cutting-edge research facilities and a vibrant scientific community. This would provide him with an opportunity to become a leading scientist in his field.

However, something was missing.

Five years after coming to this country, he still could not integrate himself into society. He did not enjoy the football homecoming events, had difficulty communicating with Americans outside of his technical field due to his limited vocabulary, and did not like American food. Worst of all, the glass ceiling for Chinese immigrants seemed to be quite low. In his school, no Chinese Americans had ever held a prominent position.

He wrote to his brother for his suggestions. Two weeks later, he was awakened by his phone at about three o'clock in the morning. He rubbed his eyes and picked up the phone, wondering who called him at such an odd hour. "Hello?"

"Brother, it's me."

"Shan?" Xiang's hand jerked, afraid something was wrong. Calls from China were extremely expensive, and his brother had never done so before.

"Yes, it's me."

"Let me call you back. It's too expensive for you."

"Don't worry."

"Why?" Xiang blinked.

"I'm using my friend's phone. It's free."

"Free? Who is your friend?"

"Yes, it is free. He is the chief editor of the *Xihe*

Daily. They have a big budget for international communication. I won't put a dent in their budget."

"You scared me. I thought something happened to our parents." Xiang sat back to the edge of his bed.

"No, not at all. Last week, I received your letter. It says that you're graduating this semester and trying to decide whether to stay in the United States or return to China."

"That's right. It's hard to decide."

"What's so difficult about it? Come back. Economic reform has created many opportunities for our generation. With a doctorate from the United States, you can get a good job and have a great future. America is not your home anyway. As a foreigner, you can't compete with Americans."

"You are right, but the political situation in China worries me. I heard the news about student demonstrations in Huadu, demanding political reform from the government. I'm also concerned that the Great Cultural Revolution will repeat itself."

"Forget about the demonstrations. They change nothing. Look at America. There are many more demonstrations in the United States, but the country is still advancing steadily. Come back. Our country is changing, and many important people will retire in the next five to ten years. If you return now, you can quickly be promoted into a key leadership position. This is a once-in-a-lifetime opportunity for you. Don't worry about the Great Cultural Revolution. It's history now, and no one wants it to return."

"You are too optimistic. Don't you remember that you were kicked out of the Communist Party when you were in college?"

“That’s history too. People encounter difficulties at some point in their lives. You just have to learn how to deal with it. If you fall, you have to get back up and move on. I was lucky that the incident occurred while I was still a student. I have started a new life.”

Following a conversation with his brother, he was convinced that the time was right to take advantage of the economic reforms taking place in China. Returning home would not only allow him to realize his ambition but also give him financial freedom. The average salary of professors in China was less than twenty dollars per month. During his five years in the United States, he saved about thirty thousand dollars, which was equivalent to a professor's lifetime salary at the time.

So, he wrote to universities and research institutes in China to inquire about possible job opportunities. Just a month later, he received warm responses from all of them. Some offered him the position of associate professor with the possibility of promotion to full professor in one year, and others expressed interest in immediately appointing him to leadership positions such as an associated department head.

Upon receiving the exciting offers, he wrote to his parents, telling them that he would return to China right after his graduation. Two weeks later, he got a call from his mother.

“Xiang, we received your letter. Father and I are pleased that you are going to graduate soon. Congratulations.”

“Thank you. I—”

“But don't come back.” She sounded frantic.

“What?” He froze, his mouth hanging open in confusion.

"Our country is facing too many uncertainties. If you come back now, you may regret it for the rest of your life."

"What happened?" Xiang blinked. "A few weeks ago, Shan told me that now is the best time to return to China. Now, you are telling me not to go back. What exactly is going on?"

After receiving conflicting advice from his parents and brother, Xiang decided to visit China. Two months before graduation, he left Atlanta for Huadu without informing his parents, intending to surprise them.

Thirteen hours later, the airplane landed at Huadu airport, and he took a taxi to the Yangtze River International Hotel near his parents' home. He intended to stay there for a few days to recuperate from jet lag before moving into his parents' apartment for the rest of the trip.

In the car, he gazed out the window at the city, attempting to connect it with his memories as if putting together a puzzle. He was, however, unable to do so because the city had changed so much. Four years before, the road had been a two-lane street in farmland, but now it was a six-lane highway with high-rise offices and commercial buildings on both sides. They were so tall that he had to tilt his head against the window to see their tops.

Fifty minutes later, the taxi exited the highway to the intersection of Fujie Street and Guanhua Road, the place where he had grown up. However, he soon began to wonder whether he was in a different place with the same street names. When he had left for America, it had been a quiet suburb, but now it was filled with neon-lit buildings, shops, and bustling nightclubs. Upon reaching the traffic light, he bowed low to peer out the front window at a tall building on the opposite corner of the road. On top of it was a giant glowing red sign that read *Aerospace National Lab*. Yes, he was at home. That was the place where his father had been working for over forty years.

"Excuse me." He turned to the driver. "Could you go to the subdivision of the national lab first rather than the hotel? My parents live there. I want to have a quick look from outside."

"Sure."

When the traffic light turned green, they drove across the road to the community. After passing through a security gate and making several turns, they stopped in front of a fifteen-story building. Xiang stepped out and looked up at a small, dark window that he had not seen for four years.

How are they? Has the apartment been renovated? How does it look?

He wondered what kind of refrigerator they were using and what type of air conditioner they had installed. He imagined new furniture and a large television in the improved living room. With the money he had sent to them, they should be living a very comfortable life.

After a while, he got back into the taxi and asked the driver to take him to the hotel.

The next morning, after waking up, he went to the window and gazed outside. Through the morning mist, the sun cast its light onto the city. The area that had once been surrounded by farmland had become a land of skyscrapers and highways. Four years, only four years, the mighty force of economic reform had transformed the place into a modern business district.

No wonder Shan told me to come back. The country is indeed developing rapidly.

Xiang turned around, grabbed his backpack, and walked out of the room to see his parents. He soon got lost in the neighborhood where he had grown up. Farmland has been replaced with shops and restaurants, and narrow bicycle streets have become wide four-lane roads. Skyscrapers were erected on the spot where a row of one-story homes previously stood. He had to ask for directions several times before reaching the east entrance of the national lab.

On his way to his parents' apartment, he noticed that the campus had not changed much. A cement ping-pong table that he had used frequently still stood in the sports area. The grocery store where he had bought salt and soy sauce regularly remained unchanged. He bought some oranges and apples and headed home. Taking the elevator to the thirteenth floor, he knocked at the door.

"Who is it?" It was his mother's voice.

"Delivery." He faked his voice to mislead her.

"I'm coming."

The door opened, and his mother gazed at him for several long seconds before speaking in an uncertain tone. "Xiang?"

"Yes, it's me!"

She immediately turned her head and called out, "De, your son is home!"

"Who?" Father asked.

"Your son."

"Why did he come home today? He said that he would come back next week."

"It's not Shan. It's your elder son."

"Are you all right, my old lady? That's not funny."

"I'm not joking."

Xiang heard footsteps and then saw Father standing right behind Mother, eyes wide open.

"When did you come back?" Father asked. "Where is your luggage? Why do you come back?"

None of his parents appeared to be excited. Xiang had expected that they would give him a big hug and say in tears, "Oh my dear, we are so happy to see you." However, none of these things happened. Although he was a little disappointed, it did not bother him. He understood that the country could change dramatically in a few years, but not the people. Like most Chinese, his parents were still introverts. Hugging and expressing love in words were simply not part of the culture.

"I've come back to see you. My luggage is still in the hotel. I'll stay there for a few more days to recover from jet lag so I don't disturb your routine."

"You should come back home. We are fine." Father stepped aside to let Xiang in.

The apartment was almost the same as it had been when he had left for the United States four years ago, aside from the addition of a refrigerator.

"Why didn't you buy new furniture?" Xiang asked.

Father approached the old couch. "They all work. There is no need to buy new ones. It is a waste of money."

"You don't have to worry about money. I have far more savings than you need."

"Never only consider the present." Father sat down. "You must be prepared for the future. No one knows what will happen in ten years, twenty years, or even longer."

Mother came from the kitchen with two cups of hot

water and set them on the old worn tea table. "After paying off our debt and buying that refrigerator, we have deposited all the money you sent back into an account for you. It's your money, and we don't need it. Our salaries are more than we can spend."

"The purpose of sending you money was to improve your living conditions so you could remain healthy and enjoy life."

Father took a drink of water. "Xiang, you are doing very well now, but you don't know what can happen in the future. You should save money in case of an unexpected disaster. When I returned to China thirty years ago, I was in good financial condition and had a promising career. I thought the country would prosper each day and never expected that the Great Famine could happen. At that time, more than thirty million people died, and we were lucky to survive. You should always prepare for the worst."

No wonder his parents and his brother had given him contradictory advice. That bitter history had eroded the courage of the older generation. As a young man, he must look forward, not backward.

Chapter 55

Three days after returning to China, Xiang went to Huadu University for a class reunion arranged for him. To avoid getting lost, he took a taxi to the school instead of biking as he had always done when he had been a college student. As they neared campus, the traffic clogged, and they crawled along like turtles. This area had once been quiet, with two-story brick houses and small businesses along the two-lane street. Now, new office towers with dark blue glass walls and large shopping malls had sprung up, turning this place into a bustling business zone. Pedestrians scooted between cars to cross the jammed-up streets, and bikers rode between the vehicles.

The cab crept along for twenty minutes before arriving at the gate of the school. After checking in with campus security, the driver drove Xiang to a parking lot in front of a white two-story building.

"Here it is," the driver said.

Xiang looked at the building and then at the driver. "I meant Yanchun Restaurant, not here."

"This is it."

"No, it should be a one-story gray building." Xiang shook his head.

"It used to be a one-story building, but about a year ago it was renovated into a two-story one."

Xiang paid the taxi driver, got out, and walked into

the building. After passing through the glass doors and entering the lobby, he approached a young woman standing behind a wooden counter. "Excuse me, could you please check which room we have reserved? It's under Dong An."

She looked at her paper and then gestured at the stairway. "Room Mount Emei. Second floor."

He thanked her and walked toward the stairs. As he looked around, he noticed that the place was so much different from what he remembered. Once a small, dimly lit restaurant, it had been doubled in size, with a high ceiling and exquisite chandeliers. Four years before, only the elderly who could afford the expensive fare had dared to dine here. Now, it was packed with young people. He climbed the stairs to the room. As he pulled open the door, he saw a group of his classmates sitting around a large round table, chatting.

"Sorry, I'm late." Xiang went to the only empty seat next to Dong. "I didn't expect the traffic to be so bad. It took me nearly an hour by taxi to get here."

"That's not a surprise," someone said. "This area has become one of the city's busiest districts."

After sitting down, he looked at the Sichuan-style boiled fish, lobsters, and many other delectable dishes. Then he turned to Dong. "I haven't had a meal like this in four years. It reminds me of the little restaurant across the street from the school." He paused for a second. "I think it was called Little Emei."

"That little family-owned restaurant has long gone," Dong said.

"Too bad. It was my favorite. What happened to it?"

"It has grown into a company with over thirty employees. This cafeteria is operated by it."

Xiang's eyes widened in disbelief. “Seriously? How is that even possible? How could a small restaurant with only ten tables take over this high-end university cafeteria?”

His friend laughed. “Anything is possible nowadays. After losing money for three years, the university outsourced all its dining services. Little Emei took over this one. Since then, the business has been booming.”

“How did the owner accomplish this?”

“I don’t know. But everything is possible in this economic transformation if you’re willing to take a risk and work hard.”

Another friend leaned toward Xiang. “What are you going to do after getting your PhD?”

“I haven’t decided yet. I’ve been debating whether to return to China or remain in the United States.”

“Staying in America,” the classmate said. “Everyone wants to go there. It —”

“I think it’s better to come back.” Another friend cut in. “Look at Yiming. She earned her doctorate from a small French university. Because of France's restrictive immigration policies, she had no choice but to return to China after graduation. It turned out that she benefited from the move. She was immediately appointed as an associate professor and was promoted to full professor a year later.”

Throughout the dinner, Xiang received conflicting advice again. Some suggested he stay in the United States, where the research facilities and living conditions were far more advanced. Others urged him to return to China as soon as possible because the economic reforms were offering his generation a once-in-a-lifetime opportunity.

The dinner lasted for hours until the cafeteria closed. Dong offered to drive Xiang home. When they came to a stop at a traffic light, Dong asked, "Would you like to go for a drink? It is far too early to go to bed."

"Sure." Xiang needed some personal time and in-depth chats with his old buddy.

They went to the lake, where, along the shore, street after street of bars faced the water, with people drinking, dancing, and singing along to the loud music. After they had each ordered a beer and sat down at an outdoor lakeside bar, Xiang shouted over the din, "Where is this? I don't remember such a lake near our school."

"We're at Yuanyang Lake."

"Seriously?" Xiang glanced at the street filled with young people and neon-lighted bars. "It's hard to believe. When I left for the United States, the lake was almost a deserted place."

"Things have changed so fast. If I were you, I would return. Just look at Ping and Yiming. Ping is now an associate department head, and Yiming is a full professor. They're going to move up the ladder very quickly. How long will it take you to reach their levels in America?"

"Maybe never." Xiang gazed up at the unreachable stars and then back at his friend. "I don't understand how Ping became an associate chair. When we were in college, he wasn't a particularly bright student."

"He wasn't, but after all the top students went overseas to study, he became the best. When the university tried to promote young people to leadership positions, no one was better than him."

Three young women in their twenties passed by,

their short, thin skirts revealing their thighs.

"Pretty girls," Dong stated. "Which one do you like the most? I prefer the one on the right. Look at her hourglass figure."

Xiang smiled. "Buddy, you are married."

"Yes, but that doesn't preclude me from admiring beautiful women." Dong took a drink. "Did you notice the young lady sitting next to Shenyi at the dinner?"

"Yes, is she his wife? She looks rather young."

"No. She's his lover. Having young and beautiful lovers is a status symbol." Dong leaned back.

"What does Shenyi do?"

"He is in the real estate business. His company is probably worth tens of millions of yuans."

Xiang blinked. "A person with a physics background becomes a real estate developer?"

"Surprise? Everything is possible now."

Feeling a pang of envy rising within him, Xiang said, "In college, Shenyi struggled to keep up with his schoolwork, barely talked to anyone, and had no friends. Besides, he was from the poor countryside with no connections. How could he be so successful?"

"Luck, sharp eyes, and a willingness to take risks."

"Oh?"

Dong took another drink. "After graduation, unlike the rest of us who were allocated to universities, research institutes, or state-owned companies, he worked for a middle-sized local company. A few months later, he sensed a big profit opportunity in the computer business. At that time, even though China opened its doors to Western countries, we were far behind in manufacturing computers, and all imports were strictly regulated by the government. So, he smuggled computer motherboards with a coworker who had relatives in Taiwan. They instantly earned a profit of more than 500 percent."

"Wasn't he afraid of getting caught?"

"I'm sure he was. That's probably why he managed to kick that partner out and transition to real estate." Dong leaned toward Xiang. "If I were you, I would come back after getting a doctorate. The older generation is leaving the stage, and it's our turn. That's a once-in-a-lifetime opportunity."

Xiang nodded and turned to gaze at the lake. In the dark, a crimson and orange lights decorated boat bumped gently against the dock nearby. The wind wafted the mingled strains of music and laughter along with the delicate perfume of the women down to him.

Chapter 56

Xiang was invited to give a talk at the Huadu Institute of Applied Physics where he had studied for his master's degree. After checking in at the front desk, a tall, young man with a round, pleasant face, in his early thirties, came forward to shake his hand. "My name is Fang. I'm the vice president of the institute. Thank you for visiting us."

Vice president? He was so young.

An envious feeling rose in his mind. Although Xiang knew that people with doctorates from Western countries could get rapid promotions, he was still astounded that the young man standing right before him was the vice president of a major national research institute.

"Thank you for inviting me. Huadu has changed so much. If I hadn't taken a taxi here, I would have gotten lost."

"Yes, it has changed dramatically in recent years, particularly the research zone here. I returned two years ago after completing my PhD in Canada and am continually amazed at how quickly things change.." He looked at his watch and then back at Xiang. "We have some time left before the presentation. Let's go to my office first."

The office was located on the second floor of a six-story building, about the same size as the one that Xiang had shared with five other researchers prior to leaving China. Near a large window, a polished brown desk was piled high with books and stacks of papers. The sunlight streamed through the window and illuminated the bookshelf, which was brimming with hardcovers. The foreign language on the covers emphasized the book owner's knowledge and level of education.

"Have a seat." Fang indicated one of the two wooden chairs in front of his desk. He sat himself down in one of them, rather than in the black leather high-back executive chair behind the desk. Smiling and friendly, he talked to Xiang like an old friend about his life in Canada and his trip to the United States during his PhD studies. About twenty minutes later, he glanced at his wristwatch. "Time for the talk. Let's go to the auditorium."

When they arrived, they proceeded to the podium together. After a brief introduction about Xiang, the vice president exited the stage and sat in the first row along with other institute officials.

Looking at the distinguished and important people in the front row and the packed auditorium, Xiang remembered the old days. Four years before, he had sat far back in the hall as a graduate student of the institute, looking up at the speakers on the stage and listening to their lectures. Now, the world had flipped. For the first time, he felt the real impact of studying abroad.

Xiang placed a color slide on an overhead projector and started to give a presentation using English. The audience was quiet and attentive, like elementary students listening to their teacher. He felt a little uneasy at the beginning but soon got used to it. After the talk, he was surrounded by people asking questions, and one of them was Yu, a very senior female scientist. He had known her during his time as a graduate student at the institute but barely had had a chance to talk to her because she had always been extremely busy and far out of his reach.

"Xiang, your presentation was excellent. I wonder if you have time to come see me today," she said after the others had finished their questions.

"Sure. I'll have a lab tour now, but I'll stop by after that."

The lab tour was to see the semiconductor device fabrication and research facilities of the institute. When he followed Fang into the entrance of the lab, the vice president fetched two white lab coats hanging on the blue wall and gave one to Xiang. "This is the best cleanroom facility in the nation. Before entering it, everyone is required to put on cleanroom coats and slippers."

The best cleanroom facility in the country? Xiang blinked, hard to believe.

He stared at the slippers, feeling as if he were entering a bathhouse rather than a high-tech laboratory. Fabricating advanced semiconductor devices required a high-quality cleanroom. Even the dust of a fraction of the thickness of hair could destroy the devices. Back at the University of Georgia at Atlanta, before entering his lab, he was required to put on a hood, a gown, and boot covers to ensure no part of his body was exposed to the environment. He also had to wear protective glasses. But here, just a white coat and a pair of slippers.

After changing into his cleanroom suit, Xiang followed the vice president into the lab. As the man showed him the equipment that was so far behind what was used in the United States, he wondered how Chinese scientists were able to produce high-quality semiconductor devices and publish papers. The failure rate of experiments must be very high under these difficult experimental conditions. He felt a surge of admiration and respect for the scientists. They must have worked hundreds of times harder than their counterparts in America.

As the tour ended, Fang said, “We will have a welcome lunch in forty minutes. You might want to visit your colleagues and old friends here and join me in my office at eleven-thirty.”

They parted, and Xiang went to see Yu. When he arrived at her office, her door was open, and she was sitting behind a desk piled with papers and books. He knocked.

She raised her eyes, then walked around the desk to meet him, shaking his hand. “Thank you for coming. Please have a seat.”

As opposed to returning to her chair behind the desk, she sat next to Xiang and fetched a manuscript from her desk, showing it to him. “I’m working on a paper about a new alloy. It has some very interesting properties.”

Why was she showing him this? Did she want to collaborate with him? She had heard his talk and should know that their research was totally different.

Yu kept talking about the alloy and its properties. After she finished, she asked, “What are you going to do after you get your PhD?”

“I haven't decided yet. I'm debating whether I should come back to China or stay in America.”

“If I were you, I wouldn’t come back. America has the best scientific research environment and equipment. You can conduct interesting research and publish papers in top journals.”

"I know, but the institute has given me a very attractive offer."

"Of course they do. To the institute leaders, bringing a Western-educated PhD back to the country is a huge accomplishment. It helps them get promotions."

As they were talking, a young man knocked on the door. "Dr. Yu, people are waiting for you in the conference room."

"Oh, I forgot about it." She put her document back on her desk and turned to look at Xiang. "Sorry, I have to run. It was so nice to see you again."

Xiang stood up and followed her out of the office. When they reached the door, she stopped and turned to him. Her mouth opened a few times without a word, as if she wanted to say something but found it hard to get the words out. After a few seconds, she finally said, "By the way, my son will graduate from college this year. He wants to go to the United States. Can he contact you?"

By the way?

Xiang realized her true motivation for hosting him was to help her son go to America.

"Sure." He went back to her desk, wrote his phone number and mailing address on a piece of paper, and handed it to her. "If he needs help, just let me know."

Chapter 57

Shan flew back to Huadu from Xihe and took the whole family out for dinner at an upscale restaurant famous for its Hong Shao Jiayu, namely braised soft-shell turtles, a very expensive delicacy in China. From the outside, the restaurant looked like a plain one-story building made of old gray bricks, but the inside was quite different. It had a man-made lake with ten small fishing boats.

"Welcome to Jiayu Village," a young woman standing behind a large tree trunk-like counter said. "What name did you use for your reservation?"

"Shan."

She looked down at her reservation sheet for a moment, then led them across an arched wooden bridge to the only available boat.

After everyone sat down at a round table on the boat, Shan took out a pack of cigarettes and offered one to Xiang. "How do you like this place?"

"I don't smoke." Xiang waved his hand. "This place is amazing. It gives me the impression of a small fishing village."

"That was the idea. I like Hong Shao Jiayu. It's very delicious. They cook soft-shelled turtles for eight hours with special seasoning to let the flavors get into the bones."

A waitress came to fill their teacups and left.

"Brother," Shan continued. "Having not seen you for four years, I wish I could spend more time with you, but I can only be in Huadu for one night. Tomorrow, I must return to Xihe."

Mother's eyes widened and asked in a quick voice as if alerted. "Why the rush?"

"The company is being privatized. I need to get there before the bidding begins."

"You mean privatizing state-owned enterprises?" Xiang was shocked at the extent of China's economic reforms. Since the Communist Party had taken over the country, private enterprise had been eradicated, and all businesses were owned by the state or by local governments.

"Yes, the government is encouraging private citizens to purchase troubled businesses."

"Will you lose your job?" Mother's hand jerked for a second.

"No, quite the opposite. I'm going to buy the business." Shan lit his cigarette.

"You?" Her mouth dropped open in surprise.

"Yes." Shan leaned back.

"Where did you get the money?" Her eyes grew even wider.

Shan took a drag. "Do you remember Chief Wang? I have mentioned him to you many times."

"That Jiangkai's CEO?"

"Yes. He is backing me financially."

Mother stared at Shan for a few seconds, opening her lips several times before saying, "Shan, you must be careful. Privatizing a state company is very risky. He is not a relative or someone we know well."

"Don't worry, mother. Chief Wang is already fifty-six years old and will retire in less than ten years. To take care of his interests after retirement, he needs to recruit young people, and I'm his best choice. Besides, no risk, no return."

"Does he have children?" Xiang asked, surprised that the chief had not let his offspring take over the company.

"Yes, he has two daughters, but they have immigrated to America."

Xiang nodded. "Then why did he choose you?"

"It's a long story, but if I have to explain it to you in a few words, I would say that I have taken many risks for him and always kept my mouth shut. He also likes to listen to my ideas when he has problems. Besides, I'm the only person in the company he can trust. Anyway, this is a great opportunity to make a lot of money. Anyone can see that."

"You told us that your company has been losing money for years and is on the verge of bankruptcy," Mother said. "You'll lose every penny you have invested in it. Don't do it."

"The situation will change after privatization. Working for a state-owned company, people get their full salaries regardless of their performance, not a penny less, not a penny more. People have no motivation to work. That will have to change."

"What about the massive debt the company owes?" Mother scowled.

"We are negotiating with the government, trying to reach a mutually agreeable solution. I'm sure we'll make it. Chief Wang's father is a senior official in the central government."

"What will be your position in the new company?"

Xiang asked.

"President of the company."

"You?" Mother's eyes widened again. She turned to Father, who had been quietly listening to the conversation all along.

Father sipped the tea. "Don't be too ambitious. You're only twenty-seven, too young to lead a company. You don't know what is behind the takeover and what is waiting for you down the road."

"Yes, I'm young, but that shouldn't be a problem. During the civil war before 1949, many of the Communist generals were under thirty."

A waitress came with their orders, set the food on the table, and then walked away. Shan drew a drag on his cigarette and looked at Xiang. "When are you going to come back?"

"I'm still debating whether I should return or stay in the United States."

"Don't be so indecisive. Come back. The economic reforms present us with a great opportunity. With a doctorate from America, you are way ahead of everyone else."

"My main concern is the instability of the country. Look at the students. They demonstrate in the streets, demanding democracy."

"That's not a big deal. In the United States, people protest all the time. Just a few days ago, there was a massive march in Washington, DC, demanding the right to abortion. Not long before that, tens of thousands of people rallied in the capital, calling for gun control." Shan stubbed out his cigarette in the ashtray. "I don't understand why the U.S. government wants to take away women's rights to abortion. It should be a woman's choice, not the government's decision."

"Speaking of abortion," Xiang replied. "It is cruel to force each family to have only one child, and to force women to undergo abortions regardless of their pregnancy stage."

"What are you talking about?" Shan raised his voice. "Are you referring to the one-child policy? That's completely different. China has the largest population in the world. To lift people out of poverty, the government has to control the population. Sometimes society has no choice but to sacrifice some individuals for the betterment of the majority."

"I don't think so. Everyone is born with certain fundamental rights that cannot be revoked by the majority without due legal process." Xiang responded.

"What should a society do if the sacrifice of one person saves millions of lives?" Shan asked.

Mother clucked her tongue. "You two haven't seen each other in four years. Don't get into a fight."

"We're not fighting," Xiang said. "We're debating."

Father shook his head. "Let's eat, not talk about politics. We are just ordinary people."

Xiang glanced at the forks and knives sitting on the table and instinctively picked up the utensils while the others reached for the chopsticks.

****

Two days later, Xiang left Huadu for America. He gazed out the small oval window of the airplane as it taxied down the runway and lifted off from Huadu Capital Airport. As the city where he had been born and raised receded below him, he felt a sudden loss, a sense of disorientation as though he no longer belonged anywhere.

The previous night, he and his parents had sat up in the same chair in the same room by the same tea table as they had done the very night before he had left for America. They turned off all the lights except for the tea stand lamp to recreate the scene of that night. The moonlight cast a dark cross onto the suitcase on the floor, which contained his diaries and family photos.

"Have you made a decision yet?" Mother asked.

"Not yet, but I am leaning toward coming back."

Mother looked at his father as if passing the opportunity on to him.

Father adjusted himself in the chair. "I have noticed that you like to express your opinions. That is very dangerous. Your grandfather was killed during the Cultural Revolution for speaking out."

Mother intervened. "Don't just lecture your son. What is your suggestion?"

Slowly, Father shifted his weight to his right. "Like many other scientists, your uncle returned to China from the United States in the early 1950s with the zeal of building a new nation. Nevertheless, he was accused of being a spy simply because he was educated in America and nearly lost his life during the Great Cultural Revolution."

"Father, that time is over. The political climate has changed. The government has vowed that it will never allow the Great Cultural Revolution to repeat itself."

"Maybe I'm getting old." Father shifted his body. "But I will tell you this. If you decide to return, you should consider both the positive and negative aspects. It is important to ask yourself whether you will regret it if another political movement emerges in ten years, twenty years, or thirty years. Also, you need to control your mouth."

Xiang nodded thoughtfully.

"I am concerned about the future of the country," Mother said. "Nobody knows what will happen next." She glanced at the family portrait on the wall and then at Xiang. "I am also worried about your brother. Running such a big company is not as easy as he thinks."

The sudden vibration of the aircraft interrupted Xiang's thoughts. He closed the shade and leaned back.

But maybe I should stay in the United States. No one can guarantee that the disastrous Great Cultural Revolution will not return.

He sighed heavily.

Four years before, he had flown to the United States with the dream of returning to China after earning his doctorate. Now that the time had come, he was flying out of China to the United States, with no idea how long he would have to stay in the foreign country.

He closed his eyes and gave himself over to the long, bumpy flight. There was nothing he could do but hang on and wait to see where he would land.

A word about the author…

Li Cai was born in Beijing, China. He earned a Bachelor of Science from Peking University in Beijing, China and his PhD in engineering from Georgia Institute of Technology, Atlanta, USA. He lived through the Great Cultural Revolution and witnessed the country's dramatic change and advancement due to the Open-Door Policy that followed.

Thank you for purchasing
this publication of The Wild Rose Press, Inc.

For questions or more information
contact us at
info@thewildrosepress.com.

The Wild Rose Press, Inc.
www.thewildrosepress.com

www.ingramcontent.com/pod-product-compliance
Lightning Source LLC
Chambersburg PA
CBHW072307020726
47501CB00002B/418

* 9 7 8 1 5 0 9 2 4 9 8 5 5 *